PRAISE FOR

FATES

"A touching coming-of-age romance that
charts a fantastic course through portals of
cosmic chaos . . . spellbinding."
—USA Today/Happy Ever After

"Bross takes readers to several different
and imaginative worlds."
—Kirkus Reviews

"If you enjoy books built around mythological
concepts, magical settings and characters, and
plot lines filled with adventure and drama,
you will love this one!"
—Evie at Bookish

"Bross has done a lot right: backstory hints lend
mystery and depth to secondary characters, the
plot moves along at a good clip, and the book ends
with plenty of story left for the sequel."
—Booklist

FATES

ALSO BY

LANIE BROSS

CHAOS

DESTINED: A FATES STORY
(AN ORIGINAL DIGITAL SHORT)

FATES

LANIE BROSS

EMBER

Text copyright © 2014 by Paper Lantern Lit, LLC
Cover art copyright © 2014 Iness Rychlik (girl on rock) and Harry Pettis (background) for Trevillion Images

randomhouseteens.com

Educators and librarians, for a variety of teaching tools, visit us at
RHTeachersLibrarians.com

Library of Congress Cataloging-in-Publication Data
Bross, Lanie.
  Fates / Lanie Bross. — 1st ed.
      p. cm.
  Summary: Corinthe, a former Fate and now Executor, responsible for carrying out unfulfilled destinies on Earth, finds herself falling for Lucas, a human boy whose death she is supposed to enact as her last act before returning to Pyralis.
  ISBN 978-0-385-74282-5 (hc : alk. paper) — ISBN 978-0-307-97735-9 (ebook)
  [1. Fate and fatalism—Fiction. 2. Love—Fiction. 3. Supernatural—Fiction.
  4. San Francisco (Calif.)—Fiction.] I. Title.
  PZ7.B7995178Fat 2013
  [Fic]—dc23
  2012035297

ISBN 978-0-385-74283-2 (trade pbk.)

Printed in the United States of America

10 9 8 7 6 5 4 3 2 1

First Trade Paperback Edition 2015

To Todd.
I couldn't do this without you.

1

Principal Sylvia Patterson pulled her office door shut, checked the lock, then hitched a stack of folders slightly higher in her left arm as she made her way down the empty halls of Mission High.

The school was silent except for the sound of her own breathing and the click of her heels on the polished gray linoleum. She passed darkened classrooms behind closed doors: the desks, tables, and chairs within were just vague, silhouetted forms beyond smudged glass panes. In each window she walked by, her reflection appeared distorted.

Even after nearly two decades in these halls, she always felt scared when the school was empty.

As she rounded a corner, Sylvia stopped. A trill of alarm passed through her: a figure stood just inside the double doors at the exit, partially hidden by shadows.

No one was allowed on school grounds after hours.

Sylvia dipped her right hand into her purse, closing her fingers around the can of Mace she always kept close by. "School's closed now," she chirped, hoping the intruder wouldn't hear the tremor in her voice.

"Sorry." The girl turned, her face now illuminated by the weak light flowing in from the parking lot outside.

Sylvia exhaled. "Oh, Corinthe. You startled me." She withdrew her hand from her purse. Silly to be so jumpy. It was only the new transfer student.

Corinthe stared at her silently. She had a careless, disheveled look, despite the fact that Sylvia had been careful to emphasize the importance of one's appearance when they'd met for the first time yesterday to fill out her transfer paperwork. Corinthe might have been a very pretty girl, with her classic, well-spaced features and her pale gray eyes. Even her clothing was neat and well put-together—at least she cared about *that* part of her looks. It was the hair—the wild, tangled mess of blond that hung down her back—that told a different story.

Sylvia had been a principal for ten years and had a good eye for possibility. She sensed, after knowing Corinthe barely two days, that the girl could be a real standout if she applied herself. Unfortunately, experience had taught her that the kids in her school rarely lived up to their potential. Corinthe would probably end up just another lost child who fell through the cracks. During Sylvia's "Welcome to Mission High, Keep Your Nose Clean" speech, Corinthe had simply gazed at her, almost without breathing, her gray eyes completely flat, detached.

When children had no choices left, they all looked the same.

Corinthe shifted slightly in the doorway. "My foster mom was supposed to pick me up, but she never showed. Do you think . . . ?" Her voice trailed off and she raised her eyes expectantly.

Those eyes.

Sylvia shuffled her stack of folders from her left arm to her right so she could check her watch. It would take exactly twenty-six minutes to get home and change before Steve rang her doorbell. She couldn't be late for dinner, not after she'd practically begged him for another chance.

"Where do you live?"

Corinthe tilted her head slightly, like a curious bird. "It won't be a long drive." Corinthe spoke in a measured tone, almost like an actor reciting lines. It was a slightly strange response, Sylvia thought, but dismissed it— Corinthe was likely desperate.

"Come on, then," Sylvia said. If they didn't hit traffic, she would be okay.

They left through the main doors and Sylvia walked quickly down the sidewalk. She was tired. Too tired to make small talk. Already her mind was on Steve—what she would wear, what she would say, whether she had remembered to get her favorite blouse back from the dry cleaner's.

She turned left at the end of the block and continued toward the staff lot, Corinthe's footsteps echoing lightly behind her.

Should she wear the green blouse? Or the blue one? The green one highlighted her eyes nicely . . . but the blue one was more low-cut. . . .

"Here we are," Sylvia said cheerfully. After ten years as a teacher and ten as an administrator, she knew how to keep up appearances, even when her thoughts were a thousand miles away. She stopped next to a small black sedan parked under a flickering streetlamp. She pulled out her keys and pressed the unlock button. A quick mechanical chirp echoed in the thick spring air. She threw her things into the back and slid into the driver's seat, slightly startled by how quickly Corinthe appeared beside her.

The car growled to life and Sylvia maneuvered it onto the street. "So. Which way?" she asked.

Corinthe pointed. Sylvia eyed the girl, then turned, zigzagging the car right onto Church, left onto Duboce, right onto Castro Street, each time in response to a silent gesture from Corinthe. The pendant hanging from her rearview mirror swayed back and forth with each turn. Corinthe, Sylvia noticed, kept looking at it with a slightly troubled expression.

"It's St. Jude," Sylvia explained. "The patron saint of lost causes. Kind of a sad saint, when you think about it." She half laughed. "Still, everyone could use a miracle, don't you think?"

"Sure, I guess," Corinthe said neutrally, the first words she had spoken since she'd gotten into the car. After another minute, Corinthe raised her hand as Castro merged with Divisadero. "Keep straight here, all the way toward the water."

"You live near the Marina?" Sylvia wasn't surprised. "How do you like it?"

"It's okay for now." Her voice cracked just a little as the car smoothly rounded the slight curve.

Some emotion seemed to pass over Corinthe's face: Anxiety? Guilt? The expression was gone too quickly for Sylvia to decipher.

Suddenly, Sylvia wanted to reach out to Corinthe, to reassure her that things could be different if she only believed—if she *tried*. Sylvia knew that behind every student there was a story. That was why she kept doing this job day after day. There were moments—flashes, briefly held, like the light of a firefly—when she understood that this was the job she was *meant* for. If she could convince just one girl that her life was worth living, that she wasn't a lost cause . . . that there was someone who hadn't forgotten, who really *saw* her. . . .

"So, Corinthe," she began. "Where did you—?"

Corinthe braced her hand on the dashboard and closed her eyes. She'd already seen it happen, knew what the outcome would be, but sitting there, waiting for the car to swerve, a tiny shiver of fear had gone up her spine.

There will be no miracles today.

The car dipped into a rut and the steering wheel jerked from Sylvia's hands, spinning them into oncoming traffic. Horns blared, tires screeched, and for a split second everything froze.

Sylvia never even had a chance to finish her question.

Bright headlights illuminated the inside of the car and reflected off Sylvia's terrified face; then an enormous SUV slammed into the driver's side of the sedan. There was a loud, long howl, followed by a boom of crumpling metal. The impact sent the car spiraling wildly out of control across traffic. Corinthe threw her hands up as she was thrown forward violently. The windshield flew toward her face before her seat belt locked and she jerked back. Red-hot pain flashed through her chest.

The car glanced off a white compact that had swerved too late and finally came to rest in the opposite lane.

Then there was nothing but silence.

White powder filled the small cabin and Corinthe coughed, fighting to catch a breath. Smoke billowed from the front of the car, and the pungent aroma of burnt rubber permeated the air.

Corinthe felt a brief moment of dizziness.

Sylvia's head was resting against the steering wheel, twisted unnaturally far to the right. A tiny trickle of blood ran down her cheek from a gash in her temple and soaked into the deflated air bag. Her eyes were open so that she stared at Corinthe, unseeing.

Corinthe felt a sudden swelling in her throat. Where had she been going? Who would mourn for her? Corinthe shook her head as though to clear away the questions. Recently, she'd been overwhelmed by doubts, by questions that swirled like heavy winds whenever she closed her eyes.

But curiosity was the reason she was here, exiled to this world, in the first place. It was not her place to ask questions.

Still, she couldn't help reaching over to gently ease Sylvia's eyelids closed.

Outside the car, people had begun to shout. Cars were blaring to life again, and already, Corinthe could hear the distant wail of a siren.

Inside, Corinthe waited. Then—a tiny flicker. A firefly pushed its way free of Sylvia's hand, exactly as Corinthe had known it would. It was a Messenger. Once released, it would return to Pyralis, signifying that fate had been appeased, that order had been restored to the universe.

Corinthe gently scooped the small insect into her hand and closed her fingers around it. Relief, profound and gut-wrenching, made her limbs weak. She felt the tiny wings beat frantically against her palm, even though the firefly itself was weightless. It was like holding a tiny feather. Corinthe always worried that she would somehow harm the delicate Messenger until she could set it free near a Crossroad.

Voices rose; outside, there was an angry hiss of steam.

A blond woman in a matched jogging suit stepped out of the black SUV.

"Oh, Jesus," she said, her voice muffled by the glass.

"Oh, God. Oh, God." The woman pressed her manicured fingers against her mouth. For a brief second, her eyes passed to Corinthe. A man ran up to the woman from the sidewalk and took her elbow when she swayed. Someone screamed and several people shouted into cell phones.

Corinthe reached to unbuckle her seat belt. A stray lock of hair fell into her eyes and she pushed it away with her free hand, only to realize that blood now coated her fingers. She froze, stared at it, unblinking.

This was not possible. She didn't bleed.

She wasn't like *them*.

Suddenly, the car door was wrenched open.

"Holy shit, are you okay?"

Huge brown eyes stared at her. She nodded, tried to move, found she was still tightly secured by the seat belt. A dark-haired boy, around her age, she guessed, ducked into the car and leaned across her chest, pushed the release, then carefully untangled her arm. Even with all the smoke and the smell of burnt rubber still choking her, Corinthe was startled by the scent of the boy: spice and citrus and something irreplaceably human. He wore jeans and a Bay Sun Breakers soccer shirt underneath an army jacket. There was something familiar about him, but if Corinthe had met him before, she couldn't place where. He had full lips, an angular chin, and dark brown eyes that were wide with shock.

Too skinny, but cute.

Corinthe shook her head. She must have hit it during the accident: he was human, and she could hardly ever tell the difference between humans. But something about this boy seemed different. . . .

He started to reach behind her, to lift her out. The fog in her head cleared immediately.

"Don't touch me," she said.

"I'm just trying to help." His voice was low. For a second, his tan hand skated along her shoulder, sending a chill through her. It felt like the touch of the firefly's wings against her palm, uncomfortable but welcome at the same time. "Look—you're bleeding. You were in an accident. Do you remember anything?"

The accident. The firefly. Corinthe slid out from the car and pushed the boy out of her way with her elbow.

"Hey!" He tried to stop her, but Corinthe shoved her way through the thick crowd of people. She clenched her fist tighter around the tiny spirit, which fluttered in her palm in protest. The wail of sirens grew louder, getting closer by the second.

She had to get away.

She ran as fast as she could. She ignored the shouts, growing fainter behind her, tried to push the feel of the boy's touch out of her mind.

Her steps pounded on the concrete, taking her farther away from the disorder behind her. Her lungs burned, but she couldn't stop. Not yet.

The firefly pulsed inside her closed fist.

There was still one more thing she had to do.

2

Lucas watched as the girl disappeared into the crowd, her shock of tangled blond hair obscured by the smoke.

For a second, he was torn. He had an instinctive desire to follow her. She had the craziest eyes he'd ever seen. . . . Gray, but tinged almost with purple, like the bay reflecting the sunset.

And that streak of blood across her forehead—it looked like she'd been hurt pretty bad. Poor girl. The woman in the car . . . he hoped it wasn't her mom. Christ. She was probably in shock, running blind.

But she was already gone, lost in the throng of people that was swelling by the minute. Two police cars with flashing lights screeched to a stop at the intersection. Several people, Luc noticed, were filming the action on their phones. Sick.

Maybe he should have tried harder to stop the girl. She might have a serious head injury. She might need help.

Luc glanced back at the wreck again, really *seeing* it this time. The car still hissed like an angry snake and a figure was slumped over the steering wheel. Luc's stomach lurched. He took several deep breaths, then moved out of the way as a pair of EMTs came running past him. He wanted to walk away, but for some reason he was rooted to the spot, both terrified and transfixed.

Cop cars, sirens, accidents—they always did that to him.

In under a minute, more emergency vehicles converged, their red revolving lights casting a dim, blood-colored glow over everything. A hush fell over the crowd and Luc watched a paramedic wheel a gurney away from the car. The figure on it was covered with a white sheet.

The lights, the people in white jackets all brought back sickening memories. His chest tightened, making it hard to breathe. When he was six, he'd found his mom passed out in the kitchen and had to call 911. And just last week, it was Jasmine who'd been loaded in the back of an ambulance. She'd taken Ecstasy at a party and passed out. Thankfully, one of her friends had at least called 911. Luc didn't even remember getting the phone call, or making the drive to the hospital, half blind with fear. It wasn't until he'd reached the parking lot that he realized he'd left the house without any shoes.

Jasmine had recovered. Thank God. But Luc was still furious with her—for doing drugs, for going off her antidepressants without telling anyone.

Again.

Luc turned away from the accident. Blood pounded in his ears, making everything sound distorted. He worked his way out of the mass of people crowded around the wrecked car and the ambulances. The air drifting off the bay felt cool against his skin. He drove his hands deeper into the pockets of his army jacket to keep them warm.

The street was crowded with cars, backed up by the accident, and the blast of horns punctuated the evening.

Luc sent a quick text to his girlfriend, letting her know he was running late. Karen hated it when he was late. And she was still pissed at him for missing dinner with her parents last week. He was going to have to be extra nice tonight.

He walked toward Market and caught a bus going south, toward the Mission, and descended when it stopped at Twenty-Second Street. Bright lights illuminated window displays full of bold-colored clothing and artwork. People were crammed together at the tiny tables outside various cafes, laughing and clinking glasses. The lit windows of the high-rises in the distance looked like rows and rows of teeth, grinning down at him.

Like he was being watched.

He lowered his head and hurried toward Trinity Café. He saw her before she saw him. She sat at an outside table. Her tanned legs were crossed, and he noticed a delicate gold-and-diamond anklet encircling one of her thin ankles. A gift from her dad, probably. She had recently cut and highlighted her hair, and for one second, in the half dark, he almost didn't recognize her.

If not for the *Bay Sun Skeptic,* the school's alternate newspaper, he might never have talked to Karen. He had joined on a whim after his guidance counselor told him that even with his soccer skills, he'd have a better chance getting into UC Berkeley if he seemed more "well rounded." The *Skeptic* was the school's answer to the *Onion,* and Luc found—mostly to his surprise—that he liked writing columns and sketching the occasional cartoon.

And, of course, he liked the editor in chief: Karen.

He remembered the first time they had ever hung out. He had stuck around after a meeting at her house to help her clean up. He had been soaping up the dishes in her pristine kitchen when Karen appeared next to him, laughing.

"Luc, stop." Karen had reached into the sink to flick soap bubbles at him. "Leave them; Leticia will clean up the rest of the mess. I want to show you something. Come on."

It was the easy way she'd grinned at him—her hazel eyes had lit up with excitement—that made him set the towel down.

"Ready?" she'd asked, and grabbed his hand.

He could only nod, too distracted by the way her hand felt to speak. He followed her upstairs, where she opened a narrow door and they went up another set of stairs, this set very steep. They had to walk single file; the walls pressed so close they nearly brushed his shoulders. It was dark, too. He heard the slide of a lock and another, narrower, door creaked open.

"Where are we going?" he asked.

"Just close your eyes," she said, "and trust me."

For some bizarre reason, he did. Even though she could have been leading him straight out an open window, for all he knew. He felt wind on his skin—they had to be on some kind of deck. She led him forward a few feet. He could hear her breathing nearby.

"Open," she said.

They were standing on a small roof deck. It had an ornate wrought-iron railing on all four sides, and behind it the San Francisco skyline twinkled like thousands of fireflies in the distance.

"So, what do you think?" Karen asked breathlessly.

For a second he couldn't speak. "It's . . . amazing."

"Captains' wives used these to watch for their husbands returning from sea. They call it a widow's walk. Isn't that tragic?"

He had nodded.

"Anyway, I come up here when I just want to chill. When things get too stressful. Up here, everything is okay." As she said this, she inched closer to him, until her shoulder was touching his upper arm.

He couldn't imagine that anything about her life was stressful. She lived in a beautiful house. Her parents actually seemed to like each other. She'd already been accepted to Stanford.

"It's sort of . . . my special place, you know. Mom is scared of heights and Dad gets claustrophobic in the stairwell." She laughed and casually slid her fingers through his. "I wanted to show it to you, though."

Then she looked up at him and smiled.

That was the beginning.

Now Karen was talking on her phone and at the same time gesturing for a waiter to bring her more water. She did that a lot. Talked to people without looking at them, talked to Luc *while* talking to other people.

When she finally saw him, she muttered a quick good-bye and put down her phone. Luc leaned down to kiss her, but she barely skimmed his lips before pulling away.

Oh yeah, she was still mad.

"You're late," she said as he slid into the seat across from her.

"Sorry, there was a crazy serious accident on Divisadero. I think someone got killed."

Her eyes went wide. Instantly, he could tell he'd been forgiven. She reached out to twine her fingers with his. His pulse jumped under her touch. Her hands were so soft; she used lotion on them every day. "Smell," she was always saying. "Like cucumber and pomegranate, right?"

"Holy shit. That's crazy. I thought you were going to pull a no-show . . ."

He said nothing. His attention was still on her hands. They looked delicate next to his tan, callused fingers. Working part-time at the Marina was not glamorous by any stretch; after the first week, he'd had a blister the size of a quarter on his palm.

So different.

Karen lived in the biggest house Luc had ever seen. They had gardeners and a live-in housekeeper. Luc lived in a cramped apartment with his sister and dad, where the hot water only worked about half the time and he did his own laundry in the creepy basement of the building.

They had next to nothing in common, but for whatever reason, Karen had chosen him. He still had a hard time believing it. She was one of the hottest girls in school. And he was just . . . normal. Run-of-the-mill. Not stupid, but not too smart either. Not a dork, but not super popular. The only thing he even remotely excelled at was soccer, and recently he'd spent just as much time getting benched for bad behavior as he did on the field. That was what it felt like, at least.

Being with Karen made him forget, at least temporarily, about all the things that were bad and wrong and screwy and cramped in his life — about the dishes in the sink and the ants nesting in the cabinets, the piles of bills shoved into the TV console, the smell of weed that clung to Jasmine's clothing when she came home from hanging out with her new boyfriend, and the bags of empty beer cans Luc had to cart out for recycling every other day because his dad was too hungover to do it.

But forgetting wasn't enough — not anymore. Every day he expected to . . . feel more for her, yet the hollowness inside him never really went away.

"So," Karen said, with false casualness, "I might have a surprise for you tomorrow night. *If* you actually show on time." She quirked an eyebrow at him.

"Oh yeah?" Luc smiled at her. "Do I get a hint?"

"If I told you, it wouldn't be a surprise." She leaned forward, her T-shirt slipping down a little bit over her left shoulder so he could see the lacy black strap of her bra. The one with red hearts sewn onto it: her favorite. "Bring a toothbrush. It involves sleeping over."

Luc felt a thrill race up his spine. A few fumbling seconds of third base were as far as things had gone between them in the three months they'd been going out. But maybe she was finally ready to go further. There it was: the power of forgetting. "It's your birthday, Karen. Aren't I supposed to be getting *you* a present?"

She lowered her eyes and smiled at him. That smile made his whole body electric; he loved it when she looked at him like that. "This is a present both of us can enjoy."

Luc leaned forward. He felt a familiar surge of adrenaline. "I can't wait," he said honestly.

"*Only* if you're on time," she repeated. For a second, she looked almost pained.

They flirted through the rest of the meal—three pizza slices for him, one "skinny" slice for her—and by the time dessert arrived, a triple chocolate cake that he made her try one bite of despite her halfhearted protests, Luc felt totally relaxed. More than relaxed—happy.

Until he looked up and saw T.J. sauntering down the street. T.J. was a deadbeat DJ Jasmine insisted on calling a friend, even though he was at least twenty. Instantly, Luc's nerves were on edge again. T.J. had that effect on him: every time T.J. came around, Luc felt like somebody had jump-started his body with the wrong cables.

17

It was those stupid wannabe gangster clothes, the lazy smile, the hooded eyes that reminded Luc of a reptile. He knew T.J. dealt, knew that T.J. had probably given Jas the Ecstasy that sent her to the hospital. She denied it, said she'd bought it from some random guy at the party, but Luc didn't believe her.

When T.J. caught Luc's eye, he lifted a hand lazily in greeting. "Dude. What's up?"

"Screw off, T.J." It took a conscious effort not to jump across the table and crack him in the face. Karen was already giving him "the look," and starting a fight in the street would only get him into more trouble—with her, and with his coach.

T.J. smirked. "What's your problem?"

"You." Luc lowered his voice. Other diners had started to stare. "I know what you're about. So stay away from my sister."

T.J. raised both hands. "She's a big girl."

"She's fifteen," Luc said.

"She can look after herself. Trust me. The girl's grown." T.J. smiled—his lizard smile.

Luc couldn't help it. He shoved his chair back and was on his feet before he knew what he was doing.

"Luc!" Karen cried out.

"Whoa, whoa, whoa." T.J. stepped backward, nearly stepping off the curb, out of Luc's reach. He'd lost his confidence. Now he just looked sweaty, and oily, and sorry. "Look, I'm serious. I haven't seen your sister. Not for a few weeks, at least. Look, I hear she got into some trouble last week." T.J. licked his lips nervously. "I'm sorry, all right? But I had nothing to do with it."

Karen was gripping Luc's arm. He could sense her staring at him, pleading with him, but he kept his eyes on T.J.

"Just get out of here," he practically growled.

T.J. took off down the street. If Luc had been in a different kind of mood, he would have thought it was funny watching T.J. book it with his dark skinny jeans strapped halfway down his butt.

"He's right, you know," Karen said quietly, after Luc had sat down. "Your sister has to learn to take care of herself."

"You don't understand," he muttered.

"Then try to explain it," Karen said.

For a second, he imagined what he would say if he blurted it all out: *My dad's been hitting the bottle again; my fifteen-year-old sister tripped out and had her stomach pumped. I'm worried she's going to be like Mom.* Luc looked away. "I can't."

Karen crossed her arms. "Right. As usual. Come on, Luc. You're not her father."

"She's my sister. She's all the family I have," Luc said, too roughly. Then: "Sorry. I'm just in a bad mood."

Karen sighed and rubbed her eyes. "No, I'm sorry. I know you have . . . shit going on. Lots of it." Karen spun her water glass between her palms. She kept her eyes on the table. "It's just sometimes I feel like I'm on the outside of all of it, you know? Like I'm locked out."

His anger dissolved. She looked so uncertain. Karen never looked uncertain.

"I'm sorry." He took her hand and laced his fingers with hers. "I'm here now and you've got all of my attention. And I'm all yours at the party tomorrow night, too. I'll even get there early, promise."

"I hope you do." There was an emotion on her face that he couldn't quite read, but she blinked and it was gone. In its place was her trademark sexy grin. "You really don't want to miss it."

After dinner, Karen wanted to go over to her friend Margot's house, which had its own private screening room; Margot was having people over to drink and watch old horror movies. Margot's talent was inventing drinking games for every kind of entertainment.

But Luc was tired. He'd been at the gym at five-thirty that morning for weight-lifting and sprints and had run drills with the team for another hour after school. And that was *before* scrimmage—which Luc took as seriously as any real match. It went nearly two hours, and he played hard the whole time.

Karen had said nothing when they split up, just given him a hug and a quick kiss, no tongue—but he could tell he'd disappointed her. Again.

On his walk down Market Street, he tried listing constellations but got stuck after Cygnus.

The wind was picking up. He'd been dialing Jasmine's cell nonstop, but it went straight to voice mail every time. After what had happened last week, they'd made a deal: she had to check in every few hours and let him know where she was and what she was doing. And she couldn't be out past nine.

But it was already ten, and it had been at least four hours since he'd heard from her. What if she OD'd again, only this time, no one was there to save her?

He caught a bus back to Richmond, pushing through the crowds of commuters and tourists. Standing at the back of the bus, he couldn't help automatically scanning the faces, hoping for a glimpse of that small, stubborn chin and the long, familiar dark hair. But there was no sign of her. Luc held on to the overhead straps as the bus sped across the city.

It wasn't long before the bus emptied out, until only an old man in a crusty-looking leather jacket remained. Luc sat down and turned, forehead pressed against the cool glass in front of him. The rocking of the bus, minute after minute, began to tug him toward sleep. Darkness broken by streaks of light—like multicolored shooting stars— raced in and out of view, hypnotizing and rhythmic.

They past a block under construction, half-finished, littered with KEEP OUT signs and wooden barricades. Luc saw rebar protruding from cement, the spokes of unhung metal signs, chunks of concrete.

Steam hissed out from a grate just behind a section on the street. Luc stared at it, watching the steam twist and curl, as though trying to condense into a solid shape.

Then it *did* — condense, take shape, change.

The bus seemed to slow to a crawl and everything went silent. He watched a woman step into the steam, her long black hair billowing around her head. The mist undulated around her body like a serpent. He blinked. In an instant, she had faded away into nothingness, as if she had disintegrated into the fog itself.

Sound and motion returned, bringing Luc straight up in his seat. His forehead banged against the glass when he pushed forward, trying to look back at the site, toward the vanishing woman.

Nothing.

What the hell?

He turned toward the old man in the leather jacket, seeking some kind of confirmation that he wasn't crazy, but the man's eyes were closed and his body rocked in time with the motion of the bus. Luc pressed the heels of his hands over his eyes. People didn't just disappear into thin air like that.

He dropped his hands and returned his gaze to the window, half dreading another vision, but the city sped by, same as always: looming dark buildings, pinpoints of light. He must have imagined it, or fallen asleep for a few seconds.

At his stop, he jumped out and half jogged the six blocks to their apartment, sucking the cool night air deep into his lungs until it burned.

The breeze coming off the ocean carried a familiar fish smell, mixed with the unmistakable aroma of clove

smoke. Above him, on the second-floor fire escape, a figure was sitting cross-legged. Against the muted light of
the open window behind her, he could make out her familiar silhouette, her long dark hair, the flash of her ring
as she brought the cigarette to her mouth.

His sister *had* been home all along. He didn't know
whether to feel relieved or angry. For the past week,
every time he saw her, he saw the other her, too: pale,
unconscious, her dark hair scattered across the hospital
pillow, her nails blood-red against the white sheet, still
wearing some awful glittery shirt cut practically to her
belly button. A little bit of puke at the corners of her
mouth.

His sister—his baby sister.

The memory made his throat tighten. "Jas," he
called up.

She stood, then grabbed the ladder at the end of the
small platform and gave it a tug. The ladder descended,
squeaking and shuddering.

He climbed carefully, never quite trusting the way
the metal creaked under his weight, then pulled himself onto the small grated platform. Jasmine had leaned
back against the bricks, one arm slung over her knees. A
clove cigarette dangled from her fingers. He knew it was
more for show than for actual smoking, but it still killed
him. The smoke made its way into her clothing, into the
couches, into his bedroom, even—then he went to practice smelling like a hippie's ashtray.

She wore black skinny jeans and a torn, off-the-shoulder gray sweater, definitely not her usual club getup.

"Where were you tonight? I tried to call a hundred times and you didn't answer. Remember our agreement?" He sat down hard next to her.

Jasmine shrugged, trying to detangle some of her long, curly dark hair, then giving up. "I was home before nine, if that counts for anything."

She fiddled with the ring with little circle cutouts he'd won her at the carnival years ago. Then she took another drag from the clove cigarette, blowing out the smoke without inhaling it. She always fidgeted.

Their mother used to smoke the same type of cigarettes, though Jasmine probably didn't remember it. Every time he caught a whiff of the familiar aroma, it made something twist in his stomach—half longing, half nausea. They were so alike, Jas and their mom—both thin and stubborn and always moving.

Sometimes Jasmine would say something or gesture with her hands and it would bring back a memory from the dark place Luc had buried it.

He rubbed his eyes again, feeling the exhaustion sink down into his bones. The accident. The fight with Karen. Looking for Jas. Everything seemed to catch up with him at once, just like after an overtime game, and he wanted to close his eyes for a week.

"So, how come you didn't answer your phone?"

She picked at an invisible thread from her sweater for several long moments before she answered. "The ringer must have been off."

"Yeah, but you could have been hurt, or . . ." His voice trailed off as he thought about the woman slumped over that steering wheel.

About the girl with those crazy eyes.

"Dead of boredom?" She pulled her phone out and made a production of turning the ringer back on.

"Wow, Jas, thanks for the extra effort." Luc stretched out his legs on the narrow iron stairs. "You know, I heard somewhere that the point of phones is so people can actually call you." But he was relieved. "Anyway." He nudged her with his shoulder, "What the hell *did* you do tonight?"

"I rode the bus for a few hours." Jas pushed him back with her shoulder, something they used to do for hours while sitting on the couch watching cartoons when they were younger. It became a game, who could get the last nudge in. "Some crazy artist lady talked my ear off. It was kinda funny."

"Why funny?"

Jasmine didn't answer directly. An expression—almost of pain—passed quickly over her face, but it was gone before Luc could identify it. "Don't worry," she said abruptly, stubbing out her cigarette, "I'm sorta over late-night bus riding now. Besides, I've heard the real crazies hang out under the boardwalk."

"Yeah. And the serial killers." Luc rubbed his forehead. He was still wound up. Jesus. He needed to relax. "Karen's party is tomorrow," he said. "You could come with me."

"I thought I wasn't allowed out after dark." Jasmine

rolled her eyes. "Besides, Muffy and Buffy and the rest of them make me want to puke. Seriously, Luc, you could do better than Karen. She isn't going to magically make everything better, you know."

Jasmine's words — sudden, unexpected, *true* — shocked him into silence for a second. Jas was like that: flaky, fidgety, distracted one second and the next saying something that cut straight through Luc, straight past the layers of bullshit.

"I like Karen," he said shortly. Karen was smart and funny and made him feel like someone. Any guy in his right mind would be in love with her. Most guys *were*.

"What do you two even talk about? Trust funds and Jet Skis?"

Luc could feel Jasmine staring at him, but he refused to meet her gaze.

"Karen's super smart, Jas." He tried to work up a sense of outrage on behalf of his girlfriend, but he was simply too tired. "She got into Stanford on early admission, remember?"

"Doesn't her dad have some campus building named after him?" Jasmine asked. "That's how it works with rich kids, right? They don't have to earn anything. It's just handed to them."

"That's not how it is with her." He paused. "Besides, it's not a building. It's just a decorative bench."

Jasmine snorted. "La-di-da." She nudged him again, and finally, Luc couldn't help but smile. He would never admit it to Jasmine, but sometimes, he felt the same way she did. He never *exactly* felt like an outsider, but the thought was always there, in the back of his mind: *Different.*

"Just come with me," he said. "It's on Karen's houseboat. That'll be cool, right?"

"In what universe is that cool?" Jas said, raising her eyebrows.

"It's cool, trust me." Nudge. "Got you."

"We'll see." She leaned her head back against the bricks and closed her eyes. "Why not use their on-land mansion I've heard so much about?"

Luc shrugged. "Maybe they're having the tennis courts cleaned."

Jasmine cracked a smile. "Maybe they're getting the vomit cleaned out of their pool from the *last* party."

"The great thing about a houseboat is people can barf right off the balcony, no cleanup necessary."

"Well, when you put it *that* way . . ." Jasmine laughed.

This time, Luc laughed with her, and they eased into a natural silence. He gave his sister a sideways glance; at certain angles Jasmine's resemblance to their mom was striking. She tilted her chin up toward the sky with that same restless look in her deep-set eyes.

"Seems funny to care about all this bullshit," she finally said, "when the universe is so much bigger than this . . . than us."

"Funny," Luc said noncommittally.

"Seriously, though. Think there's life out there somewhere?"

God, she was so innocent. He knew Jas was attached to the idea that something must come after death. It was probably the only way she could handle what happened to their mom. "Not really sure," he finally answered. "You?"

"Oh yeah." She smiled. "It's everywhere."

3

By the time Corinthe stopped running—almost half an hour after fleeing the accident—her lungs burned and she'd nearly worn through the soles of her flats, even as the tiny firefly fluttered continuously in her palm, wings beating rhythmically like a miniature pulse.

Each time her feet connected with the pavement, spikes of pain skittered up her legs. There was no energy in this concrete place, no way for her to draw sustenance from the walls of brick and steel, the rivers of poured cement.

More than anything else, what Corinthe missed about Pyralis was the physical bond: the constant, flowing, physical sense of connection to everything and all. The energy in Pyralis *was* food; you had only to inhale to be nurtured.

When she'd first been exiled, she hadn't thought

she'd be able to survive. Her body burned all the time, as though every cell in her body had been ripped apart. She was sure the Unseen Ones wished her to die.

She hadn't died, though. And ten years later, only echoes of that excruciating pain remained, a reminder of the penance she must endure because she had been too eager, too curious, too questioning. And though the pain never truly went away, she'd grown used to it—except in times of exhaustion, when the pain seemed to double in intensity and she was consumed by a craving she couldn't name or satisfy.

Finally, she reached the massive pergola at the Palace of Fine Arts. Her footsteps echoed on the sidewalk as she slowed to a walk, sucking in deep lungfuls of air.

The soft gurgling of the fountain sounded like music. The air grew thick with the scent of flowers. For a moment she closed her eyes and inhaled. It reminded her so much of home. Regret burned her throat.

She threaded her way along the path that wound between rows of looming columns. Across the lagoon, Corinthe could see warm lights shining out of the windows that lined the buildings across Lyon Street, casting dazzling reflections over the surface of the water.

She watched it, mesmerized by the way the colors danced across the surface. This was her favorite time of night, when the day was put to rest under a sky streaked with deep purples and reds.

The sound of low voices startled Corinthe. She quickly ducked behind a column as a couple of teens wandered into view—a guy and a girl, arm in arm. A dog trotted happily in front of them, sniffing, tongue wagging.

Every few steps, the couple stopped and kissed.

Kissed. A word—a concept—she had never known until she came here, to this world.

She watched the boy's hand move up the back of the girl's white peasant blouse and into her hair. A strange tightening sensation gripped Corinthe's gut. It was the same feeling she'd had when the boy touched her in the car today. She turned away and pressed a hand to her stomach.

She heard the light pitter-patter of paws on stone, the jangle of a bell, and suddenly the dog had rounded the column and stood looking at her, panting.

Corinthe broke into a grin. She crouched down and with her free hand stroked the dog's fur, kissed its wet nose, inhaled the dog-skin.

"Hey, boy," she whispered quietly. She could sense the life, the joy, moving just below her fingertips, flowing hot through its body, but she was careful not to draw any of it.

In Pyralis, she had known and seen many animals, but she had never had one as a pet. Nothing in Pyralis belonged to anyone else, and yet everything, and everyone, belonged to the great order. Here, in Humana, she found that animals were drawn to her. It was as though they shared a common understanding, a common language of need that couldn't be expressed in human words.

The dog woofed as Corinthe stroked its head. From

the other side of the columns, a girl cried out, "Sammy! Sammy!" And the dog peeled away from Corinthe and disappeared, responding to its owner's call.

Corinthe straightened up and listened for the sound of their retreating footsteps. When she peeked out several minutes later, they were gone.

She hurried to the middle of the rotunda. The recessed lighting pulsed softly in the honeycomb ceiling. The lagoon winked at her through the arches, between breaks in the shrubs, and gold rippled across its surface. She began to relax.

Almost done.

She walked to the farthest arch, the one overlooking the lagoon, and stopped. A low buzzing filled the air, too quiet for any human to hear: the sizzle and pop of tiny Messengers dissolving into the water. The firefly's wings batted furiously against the soft flesh of her palm. She breathed a sigh of relief and opened her fingers to let the small spirit free.

The Messenger zipped straight up and joined thousands of others like it. They looked like miniature shooting stars cascading from the sky as they plummeted into the still water. There was no splash as they hit—only the slight hiss of their tiny lights extinguishing. After a few seconds, weightless opaque marbles bobbed to the surface in their places and gently floated away, disappearing into the darkness.

She felt the familiar ache of a memory, and for a moment, she was wading into the river of Pyralis again, like she did all those years ago. Back then Corinthe and her sister Fates would sort through the marbles, finding the murky, imperfect ones as the others flowed past and off the edge of the waterfall. The purple twilight made her skin glow as she swept her fingers across the glistening surface, sorting through the marbles bobbing in the lazy currents.

Most destinies would be fulfilled on their own, but the clouded marbles, the damaged ones that she and her sister Fates gathered, needed extra attention. These she would give to the Messengers. Though she never knew what happened after that, she knew that she was special—that her actions, and the actions of her sisters, kept the universe in balance.

It had been their job to sort the imperfect marbles from the river and deliver them to the Messengers, but she and her sister Fates had made it a game, too: whoever could find the most in a day won.

Her sister Fates: Alexia, Alessandra, Beatrice, Brienne, Calyssa . . . She wondered whether they ever thought her name.

Corinthe felt the sharp tug of longing. She knew that the lagoon must contain a Crossroad, a way back to Pyralis; that was how the Messengers traveled between worlds. Often she had fantasized about swimming out, trying to follow them home.

Would her sisters cry with joy? Would they even remember her after all this time?

She could do nothing but wait. She had been banished

for flouting the laws of the universe once. She could not go back to Pyralis until the Unseen Ones permitted it.

So instead, she stood at the edge of the lagoon and watched, wondering momentarily about the other fireflies, about the fates that had been fulfilled—most of them without any help at all.

During her first few days in Humana—what the humans called Earth—Miranda had taken her out to the lagoon just before the sun rose. They watched silently as two Messengers flickered green in the dawn and dove straight into the water in front of them. The light went out and weightless marbles bobbed up to the surface in their place.

"In the morning we collect them." Miranda scooped up the marbles and handed them to Corinthe. "And at night we send back the ones you've fulfilled."

"Fulfilled?" Corinthe had asked. That was before she'd heard of the Executors and what was required of them. That was before she'd learned she had become one of them herself.

Corinthe had looked at the marbles cupped in her hands. They were murky, and instantly she knew: these marbles had been sorted by her sister Fates and brought here by the Messengers. And she had known, too, that she was no longer a Fate.

"You have a new job here in Humana," Miranda said, as though reading her mind. "There aren't many marbles today, but some mornings there will be dozens—and those are the days you'll need to work quickly."

Miranda explained that when the universe was particularly in balance, there were fewer marbles arriving in the human world. It meant that destiny was taking place according to the natural order.

"Are those the other marbles in Pyralis? The ones that fall off the edge of the waterfall?"

"Don't think about them," Miranda said gently. "It's not your concern." But Corinthe *did* think about them—more and more as the years in Humana passed. Those marbles were deaths, and births, and falling in love; they were accidents and chance meetings.

It shouldn't matter, really. Her job as Executor was to carry out orders, not to consider the humans affected. Still, she always found the marbles riveting. Such tiny vessels, they held immense lives, immense possibilities.

She was too curious. Too fascinated by the Messengers, by anything forbidden. That was why she'd been banished here in the first place. The Unseen Ones—the unknown beings who controlled the whole universe, and ensured that order was maintained—had cast her into Humana to do her penance. She now had to do their bidding, carrying out unfulfilled destinies.

And yet, it wasn't just the beauty, the mystery, the power of the Messengers and the marbles that fascinated her now. She *did* think about the humans—about the lives impacted, and ended, and begun—which worried her as much as the blood on her temple.

Something was changing.

She was changing.

She had to talk to Miranda about it. Her Guardian had the answers to everything.

At the northwest pillar, she paused and glanced over her shoulder to make sure no one was watching. Carved into one of the columns was a faint rectangle, barely discernible. She pushed her fingers against it firmly and heard the familiar click. A narrow door, disguised as part of the ornate panel, swung open, and she quickly stepped inside.

Within the large column, it was almost completely dark. She made her way down the narrow stairway, tracing her fingers along the stone walls as she counted thirteen steps under her breath. She knew every cool, jagged edge of the walls.

Corinthe often wondered about the other Executors. What were their homes like? Were they hidden away like her own? And did they live together, the way humans did? She closed her eyes and tried to clear her mind; Miranda always said she was too preoccupied with things she couldn't know.

The temperature dipped; she shivered. At the bottom of the stairs, the hall opened up into a series of cavelike rooms. Corinthe turned right, into the first room, lifted an arm gracefully, found the string on her first try, and tugged. Two bare lightbulbs hung from the low ceiling, illuminating the space.

Years ago, the rooms had been used to store the Exploratorium exhibits, but no one except Corinthe and Miranda had been down here in over a decade. Corinthe

moved across the packed earth floor to the battered dea-
con's bench, which took up most of one wall. Quickly,
she lit an assortment of votives and pillar candles. A
dancing pattern of light and shadow flickered over the
walls, and she felt a warm rush of happiness.

Home. A small word for such an immense thing—just
like the marbles, so small, but vast enough to enclose a
whole life. This was her home for now. Miranda had done
her best to find the things they needed, like the hot plate
that balanced on a rickety old stand, next to a tiny sink,
to heat water for tea. Or the dented wooden cupboard
they managed to nail into a crack in the wall, which held
a mismatched collection of jars and bottles and teacups.

A month after Miranda brought her here, Corinthe
had complained that the dirt floor was too cold. Miranda
found them a large, threadbare Oriental rug that took
up most of the room. It wasn't much to look at, the colors so faded they were all the same dull wash of brown,
but Corinthe loved being able to take off her shoes and
knead her toes along its surface. If she closed her eyes
and concentrated, she could even pretend that she was
walking across a carpet of soft moss that blanketed the
surface of Pyralis.

One corner of the room was dominated by a huge
chipped claw-foot tub. Neither Miranda nor Corinthe
knew why someone would install a bathtub in an underground storage room, but the water ran hot, and it
didn't take long for them to appreciate the small luxury
of a bath.

Her gaze drifted to the painting hanging on the far wall: the only decoration in the room, it had either been forgotten or deliberately left behind. In the painting, a small boy and girl probably no more than six years old had their backs turned to the observer. They were on a cobblestone pathway that wound through a manicured garden of colorful flowers. Their small hands were clasped together as they gazed out toward the horizon, which blurred into a pale blue sky.

Were they contemplating leaving the garden? Or did they find comfort in its limits? The painting's beauty wasn't in its composition but in that question. Corinthe used to spend hours lying on the worn rug, staring up at it, wondering.

It was the only piece of sky she could see from her new home.

Corinthe turned away and caught a glimpse of her own reflection in the small cracked mirror that hung over the copper basin sink. She stepped closer and studied her reflection, gingerly touched the dried blood on her temple. Her fingers shook.

The patron saint of lost causes. Sylvia's words suddenly popped back into her mind. Humans and their strange beliefs.

Behind Corinthe, the tap on the tub squeaked and water began to run thunderously into the tub. Within seconds, steam filled the small room. In the mirror, Corinthe watched an outline shimmer through the steam, a graceful shape that resolved slowly into a hazy body.

Then, gradually, features appeared. It was like watching a rainbow form on the horizon, and Corinthe held her breath. No matter how many times she saw it happen, it was still magical.

A long, flowing white dress materialized first; then jet-black hair, a face with sharp cheekbones. Then, finally, the eyes. Those night-black eyes.

Miranda.

The water in the tub rose higher, until Miranda, fully formed from the steam, stepped out onto the floor, her white dress pooling around her and drying as the steam dissipated. Abruptly, the water stopped running, and the excess began to spiral down the drain.

Corinthe caught Miranda's eyes in the reflection. "Where have you been?"

Miranda reached out and wiped away the blood on Corinthe's forehead with her thumb. Her touch was soft, but her eyes were as dark and unreadable as stones.

She ignored Corinthe's question. "Is the task complete?"

"Yes, just like the marble showed. But . . . I bled. . . ." Corinthe's voice trembled and she turned away before Miranda could see the fear in her eyes. Fear was a weakness. It was a feeling. And feelings were for humans. "What's happening to me? I'm—I'm becoming like them, aren't I?" she blurted out. She realized the question had been raging inside her since the accident. Maybe for even longer than that.

"Shhh," Miranda said. "You aren't like them. You're

an Executor. This is just a small scrape, nothing to get upset about."

"I've never bled before," Corinthe argued.

"Don't fret," Miranda said. "You're so close to going home. That *is* what you want, isn't it?"

Corinthe bit her lip. She ached to return to Pyralis, to the twilight and the scent of flowers layered through the air, to the vast horizon of stars and the trees that whispered songs to her in the half darkness, and to her sisters, singing to the sky, running through the forests. "Of course it is."

"Then leave it be and focus." Miranda reached out and cupped Corinthe's chin. "This day has been long for both of us. But trust me, it means little in the greater picture. Remember—there is a pattern to everything. This will all be a distant memory very soon, I promise."

Corinthe nodded. *Pattern.* That word always made her feel a little happier, a little more secure. There was a meaning and a reason for everything in life—as a Fate, she knew that inherently.

"First, we fix you up." Miranda moved to the row of shelves roughly constructed of cinder blocks and planks. The shelves were packed with a variety of dusty bottles and mason jars. She eyed the collection carefully and finally selected two small jars, then brought them back to the sink. Taking a cotton ball, Miranda dipped it into the clear bottle. The cotton soaked up the translucent liquid quickly, and Corinthe flinched when Miranda smeared it across her wound. "To clean off the blood . . . I'm sorry it hurts. I should've warned you it would sting."

Corinthe shook her head, bearing the pain in silence. Miranda smiled encouragingly as she cleaned the wound. As Corinthe watched Miranda's careful hands work, she felt relieved and grateful to have a Guardian who was this thoughtful, this diligent. Without Miranda, she could not possibly have survived her exile.

Miranda then tipped a second bottle over her palm, and several dead butterflies fell out. With her thumb, she crushed them and rubbed the dusty powder into the wound on Corinthe's face. For a moment, they stood in silence, and Corinthe forced all of her questions and doubts—still thudding in her chest, behind her rib cage—down and back. All except one.

"How much longer will it be?" Corinthe asked. "I've been stuck here for years."

Miranda turned and blew the last of the powder from her fingers. Then she quietly said, "I've heard whispers between worlds. If the Unseen Ones are happy with your next two assignments . . ." She let her words trail off, let the hint hover between them. She smiled as she reached into her pocket. "Your new task. Tomorrow, at the Mission Creek Harbor." She held out a marble.

Corinthe took the marble and gazed into its murky center. Would it be a new death, she wondered, so soon after the last one? Inside the marble, images swirled: Lots of teenagers laughing. A party. Tiny lights winked—the harbor seen from a distance. Boats bobbed in the dark water. The image shifted again, and Corinthe saw two humans kissing.

Corinthe didn't understand assignments like this—

coincidences, encounters, romance. Death was cleaner, more direct. But love? The concept eluded and confused her. As far as she could tell, the feeling humans termed *love* brought uncertainty. But her job was not to question, only to perform her duty.

"A party will be fun," Miranda said with a smile. "You *are* a teenager, too, you know."

Corinthe knew Miranda was teasing her. She was not—would not—be like the humans she dealt with.

Miranda squeezed her shoulder. "You can wear one of your new dresses."

As much as Corinthe loathed many aspects of this world—the constant noise, the acrid scent of human desperation—one thing she did love was the way humans dressed: the colorful patterns; the shoes of different heights and styles; the looped, beaded, and jeweled bracelets, necklaces, and rings.

In Pyralis, the Fates all looked the same. They wove white dresses out of flower petals. By human standards, Corinthe supposed the Fates were beautiful. But humans liked color. And, Corinthe realized, so did she.

Not at first, though. Initially, this world had seemed blinding and chaotic. In the beginning, Corinthe had worn a pair of tortoiseshell sunglasses everywhere she went in San Francisco—even on the foggiest, darkest days, and even though the lenses were far too big, at the time, for her small face. But that was just one of the many subtle things that had changed about Corinthe during the past ten years. Over time, she'd somehow gotten used to the sun, to the buzz of constant movement and bright lights. Her eyes had become less sensitive. Lately, she'd even found that she liked the electric energy of mornings; the calm, flat gaze of the noon sun; the long, open yawn of a summer afternoon; the dark silence of midnight.

She wasn't just *getting used to* Humana—she was fitting into it. Taking on more and more human traits. Possibly even, she thought with a sudden pang, becoming *one of them*. But being here, in this world, still hurt her; she still felt a near-constant ache for Pyralis.

She closed her eyes, willing away the thought.

"You look tired. Have you been stitching in the gardens lately?" Miranda asked.

"No," Corinthe admitted.

"Go, then. I'll be here when you come back." She gracefully skirted a beat-up table in the center of the room. "And bring me a handful of echinacea and some Brahma Kamal petals."

Stitching. It was a word all their own, infused with a meaning only Miranda and Corinthe knew. As a Fate in Pyralis, Corinthe had been connected to the world around her. The air, sky, plants—everything held vitality, a force that nurtured her body. But in Humana, the earth *hurt.* The first time she secretly tried to draw strength from it, the suffering had been so painful it had paralyzed her for days. She had been convinced she was being punished.

But Miranda tended to a small, previously neglected garden on the north side of the rotunda that she coaxed back to life. Flowers bloomed and deep green leaves stretched out to the sun. Its brilliance had called to Corinthe, and when she found it, she ran her hands over the surface of the ground, feeling the slight vibrations emitted from below. She had sunk her little fingers into the ground, pressing hard enough to feel the cold soil fill the space under her nails. Slowly, her senses had sharpened. The vibrations grew louder and turned into a gentle, swelling hum.

Life pulsed from the ground, weakly at first, and seeped into her body. Corinthe could still feel the pain of the trees and plants outside this small, sheltered space, but it was muted. Still, the relief was indescribable. She could hear bees humming, could smell the delicate rosebushes at the edges of the garden, could feel the earth's pulse thrumming under her fingers.

She had sat for what felt an eternity before Miranda found her.

"What are you doing?" Miranda wore that same enigmatic smile Corinthe had seen so many times since.

"I—I was just . . . just stitching."

"Stitching?"

It was one of the newer words she'd learned in Humana. To thread a needle, then weave strings back and forth until they made something beautiful. It was the best word she could think of to describe a process that had always been innate, intuitive. She had stood up, suddenly ashamed, determined to explain. "Something . . . passes through me when I'm here. Like strands of color. They come up through my fingertips, stitch everything in my body together. I feel . . . *stronger* here."

"It's not wrong to do," Miranda said gently. "We take, then we give back." She tipped her pitcher over a cluster of yellow flowers poking out of the ground.

Now, when Corinthe needed strength, she knew she could go there without shame. It didn't feed her the same way Pyralis did, but at least Corinthe was able to stitch enough energy to do the jobs she was tasked with.

Exhaustion caused her steps to be heavy as Corinthe made her way out of the room and turned right, down a short hall that led to a shorter flight of steep steps. On the landing, a thick wooden door, barely a foot wide, swung open on silent hinges. The sun was gone. The sky was an inky nighttime blue, and the stars were beginning to float out of the dark.

The door opened directly into a small garden. The space was tucked at the back of the rotunda, away from the wide pathways for tourists and joggers. The garden was concealed from sight by a wall of tall, thick hedges that Miranda had planted years ago.

Though Corinthe sometimes heard voices pass close by, no one had pushed their way through the thick foliage to discover her yet. At least, not while she'd been there.

Her oasis was small, maybe five feet by five feet, but it was bursting with life. Brilliantly colored flowers crowded the ground, snaked up the trellises, burst like miniature songs from the deep, long grasses. Here, it smelled like heaven—another human concept Corinthe had learned only recently.

It smelled like Pyralis. Its scent defined who she once was, and who she would be again.

Another thing she had to thank Miranda for.

"Hello," she whispered, and sat down in the middle of the garden, where a small circular clearing had been made, just large enough to accommodate Corinthe. She brushed her fingers over delicate blossoms and inhaled the heady scent her touch released.

She only took enough strength to survive, and only from the plants she tended to.

Stealing from nature without giving back was against everything she believed in.

When she felt better, Corinthe gathered the petals Miranda had requested for her tonics, thanked the plants, then squeezed back through the narrow door.

In the kitchen, Miranda sat at the table, surrounded by vials and dried leaves. She ground something between two small flat rocks, so engrossed in her task that she didn't even look up when Corinthe set the petals down next to her.

Quietly, so as not to disturb her Guardian's work, Corinthe made her way to her bedroom. It wasn't a very big space, maybe half the size of the main room, but she had managed to make it her own. An old lamp, draped with a piece of gauzy red material, sat on a battered nightstand next to her bed. The floor was covered with oddly shaped scraps of rug. It should have been hideous—

oranges and greens and pinks all mixed together—but somehow, it worked. Corinthe kicked off her shoes and kneaded her toes into the plush rug.

She'd tacked an old sailcloth to the wall over her bed. She'd found it discarded at the Marina, tossed aside because of a small tear in the fabric, and had known at once what she would do with it. Now the plain white cloth was covered in bold blue-and-green swirls around a starburst of yellow that formed an abstract sky.

A dark, jagged steeple dominated the left side of the canvas. A postcard was taped to the wall next to the makeshift canvas: Van Gogh's *The Starry Night*. The painting reminded her of Pyralis, where the perpetual twilight stained everything purple and blue.

It was a crude rendition, but it was hers, and she loved it anyway.

Ten years ago, when she had opened her eyes and found herself on a strange rooftop in a strange world, the stars overhead were the only things she recognized. She'd stood, alone and terrified, staring up at the sky for hours, watching it begin to glow, with a mixture of fascination and dread.

When the sun had finally crested the horizon in a burst of light, she'd scrambled to hide in the dark recesses of the roof. She'd never seen the sun rise before, except in marbles. The world around her had brightened until it was blinding, until she had cried for the first time, from terror and anguish, and felt the pain of those hot tears and the humiliation of snot running into her mouth:

all of it new. Miranda had found her there, cowering in the shadow of a water tank. She had spoken to her, explained, coaxed her out of hiding. She'd given her a pair of tortoiseshell sunglasses and slipped them coolly over her face, bringing some relief to the intensity. Together, they'd sat in the sunlight and Corinthe had squinted through the tinted plastic lenses, watching the world around her emerge.

"Am I the only one?" tiny Corinthe had asked suddenly, peering up at Miranda with sudden curiosity.

"No. There are many of you," she'd explained.

"Where are they? Why can't I see them?"

Miranda had smiled. "They're all around, but you can't see them because they blend in. That's what they're meant to do—to live among humans as one of them. And that's what you're meant to do from now on, too."

Corinthe could still remember how those words had washed over her consciousness like an icy wave: exiled here, in this foreign, terrible world full of obscene noises and blasts of light.

Only the stars in the sky were the same. The stars remained constant in every alternate world, the same constellations dancing across the darkened sky. It had always fascinated Corinthe to watch them move. When she was a Fate, she could commune with the Unseen Ones simply by standing at the river of knowledge and asking a question with her heart. She had asked them once if the sky moved or if Pyralis did. The answer had come back to her in silent pulsing waves:

We exist nowhere and everywhere; therefore, we move with all and none.

The statement felt so profound that Corinthe had spent endless energy trying to make sense of it, trying to find the beginning and the end of the universe in her mind.

She knew such thoughts were pointless, though; there were infinite realms in the universe, all connected by one membrane: the Crossroad. She'd been through it once and it had nearly torn her apart.

She finished undressing and slid into a soft pink robe. Silently, she padded back out to the kitchen, where Miranda now worked over a pot of steaming water, humming. Miranda always hummed when she was lost in a task or deep in thought. Next to her, on the table, were several crumpled ticket stubs, which Corinthe recognized vaguely as belonging to the city's transportation systems. That meant Miranda had been riding again.

"Why do you ride the buses?" Corinthe asked suddenly. She had always wanted to know, but Miranda hardly ever answered a question directly.

Miranda didn't look up. "You never know where an opportunity will arise."

"Opportunity for what?" Corinthe asked.

"For anything and everything," Miranda said with a smile.

Corinthe shook her head. Miranda had strange habits. She'd been known to ride around on the city buses for hours, speaking with humans. Corinthe had tried this once, hoping she might come into contact with other Executors. But it had forced her to interact with humans—and talking to them had proved too confusing. Miranda, however, seemed invigorated after these outings. Corinthe had never understood why. Perhaps it was like Corinthe's interest in clothing—unexplainable, a fluke, a small bit of Humana that appealed to her.

Corinthe drew a bath, as hot as she could stand it. The water turned her skin pink, and she scrubbed her whole body carefully: between her toes, under her fingernails, behind her ears. Death had a way of clinging to skin, and Corinthe hated the way it felt—like her whole body was wrapped up in a cold, clammy grip.

Later, as Corinthe sat on her bed, towel drying her long hair, Miranda came in without a sound and set a steaming cup on the nightstand. She moved behind Corinthe on the bed and began to run a comb gently through her tangled waves. Miranda's fingers brushed over her scalp as she worked the sections into a neat braid.

Corinthe missed the way her hair would wind itself daily into a long, perfect braid in Pyralis. Somehow, she could never seem to tame the wild mane here in this world.

"It's getting harder to remember," Corinthe admitted.

Miranda didn't ask what or why. She just squeezed Corinthe's shoulder tenderly, stood up, and left her alone with her thoughts.

Corinthe pulled on her favorite pajamas and lay back on the bed. This was the closest she came to actual sleep,

something neither she nor Miranda actually needed —
not like humans did, anyway. The bed was simply a place
where she liked to sit and remember.

It was here that the memories of Pyralis resurfaced —
mossy, dimly lit, sweet, like the gardens themselves.

The longing rose up, threatened to choke her.

Corinthe blinked her eyes open. The ceiling was
strangely blurry.

"I'm ready to go home," she whispered.

The room was silent.

Corinthe closed her eyes and tried again to picture
Pyralis Terra. But this time, instead, she saw a pair of
brown eyes gazing at her, and felt the single skating touch
of a hand, like a butterfly's wing against her shoulder.

4

The party was in full swing by the time Luc arrived. He knew Karen would be pissed. He'd tried calling her, but she was obviously screening his calls.

After he got off his shift at the boatyard, he'd come home to change, only to find out his dad hadn't bothered shopping that afternoon. There was nothing in the fridge except some mustard and beer. And the old, cracked cookie jar where they kept extra money was almost empty.

Thankfully, Luc had been paid, and his shift money would cover something for dinner. Jas was already too skinny—and Dad, well, he'd just head down to the bar and forget he needed to eat. So Luc walked to a nearby convenience store and picked up some microwavable sandwiches and a couple of Twix.

Jas, of course, still refused to go to Karen's with him.

She had said she was going to stay home, bum out on the couch, and eat the Twix he gave her. He'd reminded her: Absolutely no going out. No T.J. No parties.

Definitely no parties.

The Mission Creek Yacht Club had rules against boat parties, noise levels, and maximum capacity—but Karen's parents were founding members, and exceptions were made.

The brightly lit houseboat was moored at the end of a private pier, and it was bigger than most people's real houses. It had three decks and a hull of gleaming chrome. Even though he was late, Luc walked slowly, enjoying the feel of the ocean breeze on his skin, the view of the thousands of stars glittering in the night sky like shattered bits of ice.

Cassiopeia, Centaurus, Corona Borealis.

Voices and bursts of laughter punctuated the night air. A strong hip-hop beat vibrated through the wooden gangway, buzzing up through Luc's feet as he crossed onto the boat from the pier.

Heat lamps had been arranged all around the deck, and the air was artificially warm, despite the breeze coming off the bay.

"Ahoy, matey!" someone called out from the roof deck as Luc shouldered his way through the crowd.

He looked up and saw a very drunk guy in a captain's hat leaning way too far over the deck. Just when it looked like he might tumble over, several hands pulled him back and he disappeared into the crowd. Saul Tompson. Life of the party. Total dumbass.

"The Duke is in the house!" Tyler shouted, appearing out of nowhere. He gripped Luc's hand and bumped his shoulder. "You ready for our five a.m. weight-training session on Monday, Your Highness?"

After Luc led the soccer team to their first shutout victory last year, the guys had started calling him Luc the Duke. The nickname stuck, and when he made captain this year, Luc found he liked being held up on that royal pedestal. It kept his head in the game—helped him to focus. Most of the time, anyway.

"Hell no." Luc took the beer Ty offered. He could use a bit of a buzz tonight. "This is why I hate losing."

"Well, maybe if our *star forward* actually kicked the ball into the goal . . . ," Tyler said, grinning.

"And maybe if our *star goalie* actually stopped one once in a while . . . ," Luc fired back. The truth was, he had been distracted. He had missed an easy goal and his shot had gone way wide to the left, not even tempting the keeper to make a save. Everyone on the field had actually stopped and stared. Luc rarely missed—he couldn't *afford* to miss, not when there were always college scouts dropping by practice.

Not when he was already in the doghouse with Coach.

Two weeks ago, Luc had pushed a member of a rival soccer team. Coach wouldn't listen when Luc argued that the guy had gone straight for his *ankle*, not the ball, when Luc was about to take a shot. Coach had simply been pissed that Luc lost his cool and had benched him for the rest of the game.

No more fighting, no more screwups, or else Luc would get booted off the team for good.

He needed to play soccer.

A soccer scholarship was his best hope of actually getting into—and being able to pay for—college. Plus, it was the only part of school he was actually good at.

"Duke! Duke! Duke!" a chorus of voices yelled, and three more players from the team pushed their way over.

"Hey, man, Karen was looking around for you about a half hour ago," Jake said. He was the closest thing to a best friend Luc had. "She didn't look too happy."

Luc heaved a sigh. Great. Another night of fighting. Just when he was starting to relax.

"Guess I should go and face the music," he said, tipping the bottle back and draining the last of the beer.

"You need a longer leash," Tyler said.

"Whatever, Finnegan. Becky's on the warpath, so I wouldn't be talking too much trash," Jake said to Tyler.

Tyler's girlfriend, Becky Waller, slid up behind Tyler just then and wrapped her arms around his waist. She was tiny, and blond, and together she and Tyler looked perfect: golden and all-American, like something out of an Abercrombie & Fitch ad.

Becky was shorter than Karen and had bigger boobs, which, Luc couldn't help noticing, were barely harnessed by her stretchy pink top tonight. But Karen had confidence that Becky didn't have, and it made her sexier.

"Sorry, guys," Becky said, giggling. She was already

slurring her words a little. "I'm stealing your goalie for a while."

She shrieked when Tyler leaned down and grabbed her around the waist, swinging her over his shoulder. He strode over to the railing.

"Who'll give me twenty bucks to toss her in?" he yelled.

"I'll give you fifty *not* to!" Becky shouted, kicking and giggling.

"A hundred!" someone shouted.

A small crowd gathered and the wager grew bigger by the second.

"Wait!" Becky shouted. She arched up and whispered something in Tyler's ear. He spun around and set her down, where she wobbled on her high heels. Ty grabbed her around the waist to keep her from falling.

"Gentlemen, I've been made an offer I can't refuse," he said, grinning widely.

Luc felt a sudden surge of envy. It was so easy with Ty and Becky—they even kind of *looked* the same.

What had Karen said about tonight? She might have a surprise for him. He knew he should feel excited—he *was* excited—but he also felt weirdly guilty, as though Karen had spent a lot of money on a present he didn't totally want.

Luc started for the stairs. Karen liked to be in the thick of it all, so she was probably waiting upstairs on the roof deck.

A huge group of people stood around, laughing

and dancing to the beat thumping out of the surround-sound speakers. Paper lanterns were strung around the railing of the upper deck, bathing the roof in a soft yellow light.

Karen never threw just any party. The beer they were drinking was actually good, and cold, not just some Coors Light that had been shoved in someone's duffel bag. There was liquor, too, all top-shelf, and the lights were just dim enough. Karen would never do anything half-assed.

She was predictable, but that was exactly what he liked about her. She grounded him, kept him focused in the right direction.

Luc smiled and nodded at random people as he pushed his way through the crowd. And then, out of nowhere, he got cornered by Hillary Greer.

Shit.

"Hey, Luc," she practically purred in his ear. She pushed her chest against his arm and leaned in as close as she could get.

Luc could smell cherries and vodka on her breath.

"Uh, hi, Hil. What's up?" Luc tried to edge his way past her, but she clamped a hand on his arm.

He'd made out with her last year at a party after the team had won states. In an uncharacteristic Luc moment, he'd gotten blind drunk on tequila shots. Turned out Hillary was one of those really pretty girls who was also really freaking crazy.

She texted him at all hours of the night, cornered him

at school, and finally bought herself a dozen roses on Valentine's Day and told everyone they were from him.

The guys thought it was hilarious and showed up in the locker room with roses the next day, claiming Luc had sent them.

He'd had to put his foot down with Hillary after that, and he half expected to find a dead animal nailed to his door when he told her that there was nothing going on between them and she needed to stop.

She seemed to take it well enough, but he tried to avoid her at school just in case. Then he met Karen, and Hillary was forgotten. Except right now, she was hanging on his arm in a *very* low-cut shirt and it was hard to even remember his own name.

"So, cool party, huh?" Hillary asked.

"Karen knows how to throw a good one," he said pointedly. At his girlfriend's name, Hillary made a face.

"You're still with her?" She ran a red-tipped nail up his arm and twirled her finger in the hair lying on the back of his neck. "Bummer." The word washed across his ear, hot and breathy.

He took a step away from her, disengaging his arm. "Have fun."

On his way across the deck, he grabbed another beer out of a huge cooler filled with ice and bottles. Hillary was psycho-killer crazy, but seeing her—feeling her near him—had made his body light up.

Why couldn't he just get his shit together? Be happy with Karen? She was funny and smart and into him. Her skin smelled like raspberries, she always matched her bra to her underwear, and she had a tiny, adorable freckle to the left of her belly button.

And she threw killer parties.

He'd chugged the beer, but it wasn't working. His mood was tanking quickly. He felt an elbow in his side, and someone knocked into him from behind. He turned around, unconsciously balling his hands into fists. Ricky Semola, the class president, grinding some girl Luc didn't recognize. She looked about five minutes away from puking, though. Her short dress seemed to have gotten caught in her thong, and Ricky pulled out his iPhone and snapped a picture.

"Nice, huh?" he said, showing Luc the screen.

Without thinking, Luc grabbed the phone and tossed it over the opposite railing before Ricky could react.

"What the hell, man?" Ricky yelled.

"Oops." Luc shrugged. Ricky glared at him, and Luc stared back, raising his eyebrows. He knew he would crush Ricky in a fight—and Ricky knew it, too, because he backed off, muttering under his breath. A freshman girl had managed to disentangle her friend's dress, and was half propping her up. Luc was about to tell them both to go home when a couple tucked away in the corner caught his eye.

A girl with long blond hair braided nearly to her waist stood with her back to him. Something about her—her back, the messy braid—struck Luc as familiar, and he felt a small thrill go up his spine. She was talking to Mike

Ditson, a junior basketball player and first-class asshole. Judging by the way Mike was frowning, something big was going down.

Maybe he was getting dumped.

That thought made Luc smile.

Mike nodded to her and said something else before turning and disappearing down the stairs. The girl stayed where she was, staring out over the bay, her shoulders rigid.

Wisps of her hair kept coming loose from her braid. She reached up to smooth them down. He could see her long, graceful fingers from where he stood, but there was no polish on her nails. All the girls he knew wore it, even Jas.

It was strangely compelling to see bare nails.

She moved closer to the railing and leaned out a little. The silk wraparound skirt she had on billowed around her legs. She smoothed it down over her hips and he forgot everything—what to think, what to say, how to breathe.

Everything about her was amazing. The way she tilted her head to the side, like she was listening for something. The curve of her neck right at the shoulder, a spot he wanted desperately to touch.

Someone jostled him from behind, breaking his train of thought. God, what the hell was he doing? What the hell was he *thinking* of doing?

Karen. He had to find Karen. He took a long drink of beer.

He was tired of being alone tonight.

He glanced back at the railing, but the girl was gone.

He headed downstairs to the hold. Hardwood floors gleamed in the light of a dozen candles, and softer music played against the background of the thumping bass from above.

Lily, one of Karen's best friends, was leaning against the gleaming chrome sink, talking animatedly to another girl with identically tan skin, blond hair, and the look of someone who spent most of her life on vacation.

"So the next time you go to the Vineyard, you *have* to check out this new art nouveau coffee shop that makes the most to-*die*-for cappuccino. You seriously can't get anything like it here."

Luc barely stopped himself from rolling his eyes. He cleared his throat.

"Have you seen Karen?" he asked.

Lily swung around to face him, her high ponytail swinging around her head like a pendulum. Sparkly blue makeup covered her narrowed eyelids. "Why would she want to see you after you *ditched* her last night? That makes, what, twice in the last two weeks? Way to be a boyfriend, Luc."

Of *course* Karen had told Lily. "Look, I had a family emergency. It's none of your business, anyway."

"She's my best friend, so yeah, it *is* my business." Lily's makeup made her look just like a bug. Like a large, skinny insect. "A word of advice, Lucas: You're not the only guy who's interested. You *might* want to try a little harder."

Heat surged up the back of his neck. Lily was one of

the few people who outwardly disliked him, although as far as he knew, he'd never done anything to make her feel that way. Usually he just ignored her, but tonight, he just wasn't in the mood to take it.

"A word of advice, Lily: Keep your nose job out of it."

"Cute. Very original." She turned her back to him.

Past the kitchen was a short hallway that led, Luc knew, to the boat's three bedrooms. A cord hung across the hallway, with a neatly lettered PLEASE KEEP OUT sign attached to it.

Everyone respected Karen's rules. Luc hesitated, debating whether he should look for her there, but in the end he decided against it. She was hosting the party. She wouldn't be hiding out in a bedroom.

He went back upstairs and wound back toward the prow, where there was a smaller deck. In the shadows, where the spiral staircase led to the upper deck, was the girl he had seen before, the one with the braid.

The same flicker of recognition tugged at him. He still hadn't seen her face, but the way the light shone behind her outlined the curves under her cream-colored shirt. She was thin—a little bony, even—but he could tell by the way she accepted a beer from one guy and at the same time easily laughed at something a different guy was saying that she was confident as hell.

Her tank top dipped low in the back, he noticed, exposing her tanned shoulder blades.

Luc swallowed hard.

Suddenly, the crowd seemed to clear. The two guys

disappeared up the stairs, leaving the girl with the braid alone in a pocket of shadows.

Something leapt inside Luc's chest, like when space opened up on the field and he knew he had a shot. There was no thought involved, just his body moving toward the goal. He had to see her face.

A breeze lifted strands of hair that had escaped the braid hanging over her shoulder. They danced wildly around her head, and this time she let them.

He smelled flowers mixed with the salty sea air as he approached.

He must have made a sound, because she spun around and pinned him with her stare. Gray eyes. A flare of hot recognition leapt in his gut.

It was the girl from the accident; the girl who had run away.

"Hey—hey again," he stammered. Shock kept his brain from telling his mouth what to say, and he stood there like an idiot with his mouth hanging half open. He had hoped to see her again, but now that she was right in front of him, all his game was completely gone. "You're here." *Idiot.*

Her eyes appeared to grow darker. Those eyes—like there were shadows moving underneath them. She said nothing.

He ran a hand through his hair and cleared his throat. *Get a grip, man.*

"So, you know Karen?" Of everything he could have asked, why had that question been the one to pop out?

He could have asked where she had run off to, if she was okay, a hundred other questions that *weren't* about whether or not she knew his girlfriend.

"I've . . . seen her before," the girl answered cautiously.

Her voice had a musical lilt to it. He found himself moving closer without intending to. She smelled like flowers—*lilac*. The word popped into his head. It was intoxicating. He wanted to bury his face in her hair and breathe her in. Do more than just breathe her in.

His gaze ran over her face, stopping at the spot on her temple where, the day before, a small gash had leaked blood. Now only a tiny mark indicated she'd even been hurt.

He had a sudden vision of that poor lady: that form he'd seen hunched over the steering wheel. He'd never seen a dead person before.

"Why did you run away yesterday?" he asked, his throat dry as sandpaper.

She frowned. "Why do you care?"

Now, *that* was a good question. He chalked it up to guilt, for not making sure she was okay . . . but standing there so close he could feel her breath against his face, he knew it wasn't guilt. Not at all.

"Why are you avoiding my question?" He inched closer. She tried to back away, but the railing kept her from going any farther. The space between them grew smaller; the smell of her, that insane smell of flowers, intensified. "Look, I was worried. The woman who was driving—"

"I didn't know her," she said quickly. "She was just giving me a ride. There was no reason to stick around. She—she just worked at my school."

Luc exhaled. He hadn't realized he'd been holding his breath. "That's so intense," he said. "I'm really sorry you had to see that."

She just stared at him wordlessly. He ran a hand through his hair. "Let's try this again, okay? My name's Lucas. What's yours?" He extended his hand. "Can we do this? Can we start over?"

The girl stared at his hand as though she'd never seen one before. Then, thankfully, she laughed. Her laugh was deep and beautiful, like a low note on a piano. "Corinthe."

He stared at her mouth and fought the intense desire to hear her whisper his name instead. Light from the paper lanterns hit the dangling crystals at her ears, and bright dots danced over her neck like tiny fireflies. She craned her neck to look past him and he almost reached up to run his fingers down the curve at her shoulder.

"Corinthe. Good. Great. Well, Corinthe, I'm glad you're okay," he said.

A look of puzzlement passed over her face. "Thank you," she said stiffly, as though the words were unfamiliar. She moved a few steps away from him, and he panicked. He didn't want her to disappear yet.

"Can I get you a drink? There's—"

"No thanks. I'm fine." She held up the beer she clearly hadn't even taken a sip from, then turned and wrapped her free hand around the railing, tipping her head back to look up.

Luc moved next to her cautiously, worried she might suddenly run off again. "What are you looking at?" he asked.

"Stars." She fell silent for a few moments. "It's amazing you can still see the stars with all the smog, but you can."

He didn't need to look up to know which constellation would be overhead, which stars would be the brightest this time of year. "Do you have a favorite?"

She glanced at him for just a second. "No. How can you choose just one? They aren't anything special alone. But together . . ." She swept her hand in a wide arc, but he kept his eyes locked on her face.

She was so beautiful.

For a few minutes, they stood in silence. Luc found, weirdly, that the lapse in conversation didn't feel uncomfortable. He was actually enjoying standing next to her without speaking, listening to her quiet breaths, watching the light trace the outlines of her hair and her throat.

Corinthe spoke abruptly. "It wasn't intense."

"What?"

Corinthe turned to face him. "The accident. It wasn't intense. And I'm not sorry I was there. Death is the balance to life." She said it matter-of-factly, but he thought he saw a flicker of uncertainty cross her face. He had a sudden image of his mother—alone, kicking in an alley. At least, that was what his father had told him once, in a drunken stupor. Neither of them had brought it up again, and Luc was thankful for that. He shoved the thought away.

"You sound like you've been around death before," he said.

She looked up at the stars again. "Yes, I have."

He didn't push her. But he wanted her to know he really understood, if she needed to talk.

"Look, Corinthe . . ." The words died on his lips as she turned toward him, her wide eyes darker than he remembered. Without really thinking, he lifted his hand and ran one finger over the spot where the cut had been.

Corinthe froze under his touch. For a second, he thought she was going to bolt. Their eyes met and an electric current ran through his whole body. He felt a humming in his ears as he leaned forward. He couldn't stop even if he wanted to. The look in her eyes made it hard to think about anything except kissing her.

Then she jerked away and stumbled a few steps backward. She looked toward the water, where a faint green light buzzed in the distance.

"I need to go." Her voice sounded hoarse. She brushed past him and started back toward the front deck.

"Wait!" Luc followed her blindly along the narrow walkway, where the music was louder. Even more people were packed onto the lower deck, and he had to push his way through the crowd to follow her. He didn't know what he was doing, could think of nothing but being close to her again.

He followed her when she went down the steps into the cabin, past Lily, who was now ranting to some other girls about how she'd almost drowned in a hot tub in Vail. He'd heard that story at least a dozen times.

When Corinthe ducked under the gold rope blocking off the hallway to the bedrooms, he hesitated.

"We're not supposed to—" he started, but she cut him off.

"You don't have to follow me," she said neutrally, with a quick glance over her shoulder.

Damn it. He was acting like an idiot. But he still ducked under the rope and went down the hall after her.

"So you didn't say before exactly how you know this crowd," he prompted.

Corinthe had stopped in front of a closed door. She didn't answer him. She turned the handle and the door swung inward silently.

"Occupied," a guy blurted out. In the darkness Luc made out that same faint glow again—a tiny pinprick of greenish light, humming and crackling as it made its way across the room.

Corinthe hit the light switch. Someone screamed. Luc froze. The images bombarded him like stills, like pictures lit up by a flash: one after the other, disjointed, senseless.

Karen.

Mike.

Together.

On the bed.

Mike's hand slid out from underneath Karen's black silk tank top. Her eyes were wide and her lips were swollen, as if she'd been kissing for a long time. Normally, her layered honey-brown hair was smooth and neat, but now it was tangled and wild.

"Luc!" Karen cried out. She looked from Mike to Luc and then back to Mike, who was now staring at Corinthe.

"What the hell are you doing?" Luc heard himself say. Everything seemed to be happening in slow motion. Even his voice sounded slow, distant.

Karen reached out to him. For a moment he focused on her hand, her perfectly manicured pink nails.

Mike sat on the bed with his polo shirt unbuttoned. There was pink lipstick smeared on the side of his chin.

Rage consumed Luc, dizzying, like a hot black tide. It roared through his body and he rocketed forward, grabbed Mike by the collar, and slammed him against the wall hard, driving an elbow against his windpipe. Karen screamed again. There were other voices, too—people shouting his name, a confusion of sounds . . .

And then a hand on his back: Corinthe, saying, "Wait."

The sound of her voice and the pressure of her touch pierced the dull fog in his brain, the blur of anger and hurt.

No more fighting. Not worth it. He released his hold on Mike, who slid down the wall and thudded to the ground. Karen immediately crouched down next to him.

"I didn't know you two were still together," Mike said, wiping the corner of his mouth. "She said—"

Karen cut him off and turned an accusatory stare at Luc.

"What the *hell* are you doing? What are you trying to prove?"

The venom in her voice caught him completely off guard.

"*Prove?* Jesus, Karen. You're my *girlfriend*—"

"Was. Was your girlfriend." Tears made her eyes shine in the soft light and a lump rose up in his throat. "You promised, Luc. Promised you'd show up on time, promised you'd actually *be* here. I can't do this anymore. You don't want to be with me and we both know it."

He swallowed. The anger slowly seeped away, leaving a deep hollow in his stomach. And, even deeper than that: A momentary lifting. A sense of relief.

It was only a flash. Then he felt empty again, as though he'd been carved out from inside.

"Karen . . ." He reached for her. She was everything he thought he wanted. Why couldn't he just love her? "Please."

"Leave, Luc." Karen choked back a sob. "Just go home."

He hesitated. Mike was watching him warily, as though he expected Luc to lunge for him at any second. But Luc just felt tired. Too tired to fight.

"Please," Karen said. Her voice was strangled.

People had crowded into the hallway, trying to get a look. The girl, Corinthe, was gone. Everyone was deathly quiet but he knew that soon the whispers would begin. Luc pushed through the crowd with more force than was necessary. By Monday, this would be all over school.

Perfect.

He needed to get out of there.

He pushed through the kitchen, avoiding Lily's triumphant gaze. He took the steps two at a time and gulped in lungfuls of cool night air when he burst onto the deck. He doubled over for a second, panting, fighting the sick feeling in his stomach. Jesus. He'd been a first-class asshole. He hadn't seen it coming.

"You okay, dude?" Tyler clapped a hand on Luc's shoulder and laughed. "Looks like you need to take it easy on the brews, man."

Luc yanked away from Tyler's touch and pushed his way through the people still laughing and partying on the deck. They'd know soon enough that the golden couple had broken up. News like that spread faster than a California wildfire.

As soon as he landed on the boardwalk, he started to run. Luc had no idea where he was going; he just needed to get as far away from everyone as possible.

There was little traffic on Marina Boulevard, and after a few minutes, he slowed to a walk. His lungs hurt, as if someone were squeezing them. The image of Karen and Mike swirled around in his head. Weirdly, he didn't feel mad anymore. He felt strangely detached, as if he were watching a movie from someone else's life. Already he regretted swinging at Mike.

Luc jammed his hands into his pockets and hurried across the street, cutting down Baker. Ahead, the lights from the Palace of Fine Arts reflected across the lagoon.

The place always felt peaceful to him. He and Jas used to go there a lot when they were younger. With

Mom. Luc hadn't been back since she left. His mother had loved the rotunda. She said it was a magical place. Jasmine would sit curled up in her lap, wide-eyed and silent, as she told stories about fairies and knights and beautiful princesses rescued in the nick of time.

After their mother left, Luc had stopped believing.

There was no such thing as happily ever after.

5

The Messenger was nestled in the palm of Corinthe's hand. Once outside, on the safety of the deck, she released it. It flew up and hummed past her, its flickering glow fading into darkness. It would make its way back to the lagoon to deliver the message: another destiny fulfilled. Corinthe leaned over the polished wooden railing of the lower deck and watched Luc until he disappeared into the darkness. She felt . . . troubled. Was that the word? Was that the *feeling*?

Humans, she thought, didn't understand that they were simply parts of a much vaster plan. Karen was fated to fall in love with someone else; Corinthe wished she could have explained it to the boy, Luc, so he would understand.

This had been an easy task — so easy, in fact, Corinthe

wondered why this particular fate had required the aid of an Executor. Corinthe had sought out Mike at the party and encouraged him to act on his feelings toward Karen. He had hesitated, sure that Karen already had a boyfriend. It took a persuasive conversation and one small lie to convince him otherwise.

Karen had been easier to sway. Her doubts had obviously been there even before Corinthe intervened.

"Where is he now?" Corinthe had asked, widening her eyes, imitating a look of *surprise* and *concern* (Was it concern? Or was it caring?) when Karen mentioned her boyfriend.

Mike and Karen had done the rest.

She grabbed a crystal flute of champagne and quickly shouldered her way out of the crowd. People were whispering and giggling, and several times she heard his— Luc's—name. It made her unaccountably *angry*—that was a word, and a feeling, she knew.

Humans concerned themselves with so much that didn't matter, with so much they had no stake in. Why?

As a Fate, she and her sister Fates had lived in perfect harmony. Each had a task and a role. They were like threads in a large tapestry. Each individual strand was insignificant, but together they made something whole and beautiful. That was the essence of Pyralis: balance, equilibrium. As an Executor, her job was equally clear: do as the Messengers instructed.

That was the beautiful thing about the universe… it was a vast mechanism, full of a billion tiny spinning parts, all of them moving in tandem, like one enormous clock with a vast pendulum that ticked back and forth between night and day, death and life.

And yet, the strange sensation crept through her even as she struggled to put a name to it. The urge to run after the boy, Luc, made her muscles tense. She wanted to know he would be okay. She wanted to comfort him in some way.

She had to take several deep breaths before she could relax. Her job was done. She was one step closer to going home, so why couldn't she just be happy and celebrate?

She took a long drink of the champagne as she made her way off the gangplank, enjoying the cool fizz of the liquid in her throat and the feel of the rough, still-warm planks underneath her feet. There were very few benefits to being exiled in Humana, but one of them was this: the vast collection of surfaces and sensations, the sting of new rain and the smooth bite of gravel. She remembered how the first time she'd ever had a drink of ice water it had brought a blinding pain to her head, directly behind her eyes—but it had made her laugh at the same time.

She turned in the direction the boy had gone, telling herself that she was not looking for him—only heading down to the water, where she could sit in the sand and watch the stars.

Lucas.

A nice human name—comfortable and rough at the same time, like the old blanket she used in her rooms underneath the rotunda. For ten years she'd been dwelling in this world, executing fates as the Unseen Ones willed, but none of the humans had made her feel this way before. What was different this time?

She had remembered the boy from the accident as soon as she'd seen him. Tasks rarely intertwined. At first, she thought surely something had gone wrong.

But something had rooted her in place, made it difficult to leave his side. She discovered that he was . . . *funny*. Humor was another human invention she still barely understood, but the boy had made her laugh, as she had that day when the ice water first slid down her throat and she had a sudden image of stars exploding behind her eyes.

She'd interacted with boys before over the course of her years in Humana. But it was work, duty, nothing more. Brief moments of contact: a push at the right moment, a whispered word, a communicated secret. And she had never actually spoken with a boy—not about anything important. Lucas had asked her about stars, almost as if he knew. . . .

He was different—he looked at *her* differently, too, as if he could see something behind her eyes.

When his arm almost brushed hers as he looked out onto the water, she had felt those electric sensations again, as she had at the scene of the accident when he had leaned in close to unbuckle her seat belt. In all her time in Humana, no one had affected her like that. What were the chances that she would see him twice in the span of two days?

The Unseen Ones guided everything in the universe. There was no chance. There was no coincidence, either.

Corinthe's hand still tingled from where she had touched him, not an unpleasant feeling at all. Luc had been funny and smart and nice to look at: His strong, lean body and handsome face. And that smile.

She had wondered before—about the woman at the flower market who had fallen in love with an older man on a bicycle, or the small boy with freckles who Corinthe had helped reunite with his mother—but she had known, instinctively, that she must never give in to the instinct to *know*. Knowing was for the Unseen Ones.

But Luc was different. She wanted to see him again. She had to. After she had checked to make sure he was okay, her success—her duty—would feel complete.

That was her excuse for pulling the knife free from its sheath. As she made her way toward the beach, she used the sharp tip to prick her finger.

Blood welled up from the small wound on her pointer finger. She squeezed until a single drop of blood fell into the glass half filled with champagne, then moved the glass in small circles until the liquid, now stained a faint pink, rolled around in the glass.

The surface went from clear to reflective, like a tiny mirror. An image wavered across its surface; then a boy materialized. *The* boy. He walked alone along a darkened street. The glow of streetlights illuminated his down-turned face. Every few minutes he looked up, his face momentarily visible—the set of his jaw, the dark eyes, and full lips—before hair obscured his face again. She saw him stop in front of an old apartment building and fumble with his keys. Corinthe overturned the liquid in the glass, letting it run into the sand.

He was okay.

She let the glass fall from her fingers into the water at the edge of the planks and strapped the knife back in place. She was exhausted. The physical strain of performing her tasks drained her energy too fast. Despite her success, Corinthe desperately wanted to recharge. Weakness scared her. She had never known weakness in Pyralis. Only peace and contentment. Not happiness, exactly, but even better: the absence of unhappiness.

The water lapped gently against the piles under her feet, and she slipped her shoes off. A tiny trickle of energy seeped up between the cracks in the rocks. The water would provide her enough strength to get back to the rotunda and then some.

She walked faster along the jagged rocks that lined the water, then lifted the edges of her skirt and started to run when she hit the main bay. Her feet flew, barely making a sound, and she could feel the sparkling earrings bounce against her neck.

The rocks came to an end and Corinthe leapt off toward the water ten feet below, arms wide, practically flying through the air, letting the colorful skirt ripple around her. She found herself laughing. Away from all the humans she could *think*, could focus on why she had to do these things.

It was all to get home. Back to her sister Fates singing in the twilight air, back to flowers that wove themselves into crowns and butterflies the color of moonlight.

She landed in a patch of beach grass, which pushed up out of the sandy dirt like long, sun-bleached hair. She jogged a few more steps before stopping at the edge of the water. The air was still and silent, the ocean ink dark. Off in the distance was the Golden Gate Bridge, lit vividly against the darkness. From this distance, the cars were no more than tiny specks of light, blinking in and out.

Corinthe set her worn purple ballerina flats on the beach and stepped into the water, letting the cold liquid lap at her feet. The stinging ocean water bit into her toes, and she soon moved back a few feet, onto the shore.

She sank to the ground, pulled her knees to her chest, and dug her toes into the gritty sand. The air blowing off the bay smelled raw, a mix of salt and night.

She had lied to Luc earlier. She did have a favorite star. The North Star. The guiding star.

She wasn't prepared when he asked her that question. No one, she realized, ever really spoke to her besides Miranda. She had felt that answering him honestly would be too intimate. Yet she almost had. She wanted to share it with him. Desperately, in fact.

Which was what kept her silent.

She began to stitch from the sky, feeling her way up and out, but the energy thrown from stars was too great—it burned, closing her out. Before she could disconnect, a flash of light exploded behind her eyes and pain seared her body.

Corinthe jerked back with a cry and landed hard on her back, the connection severed. The air left her body and she gasped, struggling to breathe. Over her head, a shooting star streaked across the darkness, followed by three more in random succession.

Her breath came out in harsh bursts as she sat up. Too close. There was a dark, acidic taste in her mouth: The taste of chaos, randomness, bursts of energy. Comets that tore through space, headed toward ultimate destruction, untamed and unpredictable. Free Radicals.

Whenever there was an aberration in the universe's delicate scheme, whenever the balance was disrupted, Free Radicals were born, like spontaneous explosions. Set off into space to float forever, they were enemies of order, the sole aspects of the universe that the Unseen Ones could not control. Like stars tearing across the sky, they were instruments of chaos and destruction and refused to remain fixed.

Once a Free Radical attached itself to another being, it would alter and morph the predetermined path of its host—just like vines that snaked themselves around vast trees, piercing the bark, feeding off its strength, slowly rendering the tree hollow and, eventually, toppling it.

Just then, Miranda materialized from the dark, as though emerging straight from the foam of the bay. She folded herself neatly into the sand, next to Corinthe, tucked her long white dress around her legs, and idly drew lines in the dirt between them.

Corinthe watched her Guardian from the corner of her eye. She seemed tense, on edge. She wouldn't stop moving.

"Is everything okay?" Corinthe asked.

Miranda turned to look at her. Then Corinthe realized she was wrong. Miranda wasn't on edge. She was happy. More than happy. What was the word? *Exhilarated*.

"Everything is exactly as it should be," Miranda said with a slow smile. "Your task has been completed, I assume?"

"Of course." It had been ten years since Corinthe's exile as an Executor, and not once had Corinthe failed to complete an assignment. "And *your* night? What were you up to this time . . . more trolley rides?"

Miranda's eyes flashed, but her smile did not fade. "My night went exceptionally well. And I have good news for you." Like a magician pulling cards, she produced a marble with a flourish. "This is your last task, Corinthe. And then you can go home."

"The *last* one?" Shock and joy swelled in her chest. Would she really be allowed to return to her home now? "Are you sure? How do you know?"

Miranda's smile became more playful. "I have my ways. You trust me, don't you?"

Corinthe nodded. Trust was another human concept, a concept she had never known or particularly needed before Humana. Miranda had *taught* her to trust.

The marble was cool in Corinthe's hand. She thought it felt even heavier than usual. She gazed at it in the soft moonlight, could see the shadows inside it shifting, resolving. The marble seemed particularly cloudy, which meant the fate had been more disturbed by chance than most. Whatever the job was, it would need her full focus.

Inside the marble's swirling dark colors, a hand became visible. Corinthe's hand—it had to be; because it held her knife. She squinted and held the marble closer. The figure in front of the knife was backlit by the rising sun, featureless.

Though she could not see a face, one thing was clear. Someone would die.

A chill went through her. Someone would die by *her* hand. Usually she only assisted in orchestrating deaths: accidents, things that would be called *unlucky*. But Corinthe knew there was no such thing as luck.

Though she'd trained for it, she'd never actually been called upon to kill. She'd never seen *herself* in a marble before. Never had her own future been closely entwined with a human's.

She swallowed against the rising wave of panic. She understood now. The Unseen Ones were testing her. This was the task that would prove she was ready to return home. She was practiced and strong. She couldn't fail now.

"When?" Corinthe asked, hoping that Miranda couldn't see how nervous she was.

"In the morning, at the first light of dawn."

"So soon?" Corinthe couldn't stop herself from saying. She had to kill someone in less than five hours?

"You're not eager to go home?" Miranda frowned.

"Of course I am," Corinthe said. A tiny spark of hope ignited deep inside her chest. All these years she'd never allowed herself to hope too much, just in case. Was it really possible? Would she finally be allowed to return to Pyralis?

The light in Miranda's eyes shifted. She grinned again, just enough to reveal white teeth, sharp as knives. Her right incisor extended down farther, sharper than the rest. She reached out and ran her hand over Corinthe's cheek. "We have done so well all these years. We deserve this. *You* deserve it."

Corinthe nodded, not trusting herself to speak.

Miranda reached into her pocket. "I have something else for you. I've been waiting a long time, until the time was right, to give it to you."

She pulled out a long chain and slipped it over Corinthe's head. On it was a tarnished silver oval the size and shape of a walnut that hung low over Corinthe's chest.

Corinthe loved pretty jewelry, especially things that sparkled. This necklace was so plain it bordered on ugly.

Still, a gift—even an unattractive one—was a gift.

"Thank you," she said politely, as she had learned was customary in Humana.

Miranda laughed. "It's not meant to be pretty." She turned it over. On the back of the oval was a tiny button.

When pushed, the walnut split in half on a tiny hinge, opening; a tinny music began to play, and the figurine of a ballerina began to pirouette.

Longing, fierce and hot, rose in Corinthe's chest. She knew that melody. It was the same one Miranda hummed every day.

"What—what is it?" Corinthe's heart pounded wildly against her ribs and threatened to burst right out of her chest. The ballerina spun, flashing, in the dark; she couldn't look away. "Where did you get it?"

"This is the compass that will guide you to the thing you want the most," Miranda said. "When you find yourself inside the Crossroad, the dancer will stop and point you in the right direction."

The thing she wanted most?

To return to Pyralis.

Home.

"Don't take it off. Above all, don't lose it. It's the only way to find your way through the Crossroad when the time comes."

Corinthe turned the small music box over and over in her hand but couldn't see any mechanisms that made the ballerina spin. "I have to cross more than one world to return?" The thought of navigating the Crossroad, something only the Messengers did, made her stomach flip. She was certainly strong enough, but still—the Crossroad was dark and lawless. The danger of it was deep and psychological; it mirrored your own state.

When she'd first been pulled through the Crossroad

into Humana, her heart had been full of chaos and confusion. She had felt as if she were getting violently torn apart. But now she was older: determined and capable. She'd earned the right to go home. . . .

"Will you become the Guardian of another Executor when I'm gone?" Corinthe's voice cracked a little. She would miss Miranda, who'd been her only friend for so long.

Miranda touched Corinthe's face briefly. "I don't know what will happen next."

Corinthe felt a tug of concern. Miranda had been almost like that special human thing: a mother. Corinthe hated the idea that Miranda might be alone after she left.

"Don't worry." Miranda smiled, as if she could see Corinthe's thoughts. "Everything will be as it should. You're ready. And as long as you have the compass, you'll find your way."

Corinthe closed her fist around the locket. Holding it in her hand, solid and real, loosened the tightness in her chest. She could travel the Crossroad. A grin spread over her face. It was finally happening. The locket was suddenly the most beautiful thing she'd ever seen in her entire life.

She jumped up and then pulled Miranda up with her.

"Shall we walk together?" Miranda said. "One last time, to celebrate? Then I, too, have an errand to perform."

"In a little while," Corinthe said. She just wanted a few minutes alone to think. To prepare for the task at hand.

"Don't be too long," Miranda said. "And, Corinthe?"

Corinthe turned to her Guardian. Miranda's eyes were as dark as the ocean. The wind blew her hair around and above her, making it appear as though she was crowned with a ring of writing serpents. She smiled, and her eyes flashed momentarily green—the vivid color of a firefly's wings.

"I'll miss you," Miranda said. "When you're gone."

6

"They won't support what you're trying to do."

Miranda ignored the girl's voice. "One cappuccino, please," she said to the barista behind the counter. Miranda didn't even drink coffee, but she enjoyed Fiend, the narrow, wood-paneled coffee shop in the Mission filled with a collection of mismatched stools and mismatched people: pink-haired, pierced and punctured, tattooed, and stinking of various human smells. It was chaotic and disorganized and everything she loved.

While she was waiting for her coffee, the girl moved to stand beside her. Miranda didn't have to turn to know exactly what she looked like. Dark hair, woven through with strips of canvas, tangled against her exposed back.

"Tess," Miranda said, trying to keep her voice light. "How have you been?"

"Why do you continue to pursue this path, Miranda?" Tess persisted in a low voice. "The Tribunal has a carefully laid-out plan. You know that. And you're jeopardizing everything. They've spoken out against you. No one will even risk your company." Tess placed a hand on Miranda's arm, so that Miranda was forced to look at her. "No one will aid you, either."

Miranda took a deep breath. She didn't want to lose her temper. "So why are *you* here, then?"

"To try and reason with you." Tess spat out the words. Now Miranda saw that Tess, too, was trying to keep from losing her temper. The idea almost made her smile. "Do you have any idea what this will do to us? It could reveal our presence. Set us back millennia . . ."

Miranda shrugged. "My issue is with the Unseen Ones. How the Tribunal is affected is not my concern."

For a second, Tess's eyes blazed, going from the dark black of a polished stone to a pure, hot white, sparking with anger. "If you do this, you will force the other Radicals against you. Is that what you want?"

"One cappuccino," droned the girl behind the counter.

Miranda took the cup that was offered to her and licked a bit of foam from her finger. Garbage. But she enjoyed the ritual of it. Tess was watching her, but Miranda unhurriedly emptied sugar into her coffee, stirred carefully, tasted again.

"My plan will work, and then *they* will be forced to admit that I was right all along," Miranda said. "There will be chaos in Pyralis, Tess. There will be *blood*. One of their own carries, even now, the seeds of destruction back to its shores. Then we can rule like we should. The Tribunal wants us to wait . . . but for what, Tess? We've been waiting too long already. It's our time now." She might have been born from chaos, but she wouldn't die like a beast, driven to her knees in the dust like a dog.

She would choose. She *had* chosen; she had chosen the day she learned of Corinthe's existence and decided to launch the plan that was now ten years in the making.

"They know what's best . . . ," Tess began to say, but Miranda waved her excuse away with one hand and walked toward a small wooden table in the corner, covered with white ring stains like a series of interlinked planets. Tess trailed behind and took the seat across from her. "So you're willing to sacrifice an innocent life for the chance to prove the Tribunal wrong?" she hissed, leaning across the table so that no one else could hear.

Miranda steeled herself against the flush of guilt. She wasn't sacrificing anyone, not really. Corinthe's fate was to die. Miranda was giving her the chance to save herself. If Corinthe chose to kill the boy, she would live. She would effectively swap fates.

And if Corinthe, the only Fallen Fate in history, chose to go against her fate, it might be enough to upset the balance.

Then the Free Radicals could regain what they had lost. There had been a time when Miranda had had the power to tear holes in the universe, to bring time to its knees and make planets spin backward.

She could still almost taste it . . . how it felt to hold the universe like one of those precious marbles in the palm of her hand . . . how it felt to smash whole worlds to pieces and watch new creations rise from their dust.

Tess had been one such creation. The closest thing to an offspring a Free Radical could have.

And Miranda knew it was Tess's daughter-like loyalty that kept her here, in this cafe, continuing to urge Miranda to return to the Tribunal.

Now Tess shook her head as though she was reading Miranda's mind. Perhaps she was. "I may not be able to come again." She almost sounded sad, and Miranda, surprised, turned around. Tess's eyes were dark again, full of shadows. "If I can't change your mind, we will be enemies."

The last time Miranda had stood before the council, she had pleaded with them to listen. Begged, almost. The threads of the universe were so tightly woven that the efforts of the Free Radicals made only tiny tears in the fabric. They were ineffectual, they were *failing*, and they would soon suffocate, crushed out by the control, by the regularity, by the stiff-necked balance that forced everything in one direction.

She had a plan to take back control.

They refused. The Tribunal wanted to coexist with the Unseen Ones and were too shortsighted to realize that by denying their very nature, they were walking into their own extinction.

Now the Radicals were dying faster than they could

be born. As they moved through space unattached, their powers gradually dissipated, like water evaporating in the sun. This was why Rhys had become so weak — his exile was draining him, allowing his powers to simply seep away. This was also why the Tribunal had so much sway: they knew that only by banding together and combining their energy could they survive in a universe that was increasingly dominated by order instead of chaos.

And it worked. The Tribunal was just like a black hole — luring other Radicals into it, terrifying in its strength. Miranda knew that the biggest risk she could ever take was going against the Tribunal. They were the one force in the universe that could easily destroy her, and her powers were diminishing gradually, just like Rhys's. She knew she couldn't survive on her own forever — no Radical could.

Two could, however. She'd forged a partnership once, born out of ambition and a mutual desire for revenge. *Ford*. He was a Radical of tremendous power. Together, they had survived without the Tribunal. But the Tribunal had gotten to him long ago, and now Miranda had no allies left.

Corinthe was her only hope. She'd banked everything on Corinthe.

She had escaped her exile in the Land of the Two Suns, only to live miserably in Humana, virtually a slave, disrupting the balance whenever she could, creating tiny moments of chaos out of order.

A small, meager, pathetic way for a Radical to exercise her powers, and she didn't even know if her plan would work, but she knew she had to try. She thought of Corinthe's face, and the music box turning and turning forever unless the girl figured out what she wanted. A horrible destiny: gripped by her own indecision, compelled to spin forever at the hands of those who wished to control everything. Miranda would not be a part of it.

"Then we will be enemies." Miranda spoke gently. "I couldn't stop it even if I wanted to."

Tess shook her head. She seemed about to argue, but at last she just said: "Goodbye, then." Tess turned and glided out of the coffee shop onto the San Francisco street. Miranda turned away so she wouldn't have to see Tess disappear.

"Goodbye," Miranda whispered.

She waited for a minute, then walked into the street holding her coffee, feeling its warmth seep into her hands. Then she dumped it out in the nearest gutter.

Soon, if everything went as planned, this would all be over.

7

Went to the Marina. Lost something.

Luc stared at the note he had found tossed carelessly on his pillow. He tried to keep himself from screaming, or hitting something. He'd forbidden Jasmine to go out. He'd made her swear. And she'd ignored him.

What the hell was so important at this hour?

The apartment had been dark when he let himself in. No surprise there. His dad was snoring on the couch. No surprise there, either. Luc couldn't remember the last time his dad had mobilized himself to make it to his bedroom instead of just passing out in front of the TV.

For a long time, Luc had hoped that one day he would snap out of it and start being a father again. Then, sophomore year, after Luc had put a fist through a locker—to be fair, he'd been swinging for Drew O'Connell's head;

Drew had been spreading rumors that thirteen-year-old Jasmine had given him a striptease in the Taco Bell parking lot—he'd been forced to see a therapist for six months.

The guy was a total prick—once Luc had even caught him sleeping during a session, and his breath always made the office smell like tuna fish—but one thing Dr. Asswipe had taught him was this: *Give up the wish.*

His dad would never snap out of it. *Give up the wish.* His mom wasn't coming back to life. *Give up the wish.*

He would always feel alone. *Give up the wish.*

Luc was on his own if he wanted to find Jas. Damn it. He punched her number into his phone and waited. When it rang and went to voice mail, he hit *call end.*

There was no way he'd sleep without knowing if Jas was okay. He crumpled the paper in his fist and stormed back to his room. A dark blue varsity soccer sweatshirt hung over a chair, and he yanked it over his head. He jerked the laces of his boots tight and then stood up, pulling a Giants cap down around his shaggy black hair.

Why did she have to go to the Marina at three in the morning? The only people who hung out there at this hour were dealers and addicts.

She had probably gone to see T.J. If she got messed up tonight . . .

Luc was going to kill him. Luc was going to kill *her.*

As if his night hadn't been messed up enough already.

Luc tried Jasmine's cell again and swore aloud when

it went straight to voice mail. Of course. Why should tonight be any different? Jasmine was always full of excuses.

Just like their mother.

Training made it easy to run the four miles to the Marina; he cut through the Presidio and made it in record time. Shoving his hands deeper into the pocket of his hoodie, he headed up to the Marina. Every creeping, creaking noise set him on edge. He could take care of himself in a fight, but he'd be at a huge disadvantage in the dark, between unlit buildings.

Three more blocks down and the buildings thinned out. Across Marina Boulevard, Luc could see lights reflecting off the water. Traffic was nonexistent this time of morning, and he jogged to the entrance of the harbor.

A breeze blew off the ocean, and Luc gulped in a lungful of fresh salty air. The quiet was broken only by the occasional metallic clang of the moorings.

During the day, tourists crowded onto shiny sailboats for gourmet picnic lunches and expensive wine tours of the bay. People packed the boardwalk and the shops along the water's edge. Kids licked melting ice cream cones while joggers darted between families pushing strollers. Everything was loud and bright and full of excitement. Alive.

He remembered he had taken Jas here when they were kids; a passing carnival had set up camp at the Marina. They'd skateboarded together through the crowds, pissing everybody off, laughing like maniacs. At the shooting gallery, Jas had spun suddenly and aimed the water straight for his hat. It had nearly taken out his eye, but man, it was funny.

It was the first time she'd laughed since their mom left.

So much had changed since that day.

And now, just before dawn, the Marina had changed, too.

This wasn't the yacht club where Karen's parents moored. It was darker, more dangerous. His footsteps echoed loudly. Security lights twisted the shadows into spindly, inky fingers. Addicts huddled under the piers. The ones in the throes of a high weren't too bad. It was the ones coming down, aching for that next fix, who were dangerous. More animal than human. Every time a chain clanged against metal or a boat bumped the pier, Luc's shoulders tensed.

A thin fog hung over the Marina, curling around the deserted buildings. He jammed his hands into the pockets of his sweatshirt and ducked his head. The air was thick with salt. The Marina was huge. He had no idea how he would find Jas, but he refused to leave before he had.

He caught a glimpse of someone huddled in the doorway darkness near the water. A haggard face looked up at him. A woman. Luc felt his throat go dry. A frantic pulse beat in his temple. When the woman looked up and hissed at him, baring yellowed teeth, she looked almost like a wild animal.

His mother was long dead, but he couldn't stop imagining her like that.

God, this had been the suckiest night ever.

First Karen, then Jas.

He headed down toward the first slip, scanning the moored boats, all of them bobbing almost imperceptibly in the water. When he reached the end of the pier, the vast bay spread out before him, the stars reflected on its smooth, glassy surface. He looked up by habit, to the northeast sky, until he found Andromeda, partly obscured by low-hanging clouds.

Jas's favorite constellation gave him a small measure of comfort. He felt closer to her by just having it in his sights.

There were seven long slips, and it took almost two hours to walk up and down each, peering into darkened boats that bobbed on the water. His eyelids felt like sandpaper scratching across his eyeballs, but adrenaline kept his feet moving across the battered wood of the docks.

By the time he got to the last slip, the sky to the east was just starting to lighten at the horizon. At the edge of the last pier, Luc paused and stared into the dark where three sailboats bobbed gently on the surface. He thought he saw a shadow move across the largest boats.

"Jasmine," he called.

No one answered. He stepped onto the deck of the first boat, the smallest. He grabbed the rail to keep his balance when it gently swayed from side to side because of his weight.

He took several small steps toward the cabin. Thank God the Marina was empty. The last thing he needed was to get busted by the cops for breaking and entering.

A groan pierced the silence, and Luc froze. All thoughts of sleep vanished in a rush of fear.

"Jas." His voice was swallowed up by the silence. Even the waves seemed to have stopped moving.

A tremendous crack splintered the air. He barely had time to register the mast flying toward his head before he leapt out of the way. Over the railing. Ice-cold water closed over his head, and for a terrifying moment, Luc wasn't sure which way was up.

Struggling, he kicked his legs as hard as he could, twisting around, desperate to find the surface, choking on the salty water. His clothing turned leaden, sucking him under. His feet hit the rocky bottom, and he shoved hard, bursting to the surface and dragging in a deep breath of air.

Coughing up seawater, he swam toward the pier and used it to guide him toward shore until his feet touched bottom. When he was able to stand in the waist-deep water, he looked back at the boat. The sun peeked over the horizon and chased the mist away, revealing the snapped mast, which had crashed across the deck where he'd stood only moments before.

Christ, I could have been killed. Adrenaline pumped through his veins, clearing his head.

The water glittered like a million diamonds, sparkling in the first stray rays of new daylight. How could it look so peaceful when he'd come within inches of death just moments ago? He stood up, his waterlogged sweatshirt iron-heavy. He took it off and tied it around his waist.

Masts didn't just snap like that, like toothpicks. The back of his neck prickled. An accident. A stupid wrong-place, wrong-time near disaster. It had to be.

The icy water lapped around his shins and thighs, and he shivered. If he didn't get out of the water, he'd freeze.

Before he had a chance to turn around, someone slammed into his back, plunging him face-first back under the water. He fought hard, twisting free, using the ground to push himself up and out of the attacker's grasp.

The moment he broke the surface, he spun, fists up and ready. He blinked hard to clear the stinging seawater from his eyes, but when he did, he had to blink again.

Corinthe.

She'd changed her clothes. She wore faded jeans that hugged her hips, a simple black T-shirt, and a fitted cotton hoodie, unzipped and now soaked through. He couldn't keep his eyes from running up and over her body.

Light caught on the dangling crystal earrings she still wore from the party, and they drew his gaze to her neck. To that curve where it met her shoulder. He swallowed hard. She'd looked hot last tonight, but now, against the early morning sun, she was more than that. Otherworldly.

"You!" she gasped. *She'd* been the one attacking *him*, so why did she look so surprised?

"Christ," he panted. He pushed his cap back off his face. "You almost—"

A knife flashed in her hand and she lunged at him. Before he could move, his back was pressed against an unyielding wooden pillar supporting the dock, and her knife pushed against his throat. She used her body to hold him there, and he didn't dare swallow for fear it would force the blade into his skin.

Heat radiated between their bodies, a startling contrast to the icy water swirling around them. He realized his hands were gripping her waist, holding on to her as if they were about to kiss. He watched the black of her eyes slowly eat up the pale irises. Her breathing came out in bursts of warm air that tickled his chin.

She moved a fraction of an inch closer. Her lips parted. All he had to do was move just a little bit and . . . God, he had to be crazy. She had a knife to his throat and all he could think about was how her lips would taste.

Insanity. It had to be.

But he wanted to kiss her more than anything right that second. Press his lips against the soft curve of her neck. He pulled her hips forward instinctively, molding them against his body.

Corinthe made a sound deep in her throat, and his pulse leapt. Fire raced through his veins.

She moved closer and the knife nicked his throat.

Luc grabbed her wrist.

"What the *hell* are you doing?" he asked, breathing hard. He tightened his grip and spun her arm around, pinning her with her back to his chest. She jammed her leg back and twisted her foot between his legs, hooking him on the ankle. When she twisted her body left and kicked out with her foot, Luc lost his balance.

Instead of letting her go, though, he took her down, under the water with him in a tangle of arms and legs. Corinthe kicked out and made contact with his shin, and even underwater, the jolt shot up his leg.

He fought to keep hold of her, and she fought harder to get away from him.

His lungs burned. The second his arms loosened, she was gone, and he surged above the water, gasping for air.

He wiped the water off his face and saw her a few feet away, poised to attack. Wet hair clung to her cheeks, and she was focused on his face. She held the knife casually, and it finally hit him: this was easy for her.

Self-preservation kicked in then, fierce and hot. She was trying to kill him. Clearly, she had lost her mind. Maybe the accident really *had* messed with her head. He lunged suddenly, grabbing the knife and driving his shoulder into her body. She stumbled backward, and he ran.

He sloshed through the shallows and scrambled over the rocks lining the shoreline. Once back on solid land, he tossed the knife as far as he could and sprinted across an empty parking lot. Water squelched in his boots, and his footsteps pounded loudly, echoing in the still dawn air. *Thud, thud, thud.*

He could hear footsteps behind him, too, half as loud but twice as fast.

No way.

He looked over his shoulder. She followed him, too close for his comfort.

His wet clothes made it hard to move. There was no way he could keep running. Not fast enough, anyway. Already his breath was rasping in his chest; his heart felt as if it would explode.

Ten feet ahead of him was a line of run-down apartment buildings. He shoved the door of the closest one and was relieved that it swung open, practically popping off its hinges.

He took the rickety stairs two at a time, not sure where he was going. There must be a fire escape off the roof, or at least a room where he could lock the door. Corinthe must have lost her mind—or she was having some kind of a bad drug trip. The faster he got away from her, the better.

He ran without thinking. The stairs stopped and he burst through a door, onto the roof. His lungs burned as he gasped for air. The fire escape was on the far side of the roof, but the only part that remained was a small portion of the rail. The ladder, the steps—everything else had been dismantled or fallen away.

It was a sheer drop straight down to the alley.

Back down the stairs, then. He yanked the rusty door back open and froze.

Corinthe.

God, she was fast.

She wasn't even winded. Her breathing was slow and deliberate, and she took several steps toward him as he backed up, raising both hands so she would know he wasn't going to hurt her. The door slammed with a bang and he jumped. Shit.

"Look. Look. Whatever's going on—we can talk about it, okay?" Luc didn't even know what he was saying. He needed time. Time to figure out a plan, time to talk her down.

Corinthe stopped and cocked her head. She had retrieved the knife from the beach, but at least she wasn't leveling it at him. She watched him with intense focus, her gaze moving with each twitch of his body. It made him feel extremely exposed, vulnerable. Jesus Christ. Her eyes were practically purple.

"Can you talk to me? Can you tell me what the hell is going on?"

She wasn't coming at him anymore. Maybe it was working—the talking. He had a sudden memory of Dr. Asswipe telling him to *talk out his feelings,* and he felt the wild urge to laugh. What he needed now was a weapon and an escape route.

"Whatever I did to offend you, I'm sorry, okay?" He watched her carefully. He had assumed she might be on something, but her eyes were too lucid, her movements too steady. So what did that leave?

Batshit crazy?

"Look—last night and this morning have kind of

sucked for me, okay? I've been looking for my sister. If I scared you, I'm sorry."

The thought occurred to him that maybe Corinthe had been sleeping on one of the boats in the Marina. Was she a runaway? Maybe he had startled her and she had come after him in self-defense. Assumed he was going to turn her in.

It had to be a misunderstanding.

Now that the hard lines of her face had softened, she looked like the girl he had talked to at the party. Luc allowed himself to relax just a little. There was some need in her eyes—something he couldn't identify. He wanted to put his arms around her; he wanted to tell her it would be okay.

Great, now he was feeling sorry for the crazy girl who just tried to stick a knife in his gut.

"Can I walk you back to the Marina?" he asked gently. "Is there someone I can call? Someone at home?"

At the word *home*, her shoulders went rigid again. She sprang forward, the knife pointed at his chest, and he barely had time to react. She forced him to back up until he was almost at the edge of the roof.

He glanced over his shoulder, feeling a moment of swinging vertigo. Wind buffeted the clothing clipped to the lines strung between the buildings. Jumping was out of the question. There was another building ten or fifteen feet away. He'd never make it over the gap.

Anticipate your opponent. Look for an opening. His coach's barked commands fired through his head. But there *were* no openings. He dodged left suddenly, then right, tried to get past her, but she anticipated every move he made.

She obviously knew what she was doing. The door to the stairs was twenty feet away, but he'd have to get by her first. Which meant exposing his back to her if he made a run for it.

She raised her knife again, pointing it at his chin.

Luc's pulse was roaring. He turned his head. He had no choice. He'd have to jump. He spotted a string of shirts and pants that hung motionless on one of the criss-crossed laundry lines despite the stiff breeze blowing off the ocean, as though they were a photograph. Goose bumps sprang up over his skin and the back of his neck tightened, as if someone were squeezing it.

That was his way out.

A certainty powered through his body, just like it did when he was on the field. He didn't know how he knew it, but it was as clear as his own name.

Jump.

Luc turned back toward Corinthe. She paused, and a gust of wind lifted strands of her hair, making it dance around her head chaotically. For a second, insanely, he wondered how it would feel to have her body pressed up against him one more time. When her hair settled back down, he noticed a tiny light darting about near her head, its glow buzzing softly in and out. He could swear it was a firefly.

"Who are you really?" he asked.

When she didn't respond, he took a small, involuntary step forward. The soft grayish-purple color of her eyes was unlike anything he'd ever seen, and he couldn't keep from staring. Her pupils dilated and the color changed, deepening to a wild violet hue that reminded him of dark storm clouds in a summer sky. The air between them felt charged with something electric.

"I'm sorry," she said, and for a moment he thought she looked troubled.

It finally registered: she was dead serious about hurting him.

Luc stepped up onto the ledge. His heart raced so hard he thought it might explode from his chest. Corinthe stared at him with narrowed eyes, releasing a small bit of air between her lips, a cross between a hiss and a sigh. It was as though she knew what she had to do but wanted to stop herself. And then her eyes went cold, her body tensed, and she arched her arm back. The blade glinted in the sunlight.

She threw the knife straight at him.

He launched off the edge of the roof. The world seemed to slow down, and for several seconds he felt as if he were flying, weightless, through the air.

Then his Giants cap whipped off and sound rushed back like a freight train. Luc knew he was falling. He reached desperately for the clothesline, stretched his arms and fingers toward it.

Panic, white-hot and blinding, raced through him.

His fingers brushed the edges of a pink blouse, and

then they were empty. The wind was rushing, roaring, all around him. He wasn't going to make it.

Suddenly, he couldn't see. Everything had broken apart into mists and vapor. He spun through the nothingness, half aware, wondering with a sudden pang if this was what death felt like.

8

Corinthe watched Luc disappear in midair. She felt as though she'd swallowed a mouthful of dust. The only thing left of him was the black-and-orange Giants baseball cap, sopping wet on a dark corner of the roof.

She knew this roof. The way the water tower's shadow grew across the south corner. The way the blacktop looked a little like it had steam rising from it where the early sun hit it. This was the place where she'd first appeared in Humana ten years ago, by the gateway she'd passed through as a child.

This was the way to the Crossroad.

The memory of it made her shiver. She'd been plucked from Pyralis and pulled through a swirling, misty darkness—tumbling through the chaos for what had seemed like hours. Every muscle in her body felt stretched to its limit, and she knew the Unseen Ones were angry, pulling her apart in every direction to see if she'd break.

Corinthe had never felt such violence or confusion, and when she landed on this roof, her body ached. Her lips were cracked, her dress torn, and a matted nest of hair replaced the precious braid she'd worn in Pyralis. This was the same roof where Miranda had found her, cowering from the sun.

She hadn't been back since—hadn't known where to find it—until now. It couldn't all be a random chance. Being a Fate had taught her one thing: there were no coincidences. Perhaps the Unseen Ones were testing her.

When she'd looked into Luc's brown eyes in the ocean this morning and realized that she would have to kill him, she'd felt as though the water had opened up momentarily, about to swallow her in darkness.

The way he had looked at her, the hunger in his eyes, made something ache deep inside of her. His square jaw. His strange half grin. That stupid Bay Sun Breakers T-shirt, revealing broad shoulders and strong arms.

She was an Executor, and feelings had no business in her life, but for one second, she wondered what it would be like to kiss him.

How could a boy she'd met only twice before make her feel like this—hot and cold and shivery, both sick to her stomach and full of adrenaline? These were human sensations. In all her time exiled to Humana, no one had affected her quite like Luc did.

It didn't matter.

It couldn't matter.

But why did it have to be *his* fate? That part still bothered her, even though she had never questioned Miranda, or any of the other fates she had had to execute before. It was why she had hesitated when she could have slashed her knife across his throat and been done.

What did it *mean*?

Was it because she hadn't stopped thinking about him, thinking that somehow, he had been chosen for her? But that was insane. Her thoughts didn't matter. That was the whole point. She must do as the marbles dictated.

She had to follow him, to find him. The Unseen Ones didn't care about reasoning or second-guessing; all they would see was that she had failed, just when she was so close to being restored to her home.

Her fingers found the locket around her neck, and she pulled it out from under her shirt in preparation. She closed her eyes. There could be no confusion, anger, or helplessness. Only one thing: determination. She would enter the gateway to the Crossroad and find him. She backed up so she could get a running start. She sucked in a lungful of air, trying to calm her pulse.

Then she ran.

Her boots thundered across the roof. Pushing up and off the small ledge, she launched herself into the air. Wind tunneled straight through her, making her gasp.

This is going to hurt.

Suddenly, she remembered the face of a terrified

woman; she'd been standing on the Golden Gate Bridge, swaying like a reed in the wind. About to jump. It had been Corinthe's job to catch her, to pull her back from the edge. She remembered how the woman had suddenly turned and started to weep, how she had thrown her arms around Corinthe, squeezing until Corinthe's chest hurt.

Corinthe had pulled away. She had not understood the touch, the rush of feelings that had overwhelmed her.

I'm sorry. The thought flashed through her mind but then was gone as a sharp burst of pain took away her breath.

Nothing else mattered.

Corinthe fell into the swirling chaos of lights and sound that was the Crossroad. Inhuman noises echoed around her: screams and howls, the laments of all the corrupted or lost souls that had been banished to the spaces between worlds. She felt as though her head would explode. She fell, tumbling out of control, into vast emptiness.

She would stay lost in the Crossroad forever unless she could calm down. Concentrate. Breathe. Still gripping the locket, she pulled at the clasp and the top flipped open. The ballerina immediately began to spin to the tinny melody.

Corinthe's heart skipped a beat when the dancer began to slow. She watched in fascination. Where would it point? To home, or to Luc?

She closed her eyes and imagined the soft moss and the twilight air buzzing with fireflies, the smell of flowers in the Great Gardens, the stone statues that jealously guarded the river that flowed into all time.

No. Corinthe wanted to go home, but to be *accepted* there required one thing: killing Lucas. She focused on him instead—his black hair, the square jaw, the way he'd held her waist when they were both knee-deep in the water.

Her eyes fluttered open and the winds lessened. She felt more stable as she willed the ballerina to find him. It slowed to a stop, finally pointing to a coil of greenish-blue mist. It wound its way to the right and Corinthe leaned in that direction. The howls began to recede; the pounding in her head began to ease.

The ground solidified under her feet. The mist ebbed, until it swirled around her legs like a lazy cat. She cautiously moved forward as the fog dissipated, searching for the right doorway. Thousands of worlds connected at the Crossroad, and if she chose wrong, she might be lost forever. *He* might be lost forever. Lucas.

Humans entering gateways and traveling the Crossroad between worlds went against the very laws of the universe. Only Messengers and Executors were allowed to travel them. One thing was clear: it was her fault Luc had gotten away.

But the coil of mist still hung faintly in the air, and she could detect his human smell—something slightly spicy but soft, like cloves. The dim outline of trees took shape in front of her. Soon she had cleared the mist, and she found herself in a forest. The air felt thick and warm and humid on her skin. Almost instantly, she began to sweat.

Corinthe had seen the world of the Blood Nymphs on the great stone maps in the garden of Pyralis, which depicted the whole layout of the universe. The stones, like the universe itself, would constantly shift and morph, but she knew each world had a different relationship to the center of things.

She didn't know exactly where this particular world existed, only that it was far from Pyralis Terra. It was dominated by forest, and beyond that, an endless mist.

The other Fates had told stories: wisdom collected through the ages from the marbles, from the whispers that reached them through the Crossroad. The Nymphs who lived here were parasites, and they were very protective of their forest. Of *this* forest. They nested in the branches of the living *Salix babylonica* trees and fed off the blood of the sentient creatures.

The sister tree of the *Salix babylonica* grew in Humana. They called it the weeping willow, as though the suffering of their kind could be felt even across the worlds. She brushed her fingers through a curtain of wispy tendrils so thin and delicate they looked like they might break off with only a gentle pull. The branches stirred, moved closer to her touch. A stem curled around her wrist, tugging gently, as if the tree wanted to play.

Corinthe knew better. While the trees appeared to be victims of the Nymphs, they could be as cruel as their bloodsucking masters. She slowly reached for her blade and remembered too late that it had disappeared into the void with Lucas.

She disentangled the vine carefully from her wrist

and took several steps away from the tree. Angry hissing filled the air and the tree shook, the ends of its branches lashed out like whips. A high-pitched whine sounded behind her. Corinthe spun around.

Nothing.

Over her head, perched among the vast canopy of branches, which barely allowed any sunlight to penetrate, dozens of Blood Nymphs were watching her, their skin different shades of blue and green, so that they blended perfectly into the shadowed branches.

The whine sounded behind her again. This time when she swung around, a Nymph stood only a few feet away.

This one was pale yellow and virtually transparent, with spidery red veins crisscrossing the surface of her skin. Her flowing hair matched the color of her skin. Her eyes were slanted and lacked eyelids; they were like amethyst marbles. The Nymph hummed again, a sound that reminded Corinthe of the whine of an enormous mosquito. It made her skin crawl.

Above them, the others joined in, and soon the air filled with a crescendo of high-pitched echoes. The noise made pain blaze in Corinthe's head. The trees swayed as if dancing along to their song.

"I'm not here to harm you. I'll be quick." Corinthe hoped that the Nymphs could not smell her fear. They fell silent again, watching her. Did they know what she was? Could Executors even perform fates here? Could she defend herself, if she needed to?

In Humana, Corinthe was an Executor. Here, though,

the lines were blurred. She had never harmed another living creature of her own will, didn't even know if she *could*. The ramifications could be catastrophic. She had lost a single marble and had been banished to Humana for it. What kind of punishment might the death of a Nymph, an unfated killing, bring?

Several more pairs of glowing amethyst eyes peered down at her through the canopy of leaves. How many were up there, watching her, waiting?

Corinthe backed slowly away from the Nymph, glad that it did not follow. Then she quickly ducked down a pathway. The Nymphs would still watch her, but Corinthe was more worried that they would find Luc before she did.

Females who wandered into this world might end up as the Blood Nymphs were—parasites, killers, transformed into the pale, evil creatures with their sharp teeth and lidless eyes. But males? Males were teased, tormented, and bled slowly, skin pierced by sharp teeth in a thousand different places. Then they were fed to the trees.

She pushed on, faster now. She had to find Luc before something happened to him. He had to die by her hand. That was what the marble had shown. Her knife.

There was no other way to interpret it.

Her fate *depended* on his.

If she did not find Luc, if she did not kill him the way the marble had indicated—the hand, the knife— she would never be allowed to return to Pyralis Terra.

Just thinking about her home sent such a strong wave of yearning through her that she almost stumbled.

Dozens of paths spiraled in different directions, dead-ended or changed orientation suddenly, only to curl around and return to where they had started. If Corinthe got lost in the mazes, she would be unlikely to find her way out and would be left to the fickle impulses of the Nymphs.

Corinthe stopped and closed her eyes. A light breeze blew tendrils of hair across her neck, and a burst of a sweet, exotic scent filled her lungs. The acrid harshness of Humana began to fade from her thoughts, and her old senses returned, sharpened. A subtle pattern emerged in her mind and she followed it, eyes still closed. Sounds filtered through the canopy: soft calls of birds, the rustle of leaves and the creak of old branches, the gurgle of the Nymphs feeding somewhere over her head. She didn't dare glance up. She didn't want to see what could not be unseen.

A lingering aroma of cloves, out of place among all the sweet smells of flowers, guided her down a narrow pathway to the right. The trail led deeper into the trees, the sunlight all but swallowed by shadow and fog. Several times Corinthe had to stop and backtrack when the scent faded, but she always found it again. Her tracking skills were rusty, but the more she used them, the easier it became.

A low hissing stopped her. The sound was lower, quieter than the calls of the Nymphs. She peered through

a tangle of vines. A dozen enormous, translucent flowers grew in a circle in the middle of a sun-filled clearing. The flowers looked almost like guards, standing with
their backs to one another. There was nothing like them,
even in the garden of Pyralis, where every flower in the
known universe grew.

Corinthe pushed her way off the path, mesmerized by
the way the light hit the petals and shifted into different
hues, as though each petal were made of a prism. Their
buds were the size of overgrown pumpkins; their petals
curled inward. It wasn't until Corinthe stepped closer to
examine a peculiar-looking vine that she saw it wasn't a
vine at all, but a slim wrist with green-tipped fingers.

Not Blood Nymphs. Not yet.

Inside each flower, a girl hung suspended, pierced
with hollow vines that slowly drained her blood. Corinthe
circled the flowers, a sick taste coating her tongue, and
saw glimpses of paper-thin skin and unseeing eyes, of
blood swirling through the hungry plant. It wasn't the
light that made the petals appear to change colors; it
was the exchange of fluids from plant to girl. She knew
vaguely how Blood Nymphs were created, but seeing the
process up close made her feel sad and sick at the same
time.

Sad. Sick.

Human feelings.

At the last flower, Corinthe stopped. This girl was
early in the transformation, because her hair was still
black—the same color as Miranda's hair, Corinthe

thought, and felt a momentary ache, wishing she had her Guardian's advice.

The flower's pistil had pierced the girl's skin right at her wrist, just below a small tattoo of a jasmine flower. Corinthe watched as the girl's blood slowly leaked out of her body, into the plant.

Was it too late to do anything for her? Corinthe couldn't be sure. As far as she knew, the process of alteration was reversible if caught early enough. But past a certain point it could not be stopped—both plant and human would die.

It doesn't concern you. Corinthe heard Miranda's voice urging her to move on. This girl's future was not in her control.

Already the girl's skin was ghostly white. Soon her skin would take on the blue tint of the flower that changed her. Her blood would slowly be replaced with a fluid that would keep her alive, but only until she could feed like the rest.

It was a horrible thing to watch, but something compelled Corinthe closer, until she was just inches away from the girl. The aroma of cloves was overwhelming now, and Corinthe realized it hadn't been Luc's scent she'd been following.

She raised her hand, hesitated, then gently pushed a tendril of hair from the girl's face. The girl stirred and moaned quietly. Her lips were blue-tinged, bruised-looking. Corinthe stared, unable to look away. A memory tugged at the back of her mind, but she couldn't make it materialize.

"Hello?" Corinthe's voice was soft as she leaned closer to the girl.

The girl's eyelids fluttered, and she opened her eyes. Corinthe couldn't look away.

She searched around the edge of the clearing and found a rock the size of her palm, smooth and tapered at one end like an ax blade. She closed her fingers around the stone and stood in front of the girl.

The vine was meaty, and sawing at it barely made a difference, but she didn't stop, gripped by something she didn't understand. The desire to free the girl was her only thought. It moved her past the pain, the sharp agony she felt in the vine, in the plant itself.

Clear liquid oozed from the cut vine and ran down her wrist. It itched, and Corinthe swiped at it. Her pulse thundered in her ears as sweat beaded her forehead.

It wasn't working.

The vine was stringy and tough, and the rock just wasn't sharp enough. She stopped to catch her breath, looked around for something sharper, and felt the air around her begin to vibrate.

A subtle rippling pattern ran through the canopy above her, and the leaves whispered words she didn't understand. Branches closed in, eating away at the blue sky.

The Nymphs' whines started quietly but crescendoed until they were nearly deafening. Bursts of pain exploded in Corinthe's head; she dropped the rock and squeezed her hands over her ears. The noise sent her to her knees. It felt as though a knife was splitting her in two, making her whole body throb.

She fought the urge to scream as the pressure built inside her head. Just when it seemed that everything in her would explode outward, the sound abruptly stopped. The silence was deafening, beautiful.

Slowly, Corinthe took her hands away from her ears and dug her fingers into the earth, pushing her body upright. Her legs trembled, and a faint buzzing still echoed in her head. The clearing was revolving slowly in her vision; she took several deep breaths. A Nymph landed soundlessly in front of her, baring its teeth.

Corinthe moved into a crouch and scuttled backward. There was a hiss behind her. She swung around: another Nymph, close enough to touch, watched her through narrow eyes.

More Nymphs dropped from the trees, until she was completely encircled.

"I'm sorry. I didn't mean to hurt anything."

What had possessed her to try to free the girl? The urge felt like a distant, foggy memory, and it had clearly been a mistake.

"I was looking for someone, but he isn't here. If you could direct me to a gateway, I will go and never return."

Low, angry humming met her request.

A tangle of vines detached from the trees and slithered along the ground like a massive green snake. The trees had begun to lean closer, to weave their branches together like a fence, and she knew she had no hope of escape. The humming of the Nymphs swelled again. The vines lashed out together, encircling her legs and yanking so hard she fell onto her back. More vines twisted around her arms, pinning her to the ground.

Suddenly, a low rumble like the sound of distant thunder reverberated through the ground. For a second the plants stilled, and a hush fell over the clearing. Even the Nymphs stopped crying. They began, inexplicably, to retreat.

The rumbling grew louder and changed into a thousand tiny beating wings. The canopy of branches above her parted, and Corinthe saw an enormous dark blot against the sky: thousands of tiny winged insects were swarming toward her. Corinthe felt her blood run cold.

Hornets.

She struggled to breathe through the panic filling her body. Fueled now by fear, she strained against the vines, kicking her legs, thrashing and pulling, but the vines only tightened their grip.

The first hornet stung her on the thigh and a searing flash of fire shot up her leg. She screamed, heard her voice sucked greedily away by the vegetation around her, as though the trees were feeding on her pain.

More fire: on her stomach, her left arm, her hand, one agonizing jolt after another. She barely noticed when the vines loosened and slithered away. The hornets' venom coursed through her body; it instantly made her limbs weak and her fingers numb. When she rolled onto her side, her vision wavered, and the trees swam in and out of her sight. The clearing grew dim. Was it nighttime already?

Her body was so heavy. . . .

She wanted to sleep. . . .

Dimly, she thought she saw a small carving in the tree just in front of her. Almost like a door . . .

Her body quickly grew numb; the fire turned to an icy cold like she'd never felt before. But in her mind, she felt calm, cloaking her fear in a softness, a quiet. She seemed to hear music playing . . . as though the locket was open and calling to her. . . . Her mind was turning slowly, like the ballerina on its stand. . . .

Corinthe realized, with complete clarity, that she was dying. This was what she got for interfering. This was her penance.

Barely conscious, she watched the carved door swing open in the tree's trunk.

A gnarled hand reached toward her.

Everything went dark.

9

Red sand.

     Luc opened his eyes and lifted his head: red sand stretched for miles and miles along the coast of a dark ocean that swept all the way to the horizon.

Dirt covered his face. His eyes, teeth, ears — everything felt gritty, as if he'd gone through a sandstorm.

His mind was fuzzy. He remembered jumping but not landing.

There had been wind. A fierce, howling wind he thought would rip him apart and a searing pain that made his whole body shudder uncontrollably. And then . . . God, why couldn't he remember? Had he actually survived the fall off the building? Had he passed out from the pain? Luc had seen it happen on the field — a guy from another team who got his shin kicked in so hard the bone broke through his skin. He'd fainted, and Luc didn't blame him.

He rolled over onto his back despite the screaming in his muscles. He rubbed the sand from his eyes, then felt around for a lump on his skull. He must have cracked it. *Really* hard.

In the sky, two identical suns were sitting next to each other.

Double vision was a sure sign of a head injury—Ty had been out for a month after a bad hit gave him a concussion last year.

Very slowly, Luc raised his hand in front of his face. One hand appeared in his field of vision, but overhead, two suns still blazed on opposite sides of the sky.

What. The. Hell.

He pushed up onto his elbows carefully. Every inch of his body hurt, as if he'd been thrown off a building. No, not thrown—*jumped*. He slowly stood up, taking deep breaths to counteract the pain. His legs were weak, and he stumbled a few steps before regaining his balance. Behind him, his shadow, or shadows—two of them?—trailed across the sand. They fell in opposite directions and had a stretched look to them, the way shadows do when the sun hangs low in the sky.

Luc blinked several times to clear his vision, but two shadows remained. He was oddly reminded of early-morning soccer practices, of endless drills across the field as the sun started to rise—and how his shadow would dribble the ball alongside him, long and distorted, as if it belonged to a man eight feet tall.

Had he been dumped in the Black Rock Desert? No, this body of water had to be the ocean, which meant he must be somewhere along the shoreline. Yet there were no boats in the water, no people on the beach, not a sign of life anywhere.

And Christ, it was sweltering, like running an oven in a heat wave.

Something tugged at the back of his mind—some deep fear he couldn't name. Something was *wrong,* even more wrong than the two suns. He pinched the inside of his arm, feeling the pain wash over him, but he didn't wake up. No, not dreaming. Maybe he was in a coma.

Maybe you're dead.

He inhaled and tried to quell the rising fear that tightened his chest. He couldn't be dead because he didn't *feel* dead. He hurt everywhere, and the sand scratched his eyes and sweat beaded on his skin.

Dead people didn't sweat like this.

So if he was alive, then where the hell was he?

To his left, cliffs rose, sheer and jagged; a purplish-blue sky swelled above them like the taut belly of a balloon. The cliffs ran alongside the beach, parallel to the ocean, trapping him on this small strip of sand.

He fumbled for his phone, but the screen was blank. It must have been water damaged.

"Hello!" he shouted.

His voice echoed off the rocks and bounced down the beach. No one answered. He slowly turned around, dreading what he already knew he'd find. Behind him, more of the same: endless miles of cliffs and sand and ocean.

Panic welled up again and this time he didn't try to fight it. Hours earlier, he'd thought his night couldn't get any worse. Wrong.

He saw something glinting in the sand. His pulse sped up. A few feet away, the blade Corinthe had thrown at him lay half buried in the ground. He spun around to see if she was there, too, then crouched and carefully extricated the knife from the sand.

Had *she* somehow brought him here? Had she dumped his body, thinking he was dead, and bolted? Maybe she had brought him here by boat. . . .

The idea brought his gaze back to the water. He watched the dark surface of the ocean and felt a prickling at the back of his neck. It wasn't right. The water. It didn't *move* right. He'd spent enough time on the bay to know that water rippled, even if there was no wind.

His feet felt weighted with lead as he stumbled to the edge of the ocean. The water wasn't dark blue at all; it was black. And it just sat there, a giant puddle of inky darkness. Shadows undulated *beneath* its surface. They almost looked like . . . eels.

Millions and millions of eels.

Luc backed away quickly, a shiver of fear sliding down his spine, despite the cloying heat.

"Looking for something?" a voice said from behind him.

He swung around, clutching Corinthe's knife. A useless move, since he had been in a total of zero knife fights before and had no idea what to do with it.

A woman stood a few yards away from him. She was barefoot on the red sand and wore a long white dress. Her hair was as black as the ocean and hung nearly to her waist. She didn't appear to be affected by the heat at all. Her pale skin practically glowed under the sun's light, and the shadows she cast stretched long and narrow behind her, giving her an eerie air.

She smiled at him. Her teeth were very pointy; one was so sharp it looked like a dagger. And her eyes—like looking into a pit of tar, inky and bottomless. They completely unnerved him.

Luc couldn't shake the feeling that he'd seen her before. That same anxiety flickered through the back of his mind—there was something he should see or remember—but it dissipated when he tried to focus on it.

"Where did you come from?"

His voice was hoarse and raw. He swallowed against the dryness. In the sand he saw his own footprints, but around her there were none. He took a step backward.

This seemed to amuse her, because she laughed. The sound, not entirely pleasant, was quickly suctioned away by the heavy air. "That's not important. All you need to know is I'm a friend. And I came to tell you: Corinthe is responsible for your sister's current . . . *predicament.*"

Luc felt his stomach seize up. Jasmine. "What—what are you talking about?" he stammered. "What do you know about my sister?"

The woman tilted her head and stared at him almost with pity. "I know she's in trouble," she replied softly.

"What do you mean?" Luc was losing it. Blood pounded in his temples; he could hardly hold on to the knife, his hand was sweating so badly. "Where is she?"

"She is imprisoned in the Forest of the Blood Nymphs," the woman said evenly. "Because of Corinthe, she's in mortal danger."

Luc felt as though someone had punched him in the chest. "The Forest of the . . . what?" He shook his head. This *had* to be a nightmare. Or everyone around him had suddenly gone insane.

"Of the Blood Nymphs," the woman said.

"Who the hell are you? Is this some kind of sick joke? Where's my sister?" Luc instinctively raised the knife until the blade was pointed directly at the woman's throat. He hoped she wouldn't see that he was shaking ever so slightly.

But she just tipped her head back and laughed. When she looked at him again, her black eyes seemed to devour the light reflected in them.

"You can't hurt me. And you don't scare me. I told you—I'm a friend. We can stand here and play games or you can go after your sister. Either way, it makes little difference to me."

Luc felt as if he might pass out. His thoughts were spinning in dizzying circles.

"How do I find her?" he asked, practically spitting out the words.

The woman shrugged. Suddenly, she seemed to lose interest in him. "Corinthe can tell you. *If* you can trust her, that is."

Rage ate away at him, made him want to punch her. Riddles. This was clearly some kind of sick game to her. "How do I find Corinthe, then? What the hell *is* this place?"

She smiled again, and the rage turned to fear. There was something vicious about her smile—it was the way a cat might look at a mouse.

"Don't worry," she said. "Corinthe will find *you.*"

Another chill went down Luc's spine, despite the sweltering heat. He took a step toward her, but she turned and then simply vanished into the thick air, which shimmered with heat. Then Luc remembered the woman he had seen when he was riding the bus, the woman who had simply materialized from the steam.

Was she following him?

Several seconds later, he thought he saw her again at the base of the cliffs. She raised her hand and waved to him. The sun glinted off her finger. A ring, maybe. The glare stung his eyes and he had to look away. When he glanced back, the light was gone, and so was she. Then a figure appeared at the top of the cliffs, silhouetted in the brightness.

How the hell had she gotten up there so fast?

It didn't matter, because she knew where his sister was, and when he caught up with the woman, she was damned well going to tell him how to find her. He wasn't going to wait for Corinthe to find him. She would probably try to skewer him again.

Crazy. This whole thing was crazy.

He had to find Jas.

Without thinking too much about what he was doing, he tucked the knife into his belt and started to climb. He wrapped his hand around a bit of rock, found a toehold, and hauled. He tried to ignore the pain from his cut and bleeding fingers.

This was far more intense than any training he'd ever done for soccer. At the Y, they'd made him strap into a harness before letting him climb the rock wall. Here, there was nothing to catch him if he fell.

Still, he climbed, hand over hand, feet scrambling for purchase. The suns beat down on his back, pushed sweat into his eyes until he could barely see, and yet he went on.

After what felt like an hour of climbing, he pulled himself onto a small ledge and took a break. The progress was agonizingly slow, a diagonal path across the sheer cliff face. One wrong step would send him tumbling down to the sand. He wiped his face, feeling the sting of salt in his torn-up hands.

The cliffs seemed higher than when he started. The hopelessness of it all made his shoulders shake. Just above him, a swollen belly of rock jutted out over the black ocean. There was no way around it. Carefully, he found handholds and curled his fingers into them. Fresh waves of pain radiated up his arms, and blood trickled down his wrists.

Judging by the heat, the sun—well, *suns*—were directly overhead now, so he kept his eyes on the gray rocks in front of him. Gray, the color of Corinthe's eyes. The woman on the beach had said Corinthe was responsible for his sister's . . . imprisonment?

His foot slipped and he barely caught himself.

Focus, damn it.

His biceps burned as he fought to keep his grip. His fingers were on fire. His foot slipped again, and it took everything he had to lift it back onto a small ledge.

He clung to the side of the cliff as rough rocks scraped his skin. Sweat rolled into his eyes, blinding him as he tried to blink away the burning sensation.

His arms shook, and his fingers slipped another inch. He fought to reclaim his balance and dug deep down into the place where survival instincts took over.

He had to hold on.

For Jasmine.

He let out a breath through clenched teeth and closed his eyes, rested his forehead against the rock. The suns weighed down on him, blistering and stifling, as if they were trying to force him into the black ocean.

Cramps seized his legs, and his left foot slipped off the ledge. The momentum pulled him off center, and his fingers began to slip.

He couldn't hold on. No strength left. His body gave

up and stopped fighting even as his mind screamed to keep going.

His other foot slipped.

And he fell.

Above him, the two suns hung side by side, twin bloated faces leering in victory. It was the last thing he saw.

He hit the water and went under. Blackness.

A water that was not like water.

He floated in it, into a creeping, airless coolness. Was this death? It was more peaceful than he ever imagined it would be.

Then . . . his lungs began to burn and instinct kicked in. He found strength he didn't know he had. He flailed. He fought for the surface. He went nowhere. The water seemed to be full of silken hands—touching him, groping him.

His entire body burned from the lack of oxygen, a new kind of pain that reached down into his core, and his mind grew fuzzy. His limbs turned heavy. He allowed himself to float through the darkness, memories swimming next to him.

"Don't worry, baby. It was just a bad dream."

Mom stood next to his bed, smoothing her hand over his sweat-covered forehead. There was a pressure on his chest—his heart felt as if it were going to burst open. Light from the hallway spilled into the room he and Jasmine shared. His baby sister stood wide-eyed in her crib, watching him.

"You were gone," Luc said; his throat felt rough and swollen. "I couldn't find you. It was so dark."

"I'm right here," his mother said. She made soft shushing noises and he began to relax back into the pillow, his heartbeat slowing to normal. Finally, his eyes drifted closed and he heard her whisper: "It was just a bad dream. . . . You're okay. . . . You're safe. . . ."

10

Hands, rough like sandpaper, jerked Corinthe awake. A rush of pain made her gasp. Her stomach rolled, and for a second, she thought she was going to be sick.

She opened her eyes. She was lying on packed dirt on the ground. A stubby candle, enclosed by a smudgy glass-topped lantern, flickered next to her.

The smallest man Corinthe had ever seen—the size of a toddler, if that—knelt over her, holding what looked like a pair of large tweezers in his fingers, muttering to himself. He reached out with his tweezers; she felt a small tug on her arm and an icy-cold flash. She gasped and tried to sit up, but found she had no control over her limbs. Panic slid down her back.

Why couldn't she move?

The man continued muttering to himself. He held up

a dirty glass jar and dropped the stinger into it. Suddenly, he began to giggle. When he looked at her, his sunken eyes were lit up with excitement. "Hornet venom," he cackled. "Small doses, they make strong. Make safe from more stings!"

He laughed until he wheezed—a raspy, wet sound that made Corinthe's stomach turn over. When he opened his mouth, he exposed rows of blackened teeth. Each one came to a dull point, and she fought against the image of him taking a huge bite out of her.

A gnome. Had to be. Corinthe had seen their likenesses only a few times, in marbles that were not her charges. And gnomes lived in the Forest of Blood Nymphs, too— she had forgotten that. They were neither good nor bad, just very self-serving. They communicated in strange, circular ways that were hard to follow. Bargaining with a gnome took a lot of skill.

"Where am I?" she demanded. Her voice, at least, was still in her control—still steady. "Who are you?"

"This my home. I be Beatis, at your service." He bowed, then stood and dragged the edge of a crusty sleeve over his dripping nose.

It was dark and smoky in the roughly circular room, which was only a few feet wider than the length of her body. Near her feet, crudely built shelves lined with dirty bottles teetered toward the ceiling. On her left was a pile of dried grass, sticks, and leaves—a makeshift bed, Corinthe imagined.

Above her, it *looked* like roots were entangled to form

a ceiling. But was that . . . was that *fur* stuck between them?

She blinked, and her vision cleared slightly. More than a dozen animal carcasses in varying stages of decay were suspended above her, strung within the web of a tree. Bones, skin, eyeless sockets.

Corinthe quickly turned away, wincing. The gnome looked at her, then up.

"Pets. They be good tests. But not always success," he said, frowning. Then he shrugged. "Feeds tree. Keeps her happy." He reached up and patted a bit of the twisted wooden ceiling affectionately; Corinthe now recognized that they were in the hollowed-out ground directly beneath the tree's vast canopy of roots. The creatures trapped in the roots were ones she didn't quite recognize—they didn't exist in Pyralis. Or Humana, for that matter. The gnome returned to his task, bending forward to continue removing the stingers from her body. There were dozens and dozens of them remaining in her legs; Corinthe couldn't stand to look.

"I always listening for the hornets. They's very hard to find. They's very hard to trap." He rubbed his hands together. "Then I hears them and—I finds an Executor! So many questions, which to ask first?"

Alarm shot up her spine. He knew she was an Executor. She tried to force her fingers to move, but the command got lost somewhere between her brain and her hand.

"You be lucky Beatis find you in time."

Something pricked her arm again. Before she could

protest, a small tube was guiding her blood into a clear glass vial, which the gnome quickly filled and corked. He tucked it into his pocket, rubbed a greenish liquid into the spot he had bled, and waddled to the other side of the room with his jar. Carefully, he placed it on a shelf lined with an eclectic mixture of bottles, cans, jars, and boxes, each with peeling labels made of leaves and paste.

He pulled the vial from his pocket and slipped it inside a wooden box, then pushed it back behind several large bottles. When he returned, he held out a clear jar full of moving black *things*. He reached into the jar and pulled out something that looked like a slug. He held it between his stubby fingers for a moment, grinning as the slimy creature twisted and turned.

"What *is* that?"

"Leeches. They be good at sucking out the poisons," Beatis said. "Don't worry, pretty thing. Beatis be taking care of you."

"Please . . ." Now she couldn't help it. Her voice quavered. Stars danced brightly behind her eyelids, and she felt herself sinking, falling back into unconsciousness. She fought to stay awake, to stay alert.

Beatis carefully placed the slimy creature over one of the welts left by a hornet's stinger. A faint tugging sensation, not wholly unpleasant, came from where that *thing* had attached to her skin. Leeches, she knew, existed in Humana as well. Often, things were blown along the Crossroad and passed between worlds this way—like litter, like dust clinging to the shoes of those who traveled through the universe's infinite realms.

He attached the creatures all over her bare arms, where ugly bruises and welts showed evidence of the hornets' attack. Inside her chest, something began to burn. Fire trickled down her arms. Her legs. She wanted to scream but couldn't drag in enough air to make more than a whimper. Was this how the earth felt when she stitched from it, sucked from it?

Corinthe's stomach rolled. The room dipped and swayed.

"Please," she moaned again, half delirious with pain.

The carcasses above her began to move, swinging, disjointed, from their heels. One grinned down at her, its face half gone with rot. She slammed her eyes closed, though the image remained burned behind her eyelids.

But then the fire inside her died down and the frantic pounding of her pulse slowed to a normal rhythm. The room stopped spinning, and the dead animals stopped dancing above her head. She tried to move again. This time, her hand twitched.

After a few minutes more, full feeling began to flood back to her hands and fingers, trickling down her legs to her toes. It was working. One by one, the leeches released and fell to the dirt floor, curled into tight black balls. Beatis carefully picked them up and returned them to the jar.

"Good test subjects, yes? Full of venom. Perhaps they die. Perhaps not." He shuffled to the shelves again and replaced the jar on the shelf.

Corinthe slowly pushed to sitting, ducking her head

to avoid bumping up against one of the half-rotted skele-
tons above her. Now that she was upright, she practically
grazed the ceiling of roots with her head.

Gnome grottoes tended to be small and sparse: holes
in the ground, literally. Now that Corinthe was thinking
more clearly, she noticed a hole in one portion of the ceiling, a tunnel barely visible beyond the roots. That must
be how the gnome came and went and how he pulled her
into the grotto.

It occurred to her that she should be grateful.

"Thank you," she said. The leeches had left faint
bruises all over her skin, but as she flexed her fingers,
she was amazed that most of the pain had abated. She
could move again. "For saving my life."

Beatis laughed until he wheezed. "Thank you, thank
you!" he parroted gleefully. "I just buy you time. No cure
for hornet's sting. You still die, just not so fast. Two days,
maybe . . ." He counted on his fat, stubby fingers. "Three,
maybe, if you're lucky."

She felt a jolt of panic. No, she couldn't die. Fates
didn't die.

But she *wasn't* a Fate anymore.

She'd been cast out into Humana as an Executor. Had
she lived there so long that she had become like them?
Finite. Mortal. She had already bled like them, had been
wounded and fatigued.

Had wanted to sleep.

The hornets' venom *had* stunned her, rendered her
unconscious. What if the gnome was right?

What would happen to her after death? Where would she go? She knew that other people, mortal people, believed in many different outcomes, but what did *she* believe?

She had never had to consider it before.

The patron saint of lost causes . . . She suddenly remembered the words of Sylvia, the principal.

But if she could make it back to Pyralis in time . . . if she was restored as a Fate before the venom took hold . . .

"Please," Corinthe said carefully. "I'm looking for someone. Do you know where I can find a gateway?"

The gnome's lips curled back into a smile, revealing those awful, jagged teeth. "Not time enough. Beatis take care until you die. Never had Executor before."

She stared at him. "How did you—?"

"Aha! Hahaha! I be right, then." He leaned forward and sniffed. "I smell human on you. But no human blood. No. Different blood." His eyes seemed to swell even larger. He picked up a bottle of a greenish fluid. "Perhaps we test some potions. This made from nectar of green bell flower. Very rare. Might be fatal. Either way, you die." He let out a raucous burst of laughter.

Corinthe pushed into a crouch. She felt stronger now. "You can't keep me here," she said. Her head bumped against the roots and a shower of dirt rained down on her.

"Oh yes. Yes, I can. I find you. You are mine now." He pulled a dirty knife with a long, blood-spotted blade from behind his back and leveled it at her. "You stay."

Corinthe tried to swallow and found she couldn't. Blood pounded in her ears. Trying to fight unarmed in this tiny space, with venom thick in her veins, would be hopeless.

It would only mean a faster death.

She would have to find another way.

"I'll pay you," Corinthe blurted out.

He froze. She had said the magic words. Gnomes were infamous barterers.

The gnome frowned, wiped his nose on his sleeve again, and lowered the knife. "Pay?"

She held up both hands, to show him she didn't intend to fight. "Yes. I'll make you a deal."

"What you have I want?" The gnome scowled.

The only thing truly valuable that she had was the locket, which she needed to find her way home. If she couldn't get to the Crossroad, though, she would never execute Luc's fate.

And she'd be trapped here until she died.

Something else. She had to have something else.

"My shoes!" It occurred to her as she watched the gnome prance back and forth on his bare feet. "Your feet must be all cut up. A nice pair of shoes would keep them safe."

He seemed to consider it. He rocked up onto his toes. "And?"

Corinthe licked her lips. They were parched. "They come from Humana. But they're not just ordinary boots. They are made of the thick skin of a magical earthly animal. They will make you run quicker than you can dream."

The gnome's eyes flashed hungrily. "And what? What else more?"

"I *have* nothing else," she said. She was losing patience. How long would the venom take to work in her blood? One day? Two? Corinthe thought of dying here, trapped underground as the venom coursed through her veins. If she could perform her last task as an Executor, she could return home—and once she was restored as an immortal Fate, none of this would matter.

Except Luc would be dead.

Beatis grunted and shook his head. "More."

She was glad that the locket was hanging safely around her neck, concealed beneath her jacket. "You took my blood. I'd say that's a fair deal already. You take my shoes, and you get me to a gateway."

"I can wait until you die. Then have shoes for me," he said, grinning.

"You could. But you have to sleep sometime. And when you do, I'll kill you." She said the words neutrally, hoping the fact that she was an Executor would give weight to her threat; the gnome couldn't know how weak she felt.

The gnome spat on the dirt floor. "Deal," he finally said. "Magic shoes for the Crossroad. You promise now. Mine, mine, mine."

Corinthe unlaced her leather boots quickly. The floor was damp, and cold seeped through her thin socks. The gnome grabbed the shoes and sat down heavily. After shoving his dirty feet into her boots, he tugged at the laces, growled again, then wiggled his long, gnarled toes inside the front of the boot.

When he stood, Corinthe almost laughed. The boots covered the entire length of his legs and gaped open, practically falling off every time he tried to take a step. She helped him work the laces, earning her a grunt of approval.

"So." Corinthe stood again—as much as she *could* stand, without cracking her head. "Where is it?"

The gnome waddled clumsily to the corner, his steps thumping on the packed earth. Corinthe looked up at the opening in the ceiling and wondered how on earth he had managed to pull her through it. Before she could ask, he shoved aside one of the cabinets to reveal a much larger tunnel.

She peeked inside, but it was too dark to see more than a few feet of sloped earth. The tunnel smelled like musty, dank ground.

"I'll follow you," she said. Gnomes weren't known for being entirely trustworthy, and for all she knew, the tunnel led to some kind of trap.

He pulled an oil lantern off the shelf and lit the wick; the smell of sulfur tickled her nose. He walked upright into the passageway, but Corinthe had to crawl on her hands and knees. Beatis turned around to glare at her periodically and urge her to go faster. After a few feet, the tunnel began to slope upward. The small lantern illuminated nothing more than his flickering outline and the tangle of roots above their heads. Corinthe could hear a soft gurgling sound, almost like a fountain.

Then she remembered where she was. Her stomach

twisted. It was blood. She was listening to the trees feed. The air hung thicker here. Heavy. It was hard to breathe. The tunnel grew narrower, and roots raked fingers through her hair, dragged across her bare arms. She felt the shift, the flood of excitement that rippled through the ground. The walls of the passageway shuddered, and dirt showered down on her head.

"Hurry," Beatis wheezed. "They find you. The trees be hungry." Beatis scampered ahead and was soon lost in the darkness.

Terror shot through her. Dirt continued to rain down on her head. The roots continued to reach for her, pull at her, trying to consume and drain her. She tried to call out, but she could barely draw breath. The earth around her was closing in, burying her.

Stars exploded behind her eyes, and strangely, it made her think about the sky over the San Francisco Bay. About standing with Lucas. About the heat that raced through her blood when he had touched her.

Enough, she told herself. Wherever he was, she would find him and kill him. There was no choice, only destiny.

Her legs were completely encased in dirt. She couldn't crawl any farther. Beatis's light had disappeared. More dirt drove down on her shoulders, pushed her head down until she lay with one cheek against the ground.

The earth pulsed like a heartbeat. She reached out one hand, desperately clawing for help that wasn't there.

And then, even as she cursed herself for trusting a gnome, she felt a rough hand close around hers. Beatis pulled her, loosening her from the earthen coffin with surprising strength.

Fresh air filled her lungs. Dirt fell away from her legs and she pushed to her knees, let go of Beatis, and threw herself at the light. She rolled a few feet down a small incline and landed on her back, gasping for breath.

The trees around them hissed softly, as though disappointed. She wondered how long it would be before they raised the alarm. Gave her away.

"Hurry, we must go fast," the gnome said.

He didn't wait to see if Corinthe followed; he just took off down a path that cut through the trees. She stumbled after him. Hard thorns bit into her feet. Finally, the trees thinned, and then in one step, she was clear of the forest.

Twenty feet in front of her, a thick wall of mist rose to the sky. It was as if the forest simply ceased to exist right at this spot. Cool tendrils of fog snaked across the ground.

"Where is it?" she asked. There were burrs stuck to the soft soles of her feet. No wonder the gnome had taken the shoes.

Beatis spun in a full circle. "Left or right, right or left . . . ," he chanted.

Then she heard it: the high-pitched whine of the Blood Nymphs.

Not again.

Panic prickled at her skin like thousands of tiny needles. Branches clacked together behind her, gnashing like enormous teeth.

The gnome took a step back. "Deal be done." He grinned. "Venom be poison in your blood. Feed on you till you die. I still win."

"*Where?*" she repeated, lunging for him. He skidded to the left and Corinthe stumbled past him, already woozy from the venom. She spun around and tried lunging at him again, but she tripped over a tree root and landed hard on her hands and knees. The locket spilled out from under her shirt and the clasp came undone. The lid opened and the clearing filled with the tinny lullaby. The gnome froze on the edge of the clearing. The Nymphs quieted. Listened. Corinthe held her breath as the ballerina pirouetted slowly.

The gnome watched the ballerina with feverish excitement. Saliva ran down his chin and dripped onto the ground.

"You say you have nothing else!" he whined, taking a step closer.

A wave of dizziness forced her to take several deep breaths. It had to be the venom, working in her blood again. Could the gnome have been wrong? What if she didn't have two or three days?

What if she only had hours?

"Show me the gateway," she said. The gnome made a leap for her locket, but she scrambled backward and stood unsteadily. She pulled the chain off her neck and held it firmly, raising it high above his head. "Tell me and I'll give you this."

Beatis licked his lips nervously, his eyes darting back

and forth between the locket in her hand and a low tree full of blue leaves to her right. Corinthe could tell at once this tree was not full of blood like the rest.

Her pulse sped up. The entrance to a gateway was there. Once she entered she'd have to navigate the Crossroad to Lucas.

Corinthe turned and ran.

"Mine!" Beatis shrieked. He produced the knife from a strap around his waist and made a leap for her. She felt a quick tug; a clump of hair came away in his hand.

The angry hum of the Nymphs swelled to a scream.

Corinthe snapped the locket closed as she hurtled toward the gateway, calling on every ounce of her strength as an Executor. She launched herself up into the tree. Waves of nausea rolled over her and she fought them back.

"Beatis will find you!" The gnome stabbed furiously at the tree as Corinthe climbed. "You be dead and I get the locket. Beatis take it from you when you be dead. Deal! It be a deal!"

She kept climbing, fighting through the fierce wind that had begun to blow. The swell of the Nymphs' howling was drowned out. She could no longer hear Beatis's threats. Her hair whipped around her head. Blue leaves swirled in and out of her vision. They looked like shattered pieces of the sky.

The wind grew stronger, like a hurricane rush. It was as if a tornado had descended on top of her, intent on ripping her apart one cell at a time. The gateway had opened, and the wind from the Crossroad rushed into the forest. The force yanked at her body, pulled her grip loose. For one second, she hung suspended in the gray nothingness.

Then she fell—up or down or sideways, she couldn't tell.

She'd been told that like a river running through an endless prairie, the Crossroad forked through and across the whole universe, constantly changing direction. The motion created a furious wind, a current that blew its travelers between worlds.

Agony ripped through Corinthe's chest, a hundred times worse than the hornet stings. She willed herself against the current, following Lucas's trail, *feeling* his presence in the universe.

Focus.

She managed to open the locket, and the ballerina spun.

Think of finding the boy.
Think of killing him.
Then you can go home.

11

The hand came out of nowhere.

How he saw it, how he managed to grab hold of it, Luc didn't know. But suddenly, the blackness fell away and he was pulled to the ocean's surface, gasping for air.

Rough wood scraped his cheek, then his chest. The hand let go and Luc rolled onto his back, coughing. He was on some kind of raft. Overhead, the two suns still blazed hot in the sky. He blinked rapidly, the brightness stinging his eyes after the complete immersion in the dark water.

No, not water. It hadn't filled his lungs or wet his clothing.

Even his hair was dry.

Luc sat up slowly, leaning against a large wooden contraption—it looked like some kind of old-school engine or steering device—fitted with various levers and gears, which were bolted to the middle of the raft. Or boat. Or whatever.

The man who had saved him grabbed one of the levers and pulled. After a few cranks, a motor coughed and groaned, and the floor under Luc's feet began to vibrate. Oars on both sides of the raft began to circle, arching in high circles above the black ocean before submerging again without a sound. With each stroke, the boat moved forward a few feet in a path parallel to the shoreline. Overhead, a triangular patchwork sail snapped and billowed.

The man who had saved Luc now seemed content to ignore him. He had a scruffy jawline and hard cheekbones, and his hair stood out at all angles. He wore what looked like a pair of aviation goggles, but a piece was missing, so they only covered one eye. The uncovered eye was a cloudy white. He had on a dark jacket that hung to his knees, but he didn't seem to even notice the stifling heat.

A huge black bird was perched on his shoulder, its glittering black eyes focused on Luc. The man tilted his head and whispered to it. The bird responded with several deep-throated caws.

"No worse for the wear, I see," the man said. For a second, Luc thought that this comment was directed at the bird. His voice was thick with an accent Luc had never heard before. But then the man turned and limped heavily over to Luc. He was holding a tin cup; Luc prayed it was a glass of water. "We were watching you. Saw you fall."

"Thank you," Luc croaked. His throat was sandpaper raw.

When the man opened one side of his coat, Luc saw row after row of tiny vials stitched into pockets that had been sewn crudely to the inside. His half-gloved fingers moved deftly over the dusty-looking bottles, over and down, until he pulled one from its place. Quickly, he dumped the milky contents of the vial into the water.

Luc hesitated, despite an intense urge to drink. His hand went to the knife still tucked tightly in his belt.

"Boy, if I wanted to harm you, I'd have left you in the shadows. No concern of mine if you die. Go ahead. Drink, before the heat starts messing with your head. You've been in the suns too long." The man thunked down the cup. Luc waited until the man had disappeared into a bright patchwork tent that dominated half of the deck before drinking greedily.

The liquid tasted cool and clean, and almost immediately, Luc felt his senses clearing.

Luc stood up carefully. He saw an endless black ocean before him, stretching to the horizon. Overhead the two suns hung high in the sky.

And suddenly, that thing that had been bugging him since arriving in this freakish place—the worry, the doubt—sharpened and crystallized.

Despite the dual suns overhead, *nothing* here had a shadow. Even Luc's had somehow disappeared.

How was that even possible?

Luc moved his arm in a huge circle. Nada. A chill went through him, though the temperature had to be over 100 degrees.

What the hell? First there were two, and now there were none?

The raft swayed. He stumbled toward the tent. Maybe the drink the man had given him had some kind of weird side effect. But no. He had known before on the beach that something was very, very wrong. He had sensed it.

Luc lifted the tent flap and ducked inside, then froze, disbelieving.

He'd been expecting a plain setup, maybe a rough bunk or something. Instead, he felt as if he'd stumbled into a fortune-teller's living room. The man was sitting in a huge ornately carved wooden armchair. Almost like a throne. There was a brightly colored Persian rug covering the coarse planks and a gleaming table laid with a silver tea set.

Hanging from the juncture where the tent's poles connected, was a brilliantly lit chandelier. A hole just above it let in enough sun to reflect off hundreds of teardrop-shaped crystals, which threw tiny spots of light all over the room.

The entire space was no bigger than Luc's bedroom but was filled so lavishly that it felt grand.

"What is this place?" Luc asked. "Who are you?"

The man stood and thumped over to a small wooden chest in the corner. He began filling a pipe. The bird

squawked angrily at being displaced and flew over to a
perch. "The name's Rhys," he said, without looking at
Luc. "And that beautiful, indignant lady over there is my
Mags. Now your turn."

"Luc." Luc watched as the man lit his pipe. Whatever
he was smoking had a clean, floral smell. Definitely not
tobacco. "I'm from San Francisco."

Rhys returned to his chair. "Don't know it. Don't
know much about Humana, actually."

"Humana?"

"The human world. I can smell it on you." Rhys
chuckled.

Human world. Luc's heart squeezed up in his chest.
"Where *am* I?" Luc asked.

Rhys moved the goggles to the top of his head and Luc
could see both his eyes now. They weren't just cloudy;
they were totally white from edge to edge.

He was blind?

Luc passed his hand quickly in front of Rhys's face.
Rhys scowled.

"I may not be able to see what you're doing, boy, but
I can feel it. I can smell it, too."

Heat climbed up Luc's neck. "S-sorry," he stammered.

Rhys waved dismissively with his pipe and motioned
for Luc to sit. There was a bright red settee also crammed
into the space—it reminded Luc of something Karen's
parents might have in one of their formal rooms. Karen.
Jesus. Was it possible that only last night, he'd been at
Karen's party?

When would he wake up from this nightmare?

Luc suddenly felt unsteady on his feet. He sat down heavily.

"To answer your first question—" Rhys stopped and directed his eyes at Luc. "I assume you have more than one question, correct?"

Luc nodded, then remembered Rhys couldn't see him. He cleared his throat. "Yes."

Rhys continued without missing a beat. "This is the aptly named Land of the Two Suns. Not terribly original, but then the Figures aren't known for being overly clever."

"Figures?"

"That your next question, then?"

"I guess."

"The Figures," Rhys said, "are what we call—"

Mags squawked suddenly, so loudly that Luc jumped, heart in his throat. Rhys cocked his head to the side as though listening—much the way his bird did. "Ah, we have a patient to tend to. Come on, then." He pulled down his goggles and moved as briskly as possible past Luc, holding open the tent flap to permit Mags to swoop through it. A few seconds later, the vibration of the engine ceased and the boat stopped its lurching movement. As Luc pushed back into the blazing light, his head hurt.

Rhys leaned over the side of the boat. He was talking to someone, but Luc couldn't make out what he was saying.

Luc advanced closer to the edge of the boat. All he saw was darkness.

Then, as he watched, the water shifted. A black hand—insubstantial, translucent—extended out of the water. Luc stumbled back a step. Mags began clucking.

Rhys pulled out a vial from his jacket and removed the cork. Now a face—*was* it a face? Luc could just make out shadowed contours that looked like eyes and a mouth—had surfaced as well. The mouth, an even deeper dark than the rest of the thing, opened; Rhys poured the contents of the vial into it. When the vial was empty, Rhys tucked it back into his pocket and the thing disappeared back under the surface.

Luc's heart was pounding. Questions spun in his head, but he couldn't make enough sense out of what he saw to form a coherent thought.

"Where was I?" Rhys rose to his feet, wiping his hands on the back of his pants, as though nothing out of the ordinary had happened.

"What—what was that thing?" Luc finally stammered.

Rhys tilted his head, looking alarmingly like the bird that perched on his shoulder. "That? That was a Figment, boy."

"A what?" Luc was getting tired of trying to decode so many unfamiliar words. *Blood Nymphs. Figments.* His head ached.

"A long time ago, everything and everybody had two shadows, on account of the suns." Rhys moved to the rowing mechanism and made a couple of adjustments. The vibration started in the floor; the oars began churning in and out of the water again. The raft lurched forward.

"The Figures and the Figments lived together just

fine. Then one day, the suns changed orbit and the Figments grew longer, stronger. The Figures got all sorts of nervous and waged war on them." Rhys's strange accent flowed like thick honey. "Eventually, the Figures drove the Figments here, to the Ocean of Shadows. The dark keeps them contained, but they want out. Naturally."

"Figments," Luc said slowly. "You mean, like, shadows?"

Rhys shrugged and spat. "They been called different things."

Luc remembered the feel of thousands of hands on him, pulling at his clothes, touching his skin. He'd thought he was hallucinating—but really he'd been feeling the touch of thousands of Figments.

He leaned over the boat and blinked hard. He scanned the ocean in disbelief. His head felt light, as if his skull were slowly filling up with helium. *This isn't real,* he told himself. But it was. There were thousands of shadows writhing their way to the surface, and the darkness below him extended to the horizon. He saw that shadows clung to the oars each time they broke the surface. The Figments stretched like rubber bands, until it looked like they would snap, before retreating into the blackness. He wondered where his own shadows were, and whether they were safe. And whether it mattered.

"Will they ever escape?" he asked Rhys.

"Suppose so. When the Figures remember, anyway." His voice had suddenly changed. It was quieter, filled with longing. He squinted toward the shore, and Luc could have sworn that—despite his blindness—he was staring off into the distance.

"Remember what?" Luc asked.

Rhys's lips curled into a small smile. "You don't know, do ya? No matter, we all get there in time. Don't look at me. I ain't gonna tell you—I'm just a Healer. Trapped out here, the shadows start to lose it. They blend. Forget who they are, forget what they were. I've developed a tincture that'll help them remember until the right time comes. It's the balance of the universe, boy, the light and dark, the earth and the sea."

Luc didn't know what Rhys was trying to say, but he didn't want to press it, either. More riddles. And riddles weren't going to help him find Jas.

"Is there a Forest of Blood around here?" he asked, and then felt his cheeks heat up. He couldn't believe any of this—it was crazy.

Rhys shook his head slowly. "Don't know that I've ever heard of it. Why?"

"I'm looking for my sister." Luc sucked in a deep breath, then blurted out, "I met a woman on the beach. She said—she warned me my sister was in trouble."

Rhys turned away from Luc and spat again. Then he swung around and abruptly jabbed a finger at Luc's chest. "This will lead you on the straight and narrow." Then he pointed at Luc's forehead. "This will lead you to the logical, which isn't always the best truth, if you know what I mean."

Luc *didn't* know what Rhys meant. Mags made a

sound, almost like a snort. Anger and helplessness built in Luc's chest, like hot oil welling there. He didn't know any more than he had when he'd been pulled onto the raft. Judging by the way the suns had moved across the sky—both looming directly overhead, side by side—time was passing quickly. As he wiped the sweat off his forehead, he moved the shaggy black hair that had fallen in front of his eyes. Christ, it was hot.

"The universe is a tricky place," Rhys said, seeming to sense Luc's growing frustration. "The roads don't always go where they're supposed to. But I might have a map that can help you find a gateway."

"A gateway?"

"An entry point to the Crossroad. Boy, don't give me that look like I'm crazy." Luc wondered again how a blind man could see the things he did. He sat silently, waiting for Rhys to continue. "I suspect you've come and gone through the Crossroad already, so you'll need to find an entry point. But the map is back on shore, so let's make our way there. . . ."

Luc was surprised; he had assumed the blind man and Mags lived there on the raft. The sail snapped as it caught the breeze, and Rhys turned the rudder so they aimed toward shore. They moved across the shadowed ocean, and Luc had nothing to do but watch the Figments undulate in rippling waves. Now that he knew what they were, he saw the sea differently. It seemed mysterious, and heavy with something like sadness.

Please, please. Let this be a dream. Let me wake up.

His alarm would go off and he'd wake up to find Jas sitting in the living room, safe and sound. She'd laugh at the crazy dream he had, especially the part where she was trapped in some blood forest, then they'd head to the Mission, get some breakfast taquitos and coffee at Philz Coffee. Cream and sugar.

Mags's loud caw pierced his daydream. Still here. Still in this awful place, with the unbearable heat of the suns and the feel of sand underneath his nails.

They were only about fifty feet from shore. The same beach, the same cliffs stretched as far as he could see. In the distance, movement caught his eye. Luc shaded his eyes and squinted. A figure stumbled along, sinking every few feet to her knees before struggling back to her feet. Blond hair flashed in the sun, like a coin under the water.

Corinthe is responsible for your sister.

The words echoed in his head. Blood pounded in his ears.

"I need to get to shore," Luc said abruptly. He couldn't let her get away. He even contemplated jumping back into the Figments and swimming.

Rhys must have sensed his intentions. "Don't try it," he warned. "They might not drown you, but they wouldn't let you out, either. We'll be there in just a minute."

Luc paced the length of the raft, impatiently watching Corinthe make her way to the cliffs. Rhys deftly managed the steering, apparently with the help of Mags's occasional caws—the man and the bird seemed to have developed some way of communicating. Within a few minutes, the raft bumped against a sandy bottom.

Luc jumped out and landed in the red sand.

"What about the map?" Rhys called.

Luc hesitated. But Corinthe was already climbing. He couldn't let her escape; she knew where Jas was. That was what the woman had said.

"Go ahead, go get her." Rhys seemed to be smirking. "I'll poke around for it. Just give a shout when you've done whatever it is you need to do. Mags will hear you."

"Thank you," Luc said, and broke into a run.

By the time he'd made it to the base of the cliff, Corinthe had already gotten halfway to the top. Framed against the looming mass of rock, she seemed so small, so fragile, and he steeled himself against a sudden twinge of pity.

Luc took a deep breath and grabbed a piece of the jutting rock over his head. His arms and hands were still aching from his earlier attempt at climbing, but he was fueled with renewed purpose. Corinthe had done something to Jas. She was obviously a psycho. He would catch up to her, and he would get the truth out of her, no matter what.

Just as he began to follow her, she turned around and spotted him.

Even from this distance, Luc could hear her short cry of surprise. Before he could react, a rock the size of his head came tumbling toward him. He jumped off the rocks and out of the way, and the rock thumped into the sand by his feet.

Several more rained down, each larger than the last.

Small and fragile. Right. Luc wouldn't make the mistake of pitying her again.

Luc ran ten feet down the beach and started to climb. Hand over hand, he moved at an angle, safely out of the way of any more rocks Corinthe might loosen.

Thanks to the drink Rhys had given him, he felt strong even though there was still a faint pounding in his head. He climbed quickly, confidently, rapidly closing in on Corinthe. She reached the top only a few seconds before he did, and he launched himself after her, scrambling to his feet before she could attack him.

Luc tried to ignore the horrible welts marring her arms. Tried to ignore the cuts on her palms that were open and bleeding. How her feet were bare and covered with dirt, her jeans and T-shirt torn. She looked thin and pale and scared. Even her shadows looked short and huddled together.

What the hell had happened to her?

His resolve weakened a little.

And in that instant, Corinthe lunged at him, her teeth bared, like a wild animal. He easily sidestepped her attack and she fell past him, stumbling to her hands and knees, crying out softly. She turned over and tried to stand, but her arms collapsed and she landed on her back.

This time, Luc didn't wait for her to recover. Girl or not, injured or not, she was still trying to kill him. He was on her in an instant, straddling her waist, the knife pulled quickly from his belt and pressed against her throat. Her knife. Neither moved. They breathed raggedly together, staring at each other.

"Where's my sister?" he spat out.

She glared at him. "Let me go."

He leaned into her a little more. "Tell me where my sister is or I'll kill you," he said.

"Then kill me," she challenged. Despite her obvious weakness, there was fire in her eyes.

"Don't think I won't," he said. But he knew that she could see it: he was not a killer.

Corinthe grabbed his hand, forced the knife against the pulse that beat wildly in her neck. Her eyes glistened in the suns, turning a haunting shade of purple. She arched her back, lifting her chin so she was even more exposed to him.

She looked alone and lost and wild and beautiful.

Protect her.

The crazy thought came out of nowhere.

"Go ahead," she said. "Because if you don't, as soon as I am strong, I will kill you."

His hand shook, making the knife wobble. It nicked her skin and a tiny bead of blood welled up underneath her chin. He watched it roll down her neck and into her hair. His stomach twisted violently and he threw the knife aside.

He couldn't do it.

"Just tell me where my sister is," he said, "and I swear I'll let you go."

A look of pain—or disappointment?—passed over Corinthe's face. Her body tensed for one moment underneath him; she opened her mouth.

And then her lovely eyes rolled backward, her body relaxed, and she lost consciousness.

"Well, now. Quite some lovers' quarrel, ain't it?"

Luc turned around. Rhys was grinning widely. Mags let out a single caw, as though in agreement.

12

A barely discernible buzzing floats through the air. Corinthe watches the fireflies in the purple twilight: thousands flicker over the river, mingling with the reflection of the stars on the water.

Sometimes, when she stares long enough, she can't tell which is which.

Corinthe takes a step closer to the water's edge. It is forbidden to touch the Messengers. But why? She thinks of the stranger who visited Pyralis once. "Don't stop asking questions," he had told her—and now she can't stop. The question seems to burn a path through her mind, like the hot trails of the shooting stars that blaze across the sky. Why why why? And why do none of the other Fates wonder the same thing?

A strange hunger grows inside her. Hunger. A word she doesn't even know yet. Why why why? Why can't I touch the light?

Then, suddenly, as though in response to her unspoken question, one of the fireflies darts past her. Before she knows what she has done, her fingers have closed around it like a Venus flytrap—a plant that grows both in Pyralis Terra and in Humana.

For one second, the wings beat against her palm. She's filled with feelings she has never known, feelings she has no words for yet. Ecstasy. Exhilaration. A sense of flying.

But then the firefly breaks free of her hand and she hears a tiny splash. A marble has fallen into the river. Bobbing along the surface, it starts to float downstream. One of the tarnished marbles. One that was not meant to stay in the river but to be rescued and sorted and delivered. This is what she is designed for, what she does. For all of eternity, she sorts the cloudy marbles from the clear—just like all the other Fates—rescuing the obscure and darkened ones, the ones that have been warped. These contain futures that may not happen on their own. They need help. That's why she culls them and gives them to the Messengers. There is an order, a set of rules. These are not broken—have never been broken.

Corinthe leaps into the water, feeling the strong pull of the current against her legs. The marble floats closer to the edge of the waterfall. She reaches out. The marble is so close. All she has to do is grab it.

Her bare feet slip on the slick rocks of the riverbed as her fingertips brush against the smooth surface of the marble . . . and just then, the current sweeps it away from her.

She watches in horror as the marble disappears over the edge of the falls, into the unknown space that surrounds Pyralis Terra.

The water continues to rush around her, but Corinthe

can't move. She is struck with an icy dread. She has lost some-one's destiny.

It might have been a death, or a birth, or a meeting, or a masterpiece. Whatever the story, it is now lost forever.

Suddenly, Corinthe is ripped from the banks of the river, flung into a swirling mass of darkness. She hears screaming. Her sister Fates: are they crying out for her?

"I'm sorry!" she yells, but her voice is obscured by the raging wind.

The pain is searing. Unrecognizable. Her skin is on fire.

Voices float around her, angry and sharp.

You have disrupted the balance.

You are the first Fate to disobey . . .

And you will be the last.

Then: she's on top of a building. A blaze behind her eyelids, scalding, terrible. Too much light. It's dizzying; it makes her want to throw up. Everything is loud. And the stench. The stench is awful.

"Come," a soft voice says, and when Corinthe looks up, she sees a beautiful dark-haired woman in a flowing white dress. The woman crouches and places an arm around Corinthe's shoulders. Corinthe has never been touched in such a way before. She doesn't know what to make of it—of the closeness. The woman smells unfamiliar—like river silt, and flowers, and the dust of distant galaxies.

"I'm Miranda," the woman says, with a smile that reveals a sharp, jagged tooth. "I've been sent here to be your Guardian."

Corinthe stares at her. "Why me?" she asks.

"Because, my dear, you are very, very special." Her new Guardian takes her hand. . . .

"Welcome back," a strange voice said.

Corinthe opened her eyes and the vision of Miranda—and before that, Pyralis—receded, like a tide being sucked back by the ocean, leaving only a huge, vast sense of loss inside of her. Overhead, a light fixture hung from the ceiling: iron pounded into strips and twisted to form holders for a dozen white candles.

Something heavy was draped over her body, and she struggled to push it aside.

"Slow down," the stranger said.

Corinthe turned her head and cringed at the sudden burst of pain behind her eyes. Bright sparks danced across her vision. He wrung out a cloth and reapplied it to her head. The coolness felt so good.

The room finally stopped spinning.

The man wore a light-colored shirt, open to reveal his tan, muscular chest. Shaggy brown hair hung to his shoulders, his cap pulled low. He wore a torn goggle on one eye, and there was a large black bird perched on his shoulder, its eyes glittering as it watched her. The bird cawed softly and the man reached up and fed it something from his hand.

"Excuse the dirt. I been out on the ocean for weeks. I need a good bath and a change of clothes." When he leaned over to press a new cool cloth to her forehead, Corinthe noticed that his uncovered eye was completely white.

"What happened?" she asked. Her voice came out raspy and she swallowed against the dryness.

"You been out for a bit. Hot as desert and kicking in

your sleep. Don't worry, I gave you something for the heatstroke."

Corinthe closed her eyes. Her mind was still cloaked in darkness; her thoughts moved slowly, and she couldn't remember how she'd gotten here.

The gnome. The tree. The Crossroad. Flashes of pain. Towering rocks.

A knife . . .

Luc!

Luc pressing her own knife against her throat

Corinthe tried to sit up, but the room spun in circles and she soon gave up.

"Whoa now, not so fast. You're in pretty bad shape. You need to rest." The man helped her to lie back, though he propped up her head with a pillow so she could finally get a good look at where she was.

"Who are you?" Her voice cracked and she ran her tongue over the sharp peaks of her dried lips. As if sensing her needs, the man handed her a small glass he took from a cart next to the bed.

"Water," he said.

She took the glass, and after the first sips of cold water ran over her tongue, Corinthe couldn't drink fast enough. She emptied the glass in two long gulps, and she extended it for a refill.

"The name's Rhys," he said as she drank greedily. "This is Mags." The bird on his shoulder cawed and spread her wings so that feathers framed the man's head. "Show-off," he muttered at the bird.

Though obviously some kind of cave, the room was

well lit, outfitted with dozens of flickering candles. The bed she lay in was comfortably soft and set into a carved-out spot in the wall, as though a portion of the cave had been deliberately hollowed to accommodate it.

Thick rugs with bright patterns covered the dirt floor. Painted onto one of the rough walls was the image of a comet streaking across the sky. Colors exploded across the wall; a trail of bright orange and yellow flames streaked toward the ground.

Corinthe felt a sick feeling building in her chest. She looked away quickly, again struggling to sit up. But her arms refused to support her weight. The pillow under her head felt so soft, so inviting. It had to be the hornets' venom, working even faster than the gnome had predicted. The weakness terrified her—it was as though her body was turning against her.

An exhaustion unlike anything she'd ever experienced made her limbs feel like lead. It was hard not to give in to the pull of the enormous bed and simply close her eyes.

Was this what humans felt like when they needed to sleep?

"How did I get here?" Corinthe asked.

"We brought you here," a familiar voice said.

Surprise gave Corinthe new strength. She forced herself to sit up and turned around. In one corner was a stone fireplace; Luc stood in front of it, backlit by the glow. It took Corinthe a minute to decipher the expression on his face.

Hatred. It had to be. The fierceness of his eyes, the way his arms were crossed, the set of his jaw.

For a second, Corinthe couldn't speak. "Why didn't you kill me?" she blurted out finally. Corinthe remembered, now, how she had all but dared him to kill her. Why hadn't he? She would have, in his place.

But immediately, a tiny flicker of doubt tickled inside her chest. *Would* she have? She had already failed to do so.

She forced the doubt from her mind. It was a mistake — nothing else.

"*I'm* not a killer," Luc said. He crossed the room and stood next to the bed, and she found herself unconsciously shrinking away from him. It wasn't fear, though. The harsh accusation in his eyes bothered her in a way nothing had before. He thought she was a killer. But that wasn't true. Not really.

She thought of all the beautiful fates she had executed: the births and the last-minute redemptions, the children she had brought home after they were lost, the kisses and the reunions and the hope given to humans who despaired.

The patron saint of lost causes . . .

"You don't know me," Corinthe said, and was surprised that her voice was trembling. "Don't pretend you do."

Luc rolled his eyes. He didn't hate her, perhaps. He just didn't care about her at all. This thought knifed through her, suddenly painful.

"Look, I'm sick of your riddles. Just tell me what you've done to my sister."

"I don't know what you're talking about." Corinthe was growing frustrated. This fate was far different from anything she'd been tasked with. Complicated. Unclear. Things were supposed to be clear; that was the point of fate. "I didn't even know you *had* a sister." Pain shot through her temples and she pressed her hands to her head, as though she could drive back the sudden ache.

Rhys bent over her and felt her forehead. "Still warm," he murmured. "How long has the poison been in your blood?" he asked her.

"What poison?" Luc broke in.

Corinthe ignored him. "I'm not sure," she told Rhys. "I—I can't remember very clearly."

"*What* poison?" Luc repeated. He sounded almost angry.

"Looks like hornets' venom." It was Rhys who answered. "Almost certainly fatal."

Rhys placed a hand on her back and made Corinthe inhale. Then he felt the pulse in her neck. His rough hands were surprisingly gentle. When he rolled up her sleeves to explore her wounds, she let out a weak, guttural cry. The leeches had left dark welts all over her skin. Mags cawed softly, and even Luc went pale, which unaccountably gave Corinthe some small satisfaction. She refused to show fear in front of him.

"Leeches, eh? Not my first choice. But they'll do in a pinch. Probably bought you a little more time."

"She's . . . she's going to die?" Luc stared disbeliev-ingly at Corinthe.

"Might do," Rhys said curtly. Corinthe's stomach tightened, but at least he was telling her the truth. "All depends." His white eye seemed to fix on her, and she felt, strangely, as though he were staring directly *into* her. "Strange for someone like you. You ain't supposed to die, are you?" He had lowered his voice, so that Luc couldn't hear.

Corinthe couldn't answer immediately. He knew what she was? Or what she *had been*. She drew her hand away. "I was exiled," she said in a whisper.

He patted her hand and leaned in close to whisper back, "Happens to the best of us."

She wanted to ask what he meant—had Rhys been exiled, too? From where? But Luc took a step closer to the bed. She noticed that he refused to look at her di-rectly. "Can't you just give her one of your vials?"

"What do you care?" Corinthe asked.

Now it was Luc's turn to ignore her. "You have to do *something*," he said to Rhys. "You said you were a healer, right?"

Rhys shoved his cap back and rubbed his forehead, frowning. "I can't stop the poison, but I might manage to slow it down," he said. "I need to head back to the raft. Got some pinches and potions out there."

"I'll go," Luc said, too quickly.

"You don't know what to look for, boy. You stay here and watch over our guest."

Corinthe was about to protest, but Rhys had already turned and stumped out of the cave. Mags swooped after him.

Luc still refused to look at her and an uncomfortable silence stretched between them. Luc began to pace. Corinthe leaned back on her pillows, keeping her eyes on him. She felt a small spark of admiration. Luc was a mortal. He had traveled the Crossroad and been thrust into this awful world of sun and dust, and yet he was okay.

She had never had much respect for humans. They were too weak, too easily swayed and broken. But Luc was a survivor, just like she was. She had sensed it the moment she saw him on the boat. It was what had drawn her to him when she should have been focused on her task.

It was also what made her hesitate at the Marina.

Luc stopped in front of the fire, stoking it with a charred stick leaning in the corner. Corinthe knew it was an excuse to avoid talking to her. She vowed she wouldn't speak first. But as the silence grew heavier, Corinthe couldn't stand the weight of it. She couldn't help it; she needed to say something—anything—but Luc spoke first.

"You're dying." His back was still to her, but she heard him perfectly.

"Rhys said he could buy me some time." Was she actually trying to reassure him? Did he need that? "The poison won't matter if I can just get home. I can regain my strength there and—"

"And try to kill me again?" When he turned to face her, his eyes were cold. "You've tried twice already, but maybe the third time's a charm?"

"I was just following orders," Corinthe said, then immediately regretted it. Too close. It was forbidden to discuss the marbles and what they revealed. Executors would have no power if humans knew what they were, and how they worked.

"Following orders?" Luc repeated. "What the hell are you talking about?"

He crossed the room fast—too fast. He was close enough that she could reach out and touch him. He smelled like citrus and salt and a little bit like sweat—and like something else, too. Something that reminded her of Pyralis. It made her want to bury her face in his neck and inhale until she was satisfied.

She curled her hands into fists and squeezed. She was confused. Her thoughts were like vapors: swirling, impossible to hold on to. It had to be the venom working its way through her veins. A wave of nausea washed over her body and she closed her eyes, feeling frustrated and helpless. How could she perform her last task if she was this weak? It was impossible. But so was failure. Going home depended on this. Seized with fear, she fumbled around her neck, checking for the locket. Thankfully, it was still there, safely tucked under her shirt.

"It's not my decision," she said, turning away from him. "That's all I meant."

He snorted. "So, what? Little green men told you to do it?"

She turned back to him. It occurred to her that he was making fun of her—thought she was crazy. "I told you," she said coldly. "You wouldn't understand."

"Please." Luc spread his hands wide. "Explain it to me."

She couldn't without telling him what she was. What she *did*.

"I knew it," he said shortly. "You can't *give* me a reason because you don't *have* a reason. You off your meds or something?" He narrowed his eyes at her. "That woman in the car—the one who died. Was that you, too?"

Corinthe said nothing. For a second, they glared at each other. Luc exhaled forcefully, a cross between a snort and a laugh.

"And now you're trying to make me crazy, too? Kidnapping my sister? Dragging me to this—place?" He was losing it. He spun in a circle, aiming a kick at a wooden chair and sending it skittering across the room.

"I *told* you." Corinthe, too, was losing it. Her chest flashed hot and cold. Anger. She'd never been this angry before. "I didn't even know you had a sister."

"You're a liar!" The words were an explosion. Luc whirled around to face her. He reached for something in his back pocket—a wallet—and then fished out an old, creased photograph. He leaned forward suddenly, and for the craziest second, Corinthe thought he was going to kiss her. Instead, he slammed the photograph on the wall, just a few inches from her head. "Where is she?"

Corinthe froze. The picture showed a girl with a long tangle of black hair, green eyes, a slightly crooked smile.

And a jasmine tattoo on the inside of her right wrist.

It seemed that the room shifted around Corinthe.

"I . . . I do know her," Corinthe whispered, even as an alarm was going off in her head. Wrong, all wrong. Too many coincidences.

Except there *were* no coincidences.

Luc's jaw hardened. He drew back and shoved the picture down into his wallet. "I knew it."

"No. I saw her. I tried to help her, but . . ." She shook her head. She remembered the blaze of hot panic that had suddenly overtaken her, the way she had hacked at the flower that enclosed the girl. "I didn't know she was your sister."

"Tell me where to find her." Luc's voice was cold again.

An idea occurred to Corinthe. It was a risk — he would know, finally and for sure, that she wasn't a mortal. But she couldn't stand the way he was looking at her — the hatred in his eyes. "I can show you," she said, licking her lips, which were dry again. "Bring me that bowl of water." She pointed to the cart Rhys had set up earlier.

Luc stared at her for several long seconds before moving to the stand next to the bed. He carefully set the bowl in front of Corinthe, then straightened up and crossed his arms. Clearly, he still thought she was — what had he said? — *off her meds. Crazy.* Another human word.

It didn't matter. She would give him this gift; she would show him.

Corinthe unfastened one of the crystal earrings from her ears — miraculously, they were still in place — and used the sharp tip to pierce her pointer finger. Luc let out a small noise of protest. A tiny drop of blood welled up. She shook it out over the water, wincing even as she did. She was so weak.

Life from life; even now, she could feel her energy swirling away.

The blood writhed across the water, dispersing. As it stilled, an image coalesced: Jasmine lying in the middle of a giant flower, encased by the bright blue petals. Vines wrapped around her arms and one pierced her skin right below the tattoo. She looked paler than before, and blue veins crisscrossed her skin.

Luc exhaled. A look of intense pain passed across his face, as though he'd been hit. He sat heavily on the bed next to Corinthe, leaning closer. His shoulder pressed against hers, and for a second she focused on the feel of him so close, on his smell.

Energy—pure and white—passed suddenly through her body, just as it did when she drew it from the gardens at the rotunda.

Her pulse sped up.

She could stitch from people, too? There had never been a need to; she had always been strong enough that the trees, the oceans, and the earth below sustained her in Humana.

Luc reached out and touched the reflection. It became distorted; Jasmine's image rippled.

"What . . . what the hell is happening to her?" Lucas could barely get the words out.

"She's being turned into a Blood Nymph."

Corinthe looked up at the sound of Rhys's voice. She hadn't heard him come back into the room. Neither had Luc, judging by the way he jumped. Mags sat on Rhys's shoulder, still, uncharacteristically silent, like an onyx statue. Corinthe stared at Rhys, who held a small vial in his hand. How was he able to see — to feel — the image in the water?

"A *what*?" Luc asked.

"It means she'll die soon." Rhys was carrying a woven basket. He set it on a wooden table, and began sorting through it. "A part of her will, anyway. Her body will live. She'll have to feed in order to survive."

"Feed?" Luc nearly choked on the word. "What does that mean?"

Neither Corinthe nor Rhys answered. Corinthe felt a pulse go through her. Pity. She had a sudden urge to squeeze Luc's hand. But she didn't.

Luc stood up, nearly overturning the bowl of water. The image of Jasmine broke apart. He raked a hand through his hair. "Can I stop it? Can I save her?"

"Maybe," Rhys said. He stood, frowning, staring at the ground. Then he said, "I've heard say the nectar from the Flower of Life can cure any poison known or unknown, though I've never had the opportunity to see it myself."

Corinthe's entire body went rigid and she pursed her lips — not daring to say a word. Her heart beat frantically, thumping against her chest so hard she was certain they'd hear.

Rhys placed the vial down and walked over to the fireplace, where he pulled something out of a recessed hole in the cave's wall. He brought it back to the bed.

The book had a faded leather cover and yellow edges, held closed by a rawhide string that wrapped around it several times. Rhys carefully unwound the string and thumbed through page after page of intricate sketches of flowers and wildlife. If it had been another time, Corinthe would have asked for him to slow down so she could study them. Whoever did them was a talented art-ist; the flowers looked like they were growing right off the page, and Corinthe felt that if she could only handle the book herself, she might be able to draw life straight out of it. She felt desperate, thirsty for a life energy to replenish what she had lost.

Rhys's fingers moved deftly over the illustrations, as though he was feeling their contours. "Grows only at the center of the universe. I have a picture somewhere. . . . Here it is. The Flower of Life." Rhys tapped his finger on the page.

Corinthe sucked in a breath. It was true. She *knew* that flower, had seen it thousands of times. Seeing the great purple petals, the fernlike leaves that feathered around the stem, made her ache with longing. There was only one growing in the Great Gardens; as a Fate, she had often stared through the heavy iron gate that guarded the Gardens to wonder at its beauty.

The Flower of Life was in constant bloom, surrounded for miles by fields of lush grass in either direction. It grew in the very edge of the Great Gardens of Pyralis Terra. But as a Fate, she was forbidden to approach it.

And she knew that anyone who plucked it would die.

"This flower will cure her?" Luc sounded skeptical.

"Any poison, known or unknown," Rhys repeated. "The nectar is the only antidote." He pointed to the center of the flower.

Corinthe's pulse sped up; already, she felt stronger as she began to formulate a plan in her head.

Luc.

Luc was the answer. He would bring her to Pyralis.

If she could stitch *his* energy—if she could draw it the way she drew it from the flowers and trees—she just might make it to Pyralis. And once they arrived at the gardens, there would be plenty of life to pull from. She could restore her former strength and finish her final task as an Executor. She could kill him *and* reclaim her rightful place in Pyralis at last. But she had to convince Luc that he needed to take her with him. . . .

Luc had returned to the bed. He pulled the book onto his lap and studied the picture of the flower intently, as if he were memorizing it. Dark hair fell over his eyes, and she had a wild urge to brush it away. He shifted a fraction of an inch closer, so their knees touched through their jeans, and she tried to ignore how good it felt to be touching him, even in this small way. Suddenly, the thought of hurting him made her feel sick.

But it was the only way.

And feelings, she knew, were a sign that she was growing weaker. They were a sign that she would die.

"I know where the flower grows," Corinthe said. "I can take you there."

Luc slammed the book shut. "Forget it," he said, without looking at her.

"You'll never find it on your own," she said neutrally.

"How do I get there?" Luc asked Rhys, as if Corinthe hadn't even spoken.

Rhys shook his head as he picked up his vial. "She's right. The pathways between the worlds are confusing and treacherous. Easy to get lost if you don't know where to go."

"But you can tell me. You know things."

"Some things aren't meant to be known, boy," Rhys said.

"More riddles!" Luc practically shouted the words, and caused Rhys to stumble. His tray tipped and the vial fell to the floor, shattering at his feet. A sweet-smelling liquid pooled on the stone floor.

"Good thing there's more where that came from," Rhys said softly. He put the tray down and stepped over the broken glass, back toward the door.

"Rhys. I'm sorry. It's just—"

"Never mind, Luc." Rhys waved his hand wearily. "Never mind."

After Rhys exited, Luc squatted and began to pick up the pieces of glass, placing them gently in the palm of his hand. He moved slowly and sullenly, like a child who had been reprimanded. He was desperate; Corinthe could feel it. Now was her chance.

Corinthe lifted the chain around her neck and pushed

the tiny button on the back of the locket. It sprang open and tinny music filled the room as the tiny ballerina pirouetted.

He turned toward her.

"The flower grows in the Great Gardens of Pyralis. My home. This key can help us to find the gateway and navigate the Crossroad. It will lead us to Pyralis." She turned to Luc. "I can help you get there quickly."

Luc snorted. "Help me?" He shook his head. "Why would you help me? How do I know you won't use the flower for yourself?"

"I don't need the flower," Corinthe said. "Like I tried to tell you, I just need to get home. My strength will be restored once I set foot on the ground." She could hear the pleading in her voice but she couldn't help herself. "You heard what the Healer said. I'm dying. I'm almost out of time. And I need you because I'll never make it alone. You need me, too. You'll never find your way without my help. We need each other now."

"What about your *orders*?" Luc asked.

Corinthe held his gaze. She needed to get to Pyralis, to regain her strength so that she could fulfill her last task, but Luc would never take her with him if he thought she'd try to kill him again. "I couldn't hurt you right now even if I wanted to," she said. It was not a direct answer to his question, but it was not a lie, either.

He stared at her as she closed the locket and tucked it back in her shirt. His gaze was unreadable.

Staring at him, trying to determine what he was thinking, she had a sudden memory of seeing a library for the first time: carved wooden shelves that held so many words, so many messages, encoded and unread, so many things humans felt they needed to say to one another. It was the first time she had ever felt the urge to cry.

The distance between them seemed to shrink. She could almost feel his breath on her cheek. Neither moved as the tension grew, vibrated between them. A tightness gripped her chest, making her lungs work extra hard to get air in and out.

"This doesn't mean I trust you," Luc said finally. He turned abruptly and stalked out of the cave, as though to prevent himself from taking back the words.

Corinthe exhaled. So. It was agreed.

Rhys cleared his throat to alert her to his presence, a small smile carved crookedly on his face. He moved deeper into the room and arranged his tray. He tipped a small vial into a glass of water. "This won't stop the poison from doing its job," he said as he stirred the mixture together, "but it will slow the process. Maybe give you enough time . . ." His voice trailed off and he handed the glass to her, his white eye unblinking.

If she didn't know better, she'd swear Rhys knew what she planned to do.

She wanted to explain but thought better of it.

"Thank you," she said. She swallowed the bitter contents of the glass. She hesitated, then spoke quietly. "I . . . don't make the decisions of the universe. They aren't up to me, you know." For a moment, she felt a wave of sadness. She would never be able to explain to Luc; she had never been able to explain to *anyone*.

Loneliness: that was the word.

Rhys reached out and squeezed her hand.

"You have a tough journey ahead. I don't envy you. But just remember—it *is* the voyage that's the test, ain't it?"

Corinthe nodded, even though she didn't exactly understand what he meant.

"Take this," he said, placing a second tiny vial into her hands. It was the same color as the liquid he had just given her.

Corinthe's chest felt tight. "Thank you," she said, fighting to find the words. "For everything." Already she felt stronger. She pushed off her blankets and managed to stand up. For a second, black clouds consumed her vision, but they dissipated quickly. She smiled—and then, struck with an idea, removed the other crystal earring and pressed the pair into Rhys's palm.

"For you," she said. There was more she wanted to say. She wanted to ask him where he had come from, and why he'd been exiled, and whether he was some kind of Guardian for this planet, like Miranda in Humana. But thinking of Miranda made her chest ache, and she couldn't get the words out.

He held up the earrings to the light. Mags hopped up and down on her perch, emitting several excited high-pitched shrieks.

"Beautiful." His voice sounded wistful as the crystals scattered bright diamonds of colored lights over the walls.

"Can you . . . can you see, truly?" Corinthe asked.

Rhys smiled. "I see with my mind," he said. "That's enough."

"Yes," Corinthe agreed, and squeezed his callused hand.

Rhys coughed. "You'll need these," he said, his voice turning gruff again. He handed her a pair of worn leather boots and a thick canvas pack. "The journey over the mountains is a rough one. The nights get bitter cold, so I packed a few things you might need to get through."

Corinthe slipped her feet into the boots and laced them up. They were a little big, but that didn't matter. Then she shouldered the pack.

"Are you ready?" Luc stood at the mouth of the cave. His mouth was set in a line. Corinthe nodded.

She was ready.

Rhys pulled a folded piece of paper from another hole in the cave wall. He handed it to Luc. "A full day's walk over the mountain, there is a river of darkness that runs in two directions. It's rumored to be a gateway, though I've never tried to use it myself. The map should lead you straight to it, as long as you stay on the path."

"Thank you," Luc said. Corinthe said nothing. She had already spoken her thanks—had spoken the words and felt them insufficient.

"I hope you *both* find what you're looking for," Rhys said. "Safe journeys, my friends."

Corinthe felt Rhys watching them, long after they had pushed out of the mouth of the cave, long after they had once again emerged into the land of blazing sun and chalky heat. She was grateful that Rhys hadn't said anything to Luc, hadn't told him who she was or what she must do.

Even though he knew—he must have known—that their journey could end only one way.

13

"I thought I might find you here." His voice was low, gravelly and familiar.

Miranda didn't turn around. She didn't move at all. She continued to stare at the arrangement of twisted metal and desiccated branches, like a gnarled hand reaching for the sky. It was, she knew, meant to represent an exploding star.

It was crudely done. Stars, when they exploded, were far more delicate, far more vast and powerful, than the statue could suggest. Still, it was a monument to her kind, and for that reason, it moved her.

Overhead, the two suns were beginning their descent toward the rust-red horizon.

She gathered a handful of brown petals and tossed them into the air. They immediately began spinning, as if lifted by powerful winds. With a flick of her wrist, Miranda directed the winds and sent the leaves off the edge of the cliff. They separated and floated away in all directions.

Just like we have.

"You take a chance being here with me," she said at last, tilting her chin just slightly toward her shoulder to acknowledge him. Now she scooped up a handful of red dirt, reminded of an hourglass as she watched it run through her fingers.

Time is running out.

This world was nearly dead. The heat was sweltering; the sun burned everything to the same uniform red dust. It was a terrible place, and Miranda thought with sudden bitterness that she would rather destroy the whole universe than be exiled here again.

"I've never been much for following rules," Rhys answered, lowering himself next to her. Bottles clinked in his jacket.

Miranda allowed herself to smile. A chemist. Once Rhys had been so powerful—a controller of winds and an exploder of worlds. But his residence in this world, and distance from the Tribunal, had taken its toll. It had sucked the energy, the will, from *both* of them. Their powers were diminished. This was the natural way of their kind—a slow, agonized dissipation, just like a comet smoothing down to dust as it flies through space.

He looked older than she remembered. More tired. Radicals could combine with other forces of chaos and grow stronger, burn fiery and bright. That was the Tribunal. Like a black hole in space, they formed a dense energy, ever increasing in its power.

But Rhys had forsaken all that to save her life. He had reversed time to save her, but at a great price.

It ate away at Miranda every time she saw him, which was why she avoided the Land with the Two Suns. The taste of guilt was bitter, like the taste of dust itself. Sometimes it felt as though she could actually see her betrayal, as if it had a physical form that floated between them. Nothing was the same after she had chosen to align her loyalties with Ford, to work with him.

Rhys had warned against it. He'd said Ford was too volatile, too dangerous—and that his strength would burn them both in the end. But Ford was the most brilliant and powerful Radical either of them had ever known.

And now she knew she'd changed too much to ever go back to Rhys. He didn't approve of what she'd become. She hated to think of what he thought of her now.

"You should have let me die," she said. "Look at you, at where you've ended up. Is this what you wanted?"

"You're alive," Rhys said. He took her hand in his rough, callused one. "*That's* all I wanted."

Miranda remembered the first time he had ever touched her, how a whole galaxy had broken apart. The memory was bittersweet.

"There's still time to change your course." Rhys turned to look at her, his white eye wide and unblinking.

Once, Rhys's eyes had been the deepest shade of blue, like the sky before a powerful storm. She could lose herself inside of them. She had lost herself, for so long.

That was before this *place* had taken his sight; taken, too, apparently, his will to fight. Now he was reduced to tending to a never-ending sea of shadows, with an overgrown pigeon as his eyes and sole companion.

In her heart, she was doing this as much for Rhys as for herself. Someone needed to pay for all the pain they'd suffered, for the loss of freedom . . . of love.

"It's too late," she said.

Old feelings, emotions long suppressed, swirled inside Miranda—fierce and hot. She wanted to laugh and cry at the same time. She wanted to burst apart into a million pieces and scream until the sky fell.

"All my charge has to do is kill a boy," Miranda said. "Once she has done it, once she has made her choice and refused the orders of the Unseen Ones, it will alter the very balance of the universe. It will topple their strength and order. It must."

Miranda had spent years guiding Corinthe, and the girl trusted her. There was no reason for Corinthe to believe the marble didn't show truth. Or to suspect that it showed a more complex truth than she could immediately decipher.

She would do as Miranda had tasked her. She was a Fate—fallen, perhaps, humiliated and exiled. But still a Fate. Obeying was what she did.

Rhys sat quietly for a long time. "Have you forgotten about the greatest force in the universe?" he asked slowly.

"Choice?" Miranda shook her head. "You don't understand. This *will* be her choice."

Rhys ran his fingers over her arm. "Not choice, Mira. Love."

Mira. A name she had not heard in over a decade. It made her heart ache with an all-too-familiar longing.

Mira and Rhys. Created from the same star. Out of death, a new purpose—born of the same energies, the same fierce will.

But not anymore.

Weariness weighed on her. This dry, dead place sucked the life out of everything. It was sucking the life out of her. Was she even capable of love anymore? Or had that, too, been sucked out of her after years in exile?

She had once believed, like Rhys, that love was the most powerful force. But she knew now that the desire to live, to thrive, was even more powerful. Corinthe would choose to kill Luc because it meant that she would live.

"Your selfishness will destroy everything." Rhys's voice grew huskier. "You're no better than *they* are, Mira. You're playing with fate now."

"Don't say that." Miranda stood up. She had had enough of this world—enough of Rhys, too. "Corinthe and the boy can still make their own choices."

"And yet the boy's sister becomes a Blood Nymph, and he travels the Crossroad as a human." Rhys stood as well. "Are you telling me you had no role in that?"

Miranda turned her back on him, furious that he still knew her so well. She *had* brought Jasmine to the Forest of Blood Nymphs; it was the only way to ensure the sister would be trapped and unable to interfere. And yet Miranda had made a mistake, not realizing she'd opened up the gateway and allowed the boy to enter the Crossroad. It was the only mistake she'd made, but it would certainly be her last. Everything else would fall into place.

Her sole thought now was on escape, on getting as far away from this awful world as possible. But immediately, she felt Rhys's hand on her shoulder: heavy, warm, and more familiar than any other hand in the universe. A familiar melody played. The same one she'd hummed to herself every day they'd been apart.

"I still have mine," he said. He had made two music boxes—one for each of them—a ballerina and an archer. Both spun on an axis and pointed to what their hearts truly desired. Before, eons ago, they had pointed the way to one another.

That longing, that need, came surging back. She wanted to swing around and throw herself into his arms, beg him to come with her.

But she didn't. She was tired of begging. She was not a dog.

She was not a *human*.

"I lost mine a long time ago," she lied. Turning to face him, she brushed his hand away. It seemed to leave a hole in her chest.

"Maybe you'll find it again and remember." His music

box was the same walnut shape as her own, nestled in the palm of his callused hand. Miranda watched purposefully as the archer spun slowly, his arrow strung and bow pulled taut. Tinny music filled the space around them.

"I hope you understand that I will have to do what I can to influence the outcome as well," Rhys said gently. He closed the music box as the archer was in midspin. "There is balance for a reason, Mira. Some rules must be broken; others must remain."

"Do what you will," Miranda said coldly, suddenly angry that the archer hadn't immediately pointed to her. She felt sick with anger and regret. Born from the same star and firmly on opposite sides, like the two faces of the moon. "And so will I."

14

By the time Lucas and Corinthe reached the mountain pass, the suns had sunk low in the sky.

Luc was having trouble judging how long they'd been walking and how much time had elapsed since he had woken on the beach. His phone was still no help. Not that he was expecting reception here . . . wherever *here* was.

The intense heat of the two suns morphed rapidly into a profound chill as both suns began to set, one just ahead of the other. Rocks quickly became dark shapes against the blazing sky above them, and the narrow mountain trail grew dimmer and harder to follow with each passing minute.

Overhead, the stars began to glimmer out of the deep darkness. Luc searched for constellations he knew—

searched for Andromeda, Jas's favorite constellation. When he picked out the cluster of stars in the inky sky above them, a deep comfort settled into his bones and he somehow felt closer to his sister.

Luc understood now why Corinthe had said she needed him. She was obviously weak, though she was trying to conceal it. For the past hour, she had stumbled often, leaning on him frequently.

His own strength was rapidly waning. He hadn't eaten or slept since the night before, and he had taken only a few sips of water, from the canteen Rhys had packed for them. His feet were so heavy, it took a huge effort to keep lifting them.

He didn't want to stop, but stumbling over unfamiliar paths in the pitch-black would be crazy. So far, they hadn't seen any signs of animals, but that didn't mean there weren't any; and the path was so steep, one misstep could send him hurtling down a rock cliff to a broken neck.

"Let's stop here for the night," Luc said. There was a small copse just off the path, in an area relatively flat and sheltered from the wind by a series of overhanging rocks. They could start a fire and stay warm.

Rocks.

Sticks.

Firewood.

He mentally checked off what he needed to gather. Back *before,* Dad used to take him camping at Big Sur, just the two of them. Luc loved those weekends. No Jas.

No Mom. Just the guys. They'd set up the tent, roast hot dogs over an open fire, and finish the night with hot chocolate. Luc had only been a little kid at the time, but his dad had shown him what to do—taught him how to survive if he ever got lost. It had just seemed like a game to Luc.

Luc felt a twist in his stomach. He wondered whether he'd ever see his dad again. He wondered whether his dad knew how much he'd enjoyed those weekends.

Luc shivered. The temperature had plummeted. "Wait here, okay? I'm going to gather some firewood."

Corinthe nodded. She dropped the pack Rhys had given them and sat down obediently, pulling her knees to her chest. Her long blond hair was a tangled mess, hanging down her back, and her jeans were splattered with red mud. But there was still color in her cheeks, and her eyes were alert.

There were still moments when he hoped—when he prayed—that this was all part of some long, screwed-up dream. He'd wake up in his warm bed, with the sun coming through his window and landing on the piles of crap all over his desk, creeping up the walls and making his old soccer posters glow. Jasmine would be sleeping soundly in her room, one arm flung across her eyes.

But that was the problem: he wasn't waking up.

He pulled on his sweatshirt to fight the chill, wishing he hadn't lost his Giants cap on the rooftop back in San Francisco. Rhys said it would be cold, but Luc had a feeling that *frigid* was more accurate. Every time he exhaled, his breath crystallized. He knew Corinthe must be freezing, not that he should care.

"I'll be back." Luc knew he didn't have much time. The two suns were sitting perilously close to the horizon, like overripe peaches ready to fall from some invisible branch.

They needed to get a fire started or they would literally freeze to death overnight.

He cut through the trees and quickly lost sight of Corinthe. He didn't want to go too far, since the light was fading fast. He gathered whatever he could find on the ground—some twigs and what looked like dry pine needles, except a silvery-gray color and much longer—and managed to break off a few low-hanging branches. Even so, by the time he was done, the suns were completely gone.

Now he could hardly see his hand in front of his face. He could only barely make out the white glow of his sneakers.

He spun in a tight circle, completely disoriented. Which way was it? He hadn't gone too far. He *must* be close.

"Corinthe?" he called out. No answer except a distant howl that drifted through the darkness.

Shit. Howls meant wolves and coyotes and other animals with teeth. Or some unusual predator he'd never seen before, fit only for this strange landscape.

He took a few steps and nearly tripped over a portion of underbrush. Stopped, inhaled, and listened. The wind had picked up; branches clacked together, arrhythmic, taunting.

He stomped his feet to keep the blood circulating. It got cold in San Francisco, but not like this. It had started to seep down into his bones, chilling him from the inside out.

"Corinthe!" He tried again. It occurred to him that maybe she'd just leave him out here to die. But no. She needed him. *She* was the one who would likely freeze without his help.

"Luc?"

The faint cry came from somewhere to his left. He inched toward the sound, stepping carefully so he wouldn't trip. This was how Rhys lived all the time, Luc suddenly realized: in total darkness. How did he do it? Luc's heart was drumming in his throat. He kept having visions of a sudden plummet down a steep hill.

And then, all at once, the sky lightened. Luc watched a covering of clouds break apart, and two crescent-shaped moons were suddenly visible over the peak of the rocks. He exhaled.

The campsite was only a few feet in front of him.

Corinthe huddled against the back of the rocky shelter, her arms wrapped around her knees. Even from a distance, he could see that she was shaking. He lowered the bundle of sticks he'd collected.

The way Corinthe looked—so small, so pathetic and afraid—reminded Luc of the first time Jas had gone off her meds. For two straight days she'd stayed up, talking a mile a minute, trying to wallpaper her room with old magazine covers. Then she'd crashed: Luc had found her curled in a corner, shivering, her fingers stained with paint and ink, the room stinking of glue and only half papered. As he sat with her, trying to coax her to her feet and to the doctor, the magazine covers kept detaching from the wall and sliding down around their heads, like some weird shedding.

The memory brought back a heavy surge of feeling: he was gripped with helplessness and grief.

"Corinthe," he said. She didn't answer. He went a little closer, cautiously—he still didn't trust her. Christ, she looked cold. Her eyes were closed. Her lips were purple. Her breathing sounded shallow and slow. Not a good sign.

"Hey, Corinthe." He squatted so that he was level with her. She didn't wake up. After hesitating for a second, he reached out and began to rub her arms.

Instantly, her eyes flew open. She let out a cry—of anger or surprise, he couldn't tell. He pulled away. He felt like an idiot.

"Hang in there," he said. He was glad, at least, that it was dark enough to conceal his blushing. "I'm going to get a fire started."

He stacked a dozen smaller branches into a neat tepee shape, just like his father taught him so many years ago, then reached into his pocket. The bright pink lighter belonged to Jas. He'd taken it from the wobbly kitchen table the morning after their talk, hoping she'd stop smoking if she couldn't find it. It was a stupid thing to do, totally irrational. She would have just bought a new one at the corner deli. It had been an impulse — powerful, deeper than words — like the time when Charlie Halley had called Jasmine a freak in fifth grade and Luc had punched him.

Love was irrational. Luc knew that. His dad knew that, too.

He wouldn't think of Jas ensnared in that horrible growth; he wouldn't think of Blood Nymphs or blood forests or blood anything. He would only think of finding her.

It took him a while to get the lighter to work. Finally, tiny flames licked at the dry sticks, catching and spreading quickly. He fed the fire more branches, watched the light grow gradually higher, felt the heat ever so subtly begin to emanate. Slow and steady. If he piled too many branches at once, he'd smother the flames and the fire would go out. Though he'd been too young on their old camping trips to actually build a fire himself, he'd helped his dad do it several times — had studied him closely. As a kid, he'd always been like that: an observer. He watched people. He noticed the little things.

How's it look, Dad? I did it myself this time.

I've never seen a better fire, Luc.

He stood up. The fire was good now, strong and hot. He stared at the flames for a while, allowed the warmth to flow through his chest, burn up his memories, turn them to ash. No point in hanging on.

Corinthe had fallen asleep again, curled up against the stone. He eased down next to her.

"Corinthe," he said. "You have to stay awake until

you're warm." He tried to ignore the strange desire to touch her, to run his fingers through her hair. When she didn't respond, he took off his jacket and draped it over her like a blanket. "Corinthe."

She moaned softly when he shook her. Still she didn't wake up. Fear began to gnaw at him. If she was too sick, if she didn't wake up . . .

Would he be able to save Jas without her help?

Gently, he reached out and eased her up and into his arms, pulling her onto his lap, keeping her wrapped in his jacket, rubbing her arms and shoulders. For a second, her head lolled heavily against his, and he could smell her breath. *Flowers.*

She smelled like flowers.

Then she stirred and shifted in his arms. He knew the moment she became aware of him. Her body tensed and she let out a startled cry, half turning in his lap. Her hands found his chest. Her eyes were huge and silvery in the moonlight.

Luc couldn't breathe.

"I—I was trying to keep you warm." His voice sounded distant, unfamiliar, as if someone else were speaking.

For one long second—time enough for him to think about kissing her, about bringing her closer to his chest, running his hands down her back and through the wild tangle of her hair—they stared at each other.

Then Corinthe pulled away, shifting off his lap. "What happened?" she asked.

He felt dizzy and—since he had given her his jacket—

cold. And yet, weirdly, there was a wild heat racing through his veins. He stood up and moved toward the fire.

"You fell asleep. You were freezing." He squatted and stoked the fire, trying to avoid looking at her.

But she came and sat next to him. The color was returning to her skin, and her lips weren't blue anymore. "You did this?"

"Yeah." Luc leaned back on his heels, watching the flames twist up toward the sky.

"How?" Corinthe asked.

He glanced at her quickly to see whether she was making fun of him; but she actually looked interested. "My dad used to take me camping," he said. He didn't like to talk about his family—had never talked about them with Karen, if he could avoid it—but here, in this crazy world, with two moons hanging above them, it didn't seem so bad.

"Dad," Corinthe repeated, as though she'd never heard the word. Then, abruptly: "Did you like it?"

Her question took him off guard.

"I did," he said slowly. "I loved it." He tossed a couple more pieces of wood on the fire, and for a while, he and Corinthe sat in silence. Luc didn't know why, but he felt oddly comfortable sitting with her in the cold and the dark.

"This one time, we hiked ten miles to these hot springs Dad wanted to see," Luc said suddenly. The memory had only just returned to him. "It took all day to get there because I was just a little kid and had to keep stopping for breaks. I was really pissed at him because he made me carry my own pack. He kept saying, 'Trust me. It's worth it.'"

Luc paused. He could practically *smell* that forest; the creeper moss and loamy earth, the smell of animals and growth, and that thick lemon sports drink he always chugged when they went camping.

"Was it?" Corinthe asked.

"What?" He had almost forgotten she was there.

"Was the hike worth it?"

He smiled. It felt like forever since he'd smiled. "Yeah, it was."

Corinthe moved a little closer. Luc was suddenly hyperaware of the space between them: barely an inch separated their arms. "Do you still go camping together?"

"Nah, it's been forever. Since my mom left." The words came out before he could stop them. He'd never told anyone about his mother. Only he, Jas, and their dad knew the truth.

"What happened?" Corinthe hugged her knees to her chest, brushing his arm accidentally with one hand. Her fingers were so small, so delicate, her unpolished nails like little seashells. He wanted to curl his fingers around hers until this stupid burning in his chest stopped. Corinthe said, "You don't want to tell me. That's okay."

Luc sucked in a deep breath. That was the problem. He did want to. "We thought she would come back," he blurted out, and immediately felt like screaming. No, his voice felt raw, burnt, as though he had been scream-ing the entire time—the full ten years since she'd left. That was the sad, pathetic truth. That for years after she walked out, Luc, his dad, even Jas—they'd all believed she would come home. For four years Luc had worn the sweater she'd given him for Christmas to school every year on picture day, even after it was far too small, in case she came home suddenly and wanted to frame his photos.

Luc had been only seven when she left, but he re-membered the day perfectly.

"Be right back," she had said, looping her ratty leather bag onto her arm, sparking up a cigarette. The cloying scent of clove lingered in the air for days after she was gone.

He'd watched her walk down the porch steps; her yel-low cotton dress looked dingy in the sun. Her dark hair, streaked with old highlights, was pulled into a messy ponytail.

She glanced over her shoulder one last time, but she didn't wave.

He and Jas had waited hours for her to come back.

Eventually, Jas had gotten hungry. She sat in the mid-dle of the playroom crying. Luc went to the cupboard—he knew Jasmine loved graham crackers, but they were too high up to reach. Climbing on the counter was not al-lowed, so he used the broom handle to knock the box from the shelf. When the box hit the floor, crackers scat-tered, broken, across the kitchen tiles.

Little fuzzy-haired Jasmine sat down in her footie pj's and started eating the graham crackers straight off the floor. After a moment, Luc joined her and started to reassemble the pieces, like a puzzle. She laughed at the new game and together they spent the afternoon right there on the linoleum.

When his father got home that night and found them still alone, found the money in the canning jar gone, it was as though he, too, vanished.

"She died." He'd never said those words. "My mom died." His eyes stung. Smoke.

Corinthe sat so quietly he thought maybe she hadn't heard. Then she reached out, very slowly, and laid her hand on his. They were warm now, and Luc swallowed against the lump in his throat.

"I'm sorry," she said haltingly, as though these words, too, were unfamiliar.

Luc cleared his throat. "Yeah, well, shit happens." He detached his hand from hers, feeling suddenly embarrassed. "So what about you? Mother? Father? Sisters and brothers?"

Corinthe shook her head. "We have no family," Corinthe said. "I did have sisters, but it was *different* from in your world." Corinthe bit her lip. "Still, I miss them."

Your world. The words reminded Luc that Corinthe was different; that he didn't know *what* she was. He wanted to ask her to explain but he found he couldn't. He was almost afraid of what she might say. He wasn't ready to hear her speak the words: she wasn't human.

But he understood, too, that he and Corinthe had one thing in common: Corinthe wanted to go home. She wanted to go *back*. Luc knew the feeling.

"So why did you leave?" Luc asked,

"I didn't leave. I . . . I made a mistake." Her voice cracked and he had to strain to hear it over the crackling fire. She looked so lost all of a sudden. He wanted to put his arms around her and keep her safe.

"What kind of mistake?" he asked instead.

She looked at him quickly, then looked back at the fire. "You wouldn't understand."

Luc had to stop himself from rolling his eyes. "Try me," he said. He knew all about mistakes. God, look at his mother. His sister. Hell, even he had more than his share of screwups. The first year at Bay Sun, he almost got kicked off the team. The opponent's right fielder had tripped him—deliberately, Luc was sure of it—and all of a sudden he'd been filled with a blind rage. He didn't even know what he was doing, didn't remember anything until Coach was hauling him backward and he saw that the other guy's nose was bloody.

"I did something no one else had done before. Something terrible." She shifted again. Now their knees and thighs were touching. He had that insane urge to put his arm around her, but he didn't have the excuse this time. She wasn't shivering anymore.

He settled for leaning back a little and resting his arm just behind her, enough that he could feel the heat from her body and shield her from the cold. There was that smell again. Flowers. It seemed to be getting stronger, seemed that as she got warmer, her skin exhaled it.

"So what?" Luc said. "They . . . like, kicked you out or something?"

Corinthe nodded. He waited for her to elaborate. When she didn't, he prompted, "So why do you want to go back so bad?"

She turned her head to look at him. A fine line had appeared between her eyebrows. "It's . . . safe. Everywhere else hurts." She frowned, and he could tell she was having trouble putting her feelings into words. "When I first came to Humana . . . to Earth . . . I hurt all the time. Now it's more of an ache. But in Pyralis I feel right, and warm. Like I belong." She looked down at her hands. "It's my home."

Home. Just that word started a slow ache in his stomach. How many times had he wished he could go home, back to how it *used* to be? When he was younger, he'd bury his head in his pillow and shout until his throat was raw, but it never changed anything.

Luc rubbed his forehead. He was trying to make the pieces of Corinthe's story slot together. "And to get back there, you have to . . . *do* certain things? Is that it?"

Again, Corinthe nodded. She picked up a handful of those strange pine needles, and fed them one by one into the fire.

Luc licked his lips. He was closer to understanding but wasn't sure he wanted to. "Like kill people?" Must be a real nice place to live.

"I've never killed anyone," she said fiercely. "I just . . . I help. I make accidents. What you would call accidents, anyway. Coincidences. And chance events."

Luc thought of how he had first seen her: the car, the woman slumped on the steering wheel, the way she had run. As the meaning behind her words sank in, he felt as if he might be sick. He closed his eyes and reopened them. "You tried to kill me," he said.

"This is the first time I've been tasked with a killing," she said, and for a moment, she looked troubled. No. More than that. Angry.

"Why? I'm not that important, so why kill me?"

Corinthe slid her hand away and tucked it into her lap. "I don't know why."

"If you don't know why, how can you just do it?" It would be like dribbling the ball down the field as fast as he could, with the goal nowhere in sight. What was the point? "How can you follow orders if you don't understand them?"

"The point is not to understand," she said simply. "The point is that it needs to happen. It's fated."

"Was that woman in the car a task?" He braced himself for the answer.

"Yes."

He was glad that she had admitted it. It was a relief, in a weird way. And something else became clear to him. At Karen's party, she'd been so determined on the boat, as if she knew exactly where to go. She'd been talking to Mike, too. He'd seen her.

"You set up Karen and Mike, didn't you?"

"Yes," she said, softer this time. "I am sorry about that."

He drew in a deep breath and let it out slowly. The thing was, he wasn't really mad about it.

"I've done good things, too," Corinthe said. "Beautiful things. Births and meetings and discoveries . . . I've given people happiness. Your people."

"What about you?" Luc asked, without knowing where the question came from. "Have you been happy?"

Corinthe turned to him. The question had obviously surprised her. The fire lit up crazy colors in her eyes — threads of silver and gold, that wild violet color — and for a second, he felt as if he was consumed by her eyes, lost in them.

"I . . . I don't know," she responded in a whisper. "I've never thought about it."

She looked totally vulnerable, totally lost. Alone in the universe. The phrase occurred to Luc suddenly, and he didn't know where it came from. Unthinkingly, he reached out and pulled her hand back into his.

It felt good to touch her.

Too good. He felt a surge of energy, and he lost his breath, as though he'd been running sprints for an hour. The world around them seemed to swirl away. There was only her: her eyes, her smell, the softness of her lips. Her skin burned under his fingers, and after a second's hesitation, she leaned into his touch and closed her eyes. He brought his other hand to her waist; he could feel the soft line of flesh just above her jeans.

They were both breathing hard. Heat radiated between them. Corinthe hesitated, then walked her fingertips over his cheekbones, to his jaw, to his neck.

"I've never . . . ," she said.

"Never what?" He could hardly breathe. He would die if he couldn't kiss her.

She shook her head. Then her expression relaxed, and she smiled. She leaned in closer, and simply laid her head in the crook between his neck and shoulder.

He hooked one arm under her legs and shifted her until she was cradled in his lap. She rested one hand on his chest, right over his heart. He didn't want to move, was afraid she'd pull away. Wanted to go further and didn't want to, too.

They'd been so close to . . . what? What the hell was he doing? He closed his eyes and took a few deep breaths.

She kept slipping under his skin in small ways, making him forget who she was. At Rhys's house, she had brushed against his arm and sent his body on high alert. She probably didn't even know she had an effect on him, but he knew it every time she got near him.

At the same time, he wasn't at all sure he could trust her. She'd tried to kill him. She'd led him into this mess in the first place.

That horrible image of Jasmine resurfaced in his mind: trapped in that awful flower, ensnared by the snaking vines. A wave of guilt overpowered him.

"Corinthe?"

She lifted her head. He pulled back a few inches so he wouldn't have to stare into those eyes—the eyes that made him forget who he was and what he was doing.

"I need to see Jasmine. I need to know she's okay."

Corinthe didn't hesitate. She carefully scooted an arm's length away and picked up the backpack Rhys had given them. In it was a flask of water. "Hold out your hands, like a cup."

He did. She poured out a stream of cold water. He knew he might need the water later, might regret using it for this purpose, but Jasmine was all that mattered right now.

Corinthe reached behind him and extracted the knife from his pocket, keeping her eyes locked on his. His breath hitched. She had the knife now. But she was so weak her hands trembled. There was no way she could kill him, even if she wanted to.

She merely pricked the end of her finger, and carefully, deliberately, she set the knife back down beside him. She held her hand over his and allowed a drop of her blood to spill into the water.

She cupped her hands under his. His skin tingled as if a small electric charge flowed from her to him. He stared at the surface of the water, but nothing happened.

Beads of sweat broke out on Corinthe's forehead, and her breathing became ragged.

The water rippled like a tiny lake in his hands, and finally, a wavy image of Jasmine appeared. She still lay inside the flower, but already he could see the changes in her. His stomach twisted. Thick veins were visible under her blue-tinged skin.

Corinthe cried out and slumped forward. Luc let the water run out between his fingers and caught her before she fell to the ground.

Her body was shaking. She felt cold under his touch.

"Corinthe?" His pulse pounded in his ears with a dull thumping beat. He wrapped his arms around her, rubbing her arms vigorously.

Her eyes fluttered open. Slowly, they focused on him. She shook her head. "I'm sorry," she whispered. "It was difficult to find her."

Dread seeped under his skin. "That's not good, is it?"

"I can connect with living things, but . . ." She didn't have to finish for him to know what she meant.

Jas was dying.

Luc wanted to jump up and hike down the mountain in the dark right that second. Wanted to tear apart the whole universe until he found her. But he knew that would be idiotic—a death trap. And his arms were like lead. He hadn't slept for almost two days. A few hours was all he needed.

Then he would find her. He would find her and save her.

No matter what.

15

Corinthe woke up, gasping, from another dream. That made two in two nights. She'd never dreamed before, as an Executor *or* as a Fate. She'd never needed to sleep.

What did it mean? What was she becoming?

The fuzziness of waking up was unfamiliar, too—she felt disoriented as shreds of the dream came back to her, weaving and melding with the events of last night:

Luc's hands on her waist, then in her hair. Luc's eyes, staring into hers. Their lips almost touching. Their bodies creating heat in the cold atmosphere. And then the two of them standing on a wooden pier, extending endlessly in both directions across the Ocean of Shadows. Gazing at the night sky. A shooting star streaking the darkness. Luc's laughter. Another star falling . . . and then another, and another. The shower of sparks becoming a downpour. Constellations collapsing. The pier catching fire, trapping them, forcing them to dive into the ocean, where Figments pulled at their limbs, pleading. Stars coming down like fiery rain, blinding. And then the stars turning into headlights, careering, heading right toward Corinthe.

Principal Sylvia's car, Luc gone. Sylvia grinning wickedly, baring one long, sharp tooth, just like Miranda's.

"What's so funny?" Corinthe's own question echoing inside her head.

Sylvia's grin. "I'm not the one driving."

St. Jude dancing wildly in the window. Corinthe looking down; the steering wheel in her own hands. Trying to swerve out of the way.

Then, the moment of impact: sudden, screeching, horrible. Jolting her awake.

The two suns were already high above the mountains, and a film of sweat lined her brow. Luc's sweatshirt was balled up under her head, and the wall of the boulder at her back barely provided any shade. She sat up slowly, trying to gauge her dizziness.

Not too bad.

She leaned against the boulder for a moment, wondering where Lucas had gone. He wasn't sleeping beside her—he must have gone to forage for more supplies.

She should never have slept, yet last night the urge had been too overwhelming to fight. Over the course of their hike yesterday, she'd managed to steal small bits of energy from Luc every time he touched her. She could draw no strength from the dry, dead terrain and was forced to use his.

It made her feel guilty.

Another feeling she had never known before.

It shouldn't matter that she was using him to get home. That she stitched strength from him to keep going—she took hardly enough for him to notice. It wasn't possible to drain another being of all its life energy anyway. At least, not as far as Corinthe knew. She could only tap into it, feel it, feed off the excess. It was barely enough for her to even stay standing. Definitely not enough strength to fulfill her task. But she had hoped it would at least be enough to get her home, where she would be healed fully.

And now he was gone, and she could feel the absence of his energy in her body. She felt brittle, exhausted: a worn shell.

When he had asked to see his sister, it had taken nearly all the power she had stored up. But she had wanted to give it to him, as a gift, to show that she was not so terrible, to show that she could do beautiful things as well as bad ones.

She wanted him to understand.

She cared what he thought of her.

The fire had burned down to a few embers. There was no sign of Luc, no evidence of where he'd gone. But then she spotted it: scratched into the hard packed dirt were several words. Corinthe began to shake as she pushed herself to her knees.

Don't follow me.

Then, as if an afterthought: *I'm sorry.*

Her chest tightened, and she suddenly felt she couldn't breathe. She fumbled inside her shirt for the reassuring weight of the locket.

Gone.

And just as quickly, a flood of anger replaced her shock, drove out every other feeling. He had taken the locket. Stolen it.

A sickening feeling opened up deep in the pit of her stomach. He had tricked her. Last night, he opened up to her, and in turn, she had told him things she shouldn't have. Things about what she did and where she was from.

It had all been an act. Getting her to let her guard down. So she would sleep. So he could steal the locket and leave her.

Corinthe wrapped the sweatshirt around her shoulders and stood up—still dizzy, still weak, but fueled by anger. The trail they had followed the previous day continued down the rocky hillside. Corinthe began to jog, half blind with fury. And some other feeling, too; one she had no words for. It was like falling backward. Helpless, out of control.

And then it came to her: *betrayed.*

Had this been his plan all along, to leave her stranded, alone without anyone to help her?

Though she had lain beside him all night, she had eked barely enough energy from him to combat the hornets' venom for a few short hours. As she wound slowly down the mountain, she could feel it pumping through her blood. Hot and thick, poisoning her slowly, making it hard to breathe, taking away her strength. Her arms and legs felt like lead, and she stumbled, fell, cursing when sharp rocks tore into her palms.

She kept trying, but she could pull no energy from this dry and desiccated world. She drove her fingers into the rocky ground, hoping to pull something, anything, but this world had very little life to give. It trickled out in tiny drops, accompanied by a pain so sharp and deep it took her breath away.

She broke the connection, trembling. There was hopelessness here, as if the very earth under her fingers had stopped trying to live.

If she didn't find Luc soon, she would die.

She thought of the vial Rhys had given her — thankfully, it was still in her possession — but she resisted the urge to drink it. As long as she could move, she didn't dare use it. Not yet. Who knew how far she had to go, how long it would take her to find him?

The suns beat down with their oppressive heat and a sudden wave of dizziness made the rocks lurch from left to right. She stumbled, then righted herself. Movement flickered along the edges of her vision, almost like people creeping through the rocks next to her, but when she turned her head, she saw only towering arrangements of stone.

She had to find Lucas. She had to get to the flower before he did.

Then, when she was strong again, she *had* to kill him. It was fate.

She'd allowed herself to trust Luc—a weakness far worse than the one caused by the venom in her veins. Perhaps living in Humana had caused her emotions to grow chaotic. She was becoming too much like humans, questioning things that she must just accept.

What would happen to the balance, to the order, if people starting choosing for themselves?

Corinthe's breath rasped in her throat, and her chest felt as if it were on fire. She thought of Pyralis, of sweet relief, a place without pain. Soon. She'd be home soon.

The path flattened out as she reached the lower foothills. With the decreased altitude it was easier to breathe now, although the tightness in her chest remained. She could see only red sand and towering, gray trees, arms twisted as though in lament. Had she somehow gotten lost? Rhys had said the river was a day's journey inland over the pass, so where was it?

Her neck was hot and sticky with sweat. She felt as if she'd been running for hours. She sat down hard on a large rock, gasping for air. There was no life under her fingers; there was no pulse left in this world.

Her vision spun in and out of focus. A wavering white form, like a mirage, moved along the path toward her, and Corinthe didn't have the will left to even stand. She reached for her knife, remembering too late that Luc had taken that, too.

The figure stopped directly in front of her, shifting so

its features became suddenly visible. Corinthe cried out.
Miranda.

Miranda would save her.

"How did you find me?" Corinthe asked.

Miranda didn't answer. "Why is the boy still alive?"
she asked.

Fingers dug into Corinthe's arms and lifted her to her
feet.

As soon as Miranda touched her, Corinthe's body
reacted. It latched on to the energy pulsing from her
Guardian and pulled. Corinthe drank. She couldn't stop.
Strength flowed through her limbs; her vision cleared
immediately.

She'd never felt anything like it before in her life. The
energy was thick and powerful and wild, and Corinthe
wanted more. Instinct took over. She opened her mind.
She pushed for a stronger connection and stitched in more.

Then she was flying through the air.

She slammed into a rock wall and breath whooshed
from her lungs. Miranda stalked toward her, eyes blazing.

"Never do that again," Miranda spat out.

Corinthe pushed easily to her feet. She felt better
than she had since leaving Humana—stronger, even,
than she did after feasting in the garden. A wild anger
flowed through her veins. She'd never felt so out of control before. Explosive. Miranda's energy writhed under
Corinthe's skin like a wild animal, fighting to get free.

"Why are you here?" Corinthe demanded. "Are you
watching me?"

"You've lost the locket," Miranda said. Her hair flowed around her head, as though charged with its own electricity. "How could you let this happen?"

Corinthe clenched her hands tightly into fists. Rage unlike anything she'd ever experienced made her body shake. Never had she wanted to strike out at someone so badly. "I'm dying. And all you care about is a stupid piece of jewelry?"

"It's not just any piece of jewelry and you know it. You *allowed* that human boy to steal it from you," Miranda said. "Maybe you don't *want* to go home after all?"

There it was: the terrible look in her eyes that Corinthe had never seen before. The anger inside fell away so quickly, Corinthe felt as if the world had been pulled from beneath her feet.

Miranda was right. She had let her guard down and allowed Luc the opportunity to take the locket. It was her own fault. She did want to become a Fate again, more than anything.

"I'll get it back," Corinthe said desperately. "But I don't know where he went."

"He's found his way to Kinesthesia already." Miranda inhaled deeply, and for a minute, they stood in silence. "I'm sorry for getting angry," Miranda said at last. "There are too many things at stake, and I only want for you to get home. Here. Take this." Miranda tossed something at Corinthe's feet.

Corinthe leaned down and picked up the heavy key. It was looped on a thick chain, as if meant to be worn like a necklace. She turned it over in her hands and made out the faint image of a spiral, tarnished by the years.

"What does it open?"

"I can't help you any more, Corinthe. I've done too much already. This has to fall to you. This is your task to complete. Go now, quickly, before he figures his way out of Kinesthesia. Do not allow him to use the locket." Miranda's voice grew soft as she closed the distance between them. "You must kill the boy. You know that, right?"

A new resolve filled Corinthe. She had started to feel too much. She had allowed herself to grow weak. She was simply the Executor of the marble, as she had been hundreds of other times. "I know," she said. "I won't fail again."

"You are so close." Miranda gently tucked a stray lock of hair behind Corinthe's ear. Corinthe was ashamed, now, for having been frightened of her Guardian, even momentarily. Miranda was the only one who had ever cared for Corinthe, cared enough to try to ensure that she return home. "Go now, before he gets too far ahead of you."

Miranda took several steps away from Corinthe, and the suns glinted off a new ring on her finger. The glare made Corinthe shield her eyes. There was a brief, blinding flash of light, and then Miranda was gone.

The energy Corinthe had taken from Miranda had restored her somewhat, and she began to run. In no time at all, she had reached the black river. The current rippled in several directions at once, an illusion that made her head dizzy.

Corinthe didn't hesitate. She took a deep breath, and she dove.

Icy water swirled over her head, knocking away her breath. She fought for the surface, but the current caught her, pulled her deeper, into the darkness and the black.

Her lungs burned.

What if there was no gateway here after all?

What if she had jumped in at the wrong spot?

Then, suddenly, she *felt* it: the river released her and her body moved freely, as if she were swimming through air. She could breathe as well. Here, the current seemed to be pulling her in one direction, so she didn't fight it. Hopefully, she would find Kinesthesia. She *must* find it.

She focused on logic and process, the very things that Kinesthesia represented. It was a world at the very center of the universe, the heartbeat that kept everything else in rhythmic harmony.

The cool rush of the river became the soothing hum of thousands of different worlds vibrating all around her like small swirling galaxies, and within reach of so many different possibilities, she momentarily wondered if Luc was right.

Could there be choice in a universe so large?

But if everyone had choice, who would maintain the balance?

Corinthe swam through a comforting, familiar buzz, as though Luc had left a trail of warmth in his wake. She was beginning to feel more comfortable in the Crossroad, remembering that if you didn't resist, you could more easily control your path. All she had to do was lean into it, stay calm, and let her instincts lead her. The water around her started to grow thicker, like molasses. But it was blacker and tasted faintly metallic. She held her breath as she found herself submerged in the thick liquid, pushing on her chest as though it were trying to suffocate her. Corinthe's arms screamed in protest at the effort it took to move, and she fought for the surface. Each stroke was harder than the last. The water was no longer water.

It was thicker—and colder, too—and felt like lead all around her.

Corinthe managed to break the surface and inhaled deeply, knowing she'd made it out of the Crossroad. She struggled to the edge of the river, where a grid framework lined the shore. The liquid metal grabbed at her legs, clawed at her waist, dragged her backward. She just managed to hook an arm over a piece of the metal frame on the banks of the river.

She pulled.

And, suddenly, thankfully, the river released her and she was out.

Liquid metal soaked her clothes and hair, impossibly heavy. She wrung it out the best she could before she stared out over the landscape of grids and vast gears, motion and thunderous noise. She had made it to Kinesthesia.

The pain here was immense. A world of metal and

fire—no nature, no growth, no life at all. Already she found it difficult to breathe. She knew she must find Luc quickly. She could not hope to last in this world very long.

Showers of brilliantly colored sparks erupted each time the enormous gears grated together, pumping out the logic of the universe, the order and the time. The world was laid out across a massive metal grid floor. Gears spun all around her, some as large as the Golden Gate Bridge, and they connected with others the size of her fist.

They moved together fluidly, shifting and changing, hooking up with new gears that rose from the ground. Some fast, some slow, but in perfect harmony. This was the heartbeat of the universe. But each pulse of the giant mechanism sent sharp pain through Corinthe's body.

The world where logic was generated.

Between the gaps in the grid, Corinthe could see more machinery churning away, and multicolored wires braided together, running between them. But beyond that, she knew, was an infinite abyss—a swirling chaos at the core of this world.

But where was Luc?

The grid was crisscrossed with metal walkways, each about three feet wide. But they seemed much narrower with spitting metal below them. The heat was intense. Steam rose from her clothing, hissed up from grates in the ground.

A low vibration shook the entire structure and gave Corinthe the impression of being on a storm-tossed boat.

She barely managed to keep from stumbling. Giant pistons pumped up and down, emitting bursts of steam. Her gaze moved along the arm that rose and fell, connecting a cog to an enormous gear.

Luc was standing underneath it.

Even from a distance, she could tell he was studying her locket, trying to figure out how it worked.

Before she could call out—or decide whether she *should* call out, whether that would make him run—he turned and disappeared behind a piston the size of a house. She began to run.

Behind the piston where she had seen Luc disappear was a suspension bridge made of steel mesh, which spanned a monstrous gap over a chasm of darkness, in which thousands of giant metal teeth were grinding and gnashing together.

On the other side of the chasm was a clock tower at least twenty stories high, whose peak was obscured by thick clouds of steam. Each time the second hand moved, a tremendous tick reverberated through the heavy air.

Luc had already crossed the bridge and had made it to the door of the tower.

She risked calling his name, but either he didn't hear or he pretended not to. The suspension bridge lacked a railing, and it swayed as she shifted her weight onto it, raising her arms for balance.

Don't look down.

She kept her gaze focused on the clock tower. As quickly as she could, one foot in front of the other, she began to walk. Each time the bridge shifted, her pulse leapt. She felt as though she were crossing a vast, dark mouth belching foul steam. She couldn't help but imagine what it would be like to be pulverized by all those metal teeth.

Fear drove through her, made her insides tight. She wondered whether any of the humans she had helped ease out of the world had felt the way she did now.

The idea made her stomach swing. She hoped not.

It seemed to take hours to cross over to the clock tower, and by then, Luc was nowhere to be seen. When she felt solid steel under her feet once more, she wanted to cry in relief. Instead, she threw herself at the door of the clock tower, grateful that it gave way easily to the pressure of her touch, and pushed her way inside.

In the middle of the small, circular room, which was filled with more machinery, more pendulums and cogs, gears and pulleys, was Luc. The noise was slightly quieter in here.

"You," he said, when he saw her. He had the decency to look guilty, at least.

"You didn't think I'd catch up with you, did you?" Corinthe kept her voice neutral, ignoring the fact that Luc was pale, that he looked exhausted and afraid. She would not make the same mistake twice.

"Look, I'm sorry." Luc raked a hand through his hair. "I need to save my sister. And I can't risk—"

"What?" Corinthe's voice faltered. She couldn't ignore the way he was looking at her: the warmth, the pleading.

"You," he said, after several seconds.

Corinthe stared at him, trying to decipher the meaning behind his words.

Luc moved, shifted closer to her. Corinthe reached for her knife that wasn't there. Could she fight him off if he attacked her? She was stronger now, thanks to Miranda. She would put up a good fight. But she didn't know whether she could kill him.

She didn't *want* to kill him.

Miranda had said she had no choice.

Of course she had no choice.

Did she?

A smudge of grease streaked one of Luc's cheeks. In that instant, Corinthe remembered a task she had once been charged with: a mechanic who was to be injured so he could no longer perform his job.

All it had taken was a jack, pushed just out of balance. Corinthe didn't question why or what would happen to the man afterward, but she knew the accident had been necessary to set him onto his destined path.

The marbles—her tasks, after all—were about balance and order.

Just like Kinesthesia.

But now she wondered what had happened to him—to that mechanic. Rob. The name resurfaced suddenly. She was shocked that she had carried it with her all this time.

"I think it would be easier if we just went our separate ways," Luc said softly. But his voice told her the opposite. His voice said *I want to go with you,* and Corinthe felt, suddenly, as if the whole shifting, spinning mechanism of Kinesthesia, as if the heartbeat of the whole universe, paused for just an instant.

"We're going to the same place," Corinthe said. "We cannot go separate ways. Our destinies are intertwined." And it was true—she knew it was true. But exactly how they'd been twisted together, and for what purpose, she didn't know.

Luc sighed and scrubbed his fingers through his hair. His dark T-shirt was torn and she got a glimpse of his stomach, the pattern of his ribs. It made her throat go dry. She wanted to touch him, to heal him.

Luc reached into his pocket and extracted the locket. Then he offered it to her.

"Why are you giving it back?" She hesitated for only a second before she slipped it over her head and tucked it safely under her shirt.

Luc looked sheepish. "I couldn't figure out how the damn thing worked," he admitted. "I jumped into the river, and the current nearly took me down. I pulled myself into this place."

"So you *do* need me after all." It gave her a stupid amount of joy to say it and to know it was true.

Before Luc could reply, a series of shuddering bangs and shrill whistles sounded in the air. Luc cried out, and Corinthe covered her ears. The gears of the clock began to shift. Pendulums swung wildly; cogs rolled loose, spinning frantically, letting off a volley of sparks.

"Watch out!" Luc shouted.

Corinthe whirled around and saw an enormous cog

bearing down on them; its steely sharp edges lit up in the flickering spray of sparks. She was temporarily stunned, frozen, and the word flashed in her head, huge, like a roar of black: *death.*

Luc yanked her out of the way seconds before she would have been flattened.

"What the hell?" He had to shout over the noise. "What's happening?"

"I—I don't know!" Corinthe shouted back. This was all wrong. Kinesthesia was a place of order, of equilibrium.

Angry blue and yellow sparks began shooting from the machinery like fireworks and a loud, steely groan shook the ground under their feet. Smoke clotted the air. Pieces of the tower came tumbling down on them, hurtling through the air like giant pieces of shrapnel, severing the wires below.

A tall spray of bright orange sparks showered up in front of them. Corinthe ducked, just barely.

The giant cog screeched and shuddered, then, with an audible snap, broke free from its anchor. Something slammed into her back and she went sprawling onto the metal floor. Luc rolled out of the way. When she pushed to her feet, she saw her knife wedged into a section of steel grating right behind them.

The floor shifted, and Corinthe fought to stay upright. The smoke grew thicker and blacker. The rhythmic ticking of the clock stuttered, then became irregular, like a malfunctioning heart.

"We have to get out of here!" Luc shouted. He jumped

over a writhing live wire and grabbed the knife handle, dislodging it from the grate. "Do you know where the gateway is?"

"No, but we can't stay down here!" The base of the clock was the least safe place to be, considering all the pieces of fiery metal falling on them. There were copper stairs spiraling along the inside walls of the clock, and they scrambled toward them.

Luc grabbed her arm and yanked her forward several feet just as a beam crashed through the grid where she'd been standing. She didn't have time to thank him.

They ran to the stairs, dodging electrified wires and crashing metal, and began to climb. Lucas took the lead. She watched him jump up several steps, over a fallen piece of bent steel, but before she could follow, a torn wire flipped into her way. There was no way around it. She turned back, only to find herself trapped by the spitting wire.

Lucas shouted her name and she saw him through the thickening smoke, climbing over the bent beam. The walls shook and the stairs became detached from the sides of the tower. She gripped the railing and then ran up, dodging the lethal end of the wire to jump over it. She landed with a jarring thump, but she made it over. Luc raced to her side and dragged his sweatshirt off her shoulders. He whipped the shirt away from them. Flames licked at the material, growing until they engulfed the entire thing. Corinthe watched, wide-eyed.

The tower shook violently, slamming her against Lucas. He held her tight against his chest, covering her head. A large gear broke free above them and crashed down, embedding itself into the stairs.

All around them, Kinesthesia was collapsing. Metal twisted and groaned under the chaotic mess. Live wires zapped and crackled like witches laughing with glee.

This place was the pulse of the universe, keeping everything outside it regulated and connected, and it was *falling apart.* All the worlds were intertwined, feeding off each other to keep balance in all. Corinthe shuddered to think of the consequences that would ripple outward because of this.

They fought their way to the top of the clock tower, where there was a narrow platform below the back of the face. The stairs came up to the platform from underneath, but the trapdoor wouldn't open. Debris had fallen onto it. Finally, Lucas managed to shove it open, and they clambered up onto the narrow ledge of grated steel.

"Now what?" he screamed over the chaos.

The air was heavy with black, acrid smoke. Corinthe's eyes stung, and she pulled the neck of her shirt up over her mouth. The smoke burned her lungs, made her cough uncontrollably.

"What are we looking for?" Luc asked. He had the crook of his arm covering the lower half of his face and black smudges marked his skin. There was an angry-looking gash just above his wrist.

"Anomalies. Disruptions in the pattern!" she shouted. Like the clothes that stayed frozen in the wind. The tree with blue leaves. Or the river that flowed two ways . . .

But as they looked around, they could see no element that seemed incongruous. For a second, Corinthe thought she could make out a figure, moving beneath the grating on which they stood . . . but then an explosion shook the entire tower again and Luc was knocked onto his back on the narrow landing, and Corinthe focused only on him. She grabbed his hand and pulled him up, just as a thick black wire danced through the air from above, writhing like a snake, spitting sparks and lighting tiny fires across dark pools of oil.

They backed up against the clock face. And that was when she saw it: the giant screw holding the hour and minute hands to the clock face did not have normal ridges—instead, the screw had a shape in its top like a keyhole.

Corinthe remembered the key Miranda had given her. "This has to be it."

She yanked the key from around her neck, but her palms were sweating and it fell to the floor. She dove after it, groping blindly through the sparks and smoke. Her heart beat wildly, and she pushed aside the pain of metal digging into her knees and elbows. Luc yelled something she couldn't make out over the noise.

Stay calm, Corinthe told herself. Blinking away the smoke, eyes stinging, she ran her hand blindly across the grating and felt something slip underneath her fingers. At that instant, her vision cleared. She watched the chain jerk down through the grating—quickly, violently, as if it had been pulled from down below.

Until she realized that the key was, miraculously, still

clutched in her right fist. It must have become detached from the chain. She stood, her hand shaking so badly she failed the first two times she attempted to insert it into the lock. Luc put his hand over hers, steadying it. Together, they turned it.

Instead of causing the clock hands to rotate, turning the key made the whole face of the clock turn. It revolved with a grinding, grating noise and came to rest upside down, with the twelve at the bottom and the six at the top, before swinging open like a door.

The winds of the Crossroad waited, almost comforting in contrast to where they were now. Corinthe stood gasping at the vision of serene turquoise light and the smell of clouds, of sky.

A deafening groan sounded above them, and the tower began to collapse into itself. Kinesthesia was falling apart. Corinthe had no idea what that meant for the rest of the universe, but she knew it was bad. Very bad.

She pulled the key from the lock just as the floor shifted underneath them. The key went tumbling downward, disappearing in the smoke.

"Go!" Luc shouted.

This is all my fault.

It was her last thought before the entire tower collapsed over them.

16

Luc gave Corinthe a push and threw himself out of the tower behind her just before it collapsed.

And then, suddenly, the tower wasn't there anymore; they were surrounded by swirling nothingness, by winds and currents. He found her hand and gripped it tightly. Although it seemed there was no ground beneath their feet, they didn't fall.

Luc opened his eyes. They were in a world of mist. Everything was a wash of gray. It was impossible to see more than a few feet in any direction. They could be on a mountain or deep in a canyon and they'd never even know it.

Corinthe squeezed his hand, as if to say she'd heard his thoughts. And despite everything, Luc was grateful she had found him. More than grateful.

In that freakish world of two suns, he had slept with his body wrapped around Corinthe's, his face buried in her hair. She had seemed surprised—and unhappy, he thought—by her exhaustion, by her desire to sleep. But soon she had relaxed, and they lay together, his arm around her, her head on his shoulder, until the first streaks of dawn lightened the sky. Waking with her in his arms had felt too good—right, almost, as if she'd been made to sleep in the hollow of his body. He'd never felt that with Karen—or with anyone.

Corinthe was a virtual stranger and he'd told her things he'd never told another soul. He and Karen had been together for three months. But he'd never been able to open up to her about his family. He'd never wanted to.

With Corinthe, it felt right.

Which was exactly why he'd decided to leave.

But with Corinthe near him, he was not so afraid—and not so alone.

A wispy finger of mist detached from the nothingness and slid toward them. Like the vines on a plant, tendrils of mist wrapped around their feet, climbed their legs. Luc's legs tingled; it felt almost as if he were being coaxed or pulled somewhere.

Luc kicked out and the mist dissolved.

"What the hell is this place?" he said.

"I don't know," Corinthe said. "I've never seen it in a marble."

Luc was about to ask what she meant, but Corinthe pointed. "Look."

The mist in front of them had cleared slightly, and a rocky pathway had appeared, extending into the distance. As they advanced along it, the ground behind them silently crumbled away to more nothingness.

The path was narrow, and they had to walk single file. He could feel the heat of Corinthe's breath on the back of his neck, a sharp contrast to the coolness of the mist.

Each step made Luc more panicked. They were lost, and Jasmine was dying. But the only choice was to keep going forward, into the unknown. There could be no turning back; the mist ate up the space behind them, and the path disappeared.

Corinthe put a hand on his back to stop him. "Wait."

The hair on the back of his neck pricked up. He turned to face her. "What is it?"

Her eyes were wide. "Listen."

Luc closed his eyes and concentrated. At first, he thought he was just hearing the wind rustling through unseen trees. But as he listened, he began to make out individual words. Whispers. Voices.

The thousands of voices that wafted up from the fog were talking, some loud, some soft, some angry, some happy.

"Hello?" he called out.

Laughter, almost directly in front of them, echoed back to them. Luc reached back for Corinthe's hand and pulled her forward along the path. Now he could see shadows passing through the fog around them.

"Hello?" he called again.

"Luc!" Corinthe called out.

He hadn't felt her pull away, hadn't seen her wander off. But she had left the path. Her outline was barely visible in the fog. He turned once in a circle. The path behind them was gone, completely obscured by the thick mist.

Goose bumps popped up along his arms.

"Luc!" Corinthe called again.

Her voice sounded fainter.

"Corinthe!" If he didn't hurry, if he didn't follow her, he'd lose her in this mess. He took a tentative step off the path, feeling ice-cold tongues of mist lapping around his ankles. The ground was soft and springy underneath him, as though he were walking on moss, but the fog was so thick, he could barely make out his own feet. He nearly collided with Corinthe before she materialized, suddenly, in the mist.

He exhaled. He felt better just standing next to her.

The fog in front of them was somewhat less dense, and he saw several sickly-looking trees. Their branches dipped down toward the earth like long fingers waiting to grab them both. Luc had a sudden image of being trapped in this world forever, of circling through the dark and the damp, of listening to the whispers of those terrible voices.

"How do we get out of here?" Luc couldn't stop himself from shivering. "What about the locket thingy? Can't you use it?"

Corinthe shook her head. "It's no use to us here."

Something occurred to Luc then—something that

made his stomach seize up with dread. "You don't know how it works, either, do you?"

Corinthe looked uneasy for a moment. Then she tossed her hair, almost defiantly. "It doesn't matter *how* it works. I'm supposed to follow it. That's all."

Luc rubbed his head, where he could feel pressure building. "Don't you ever get tired of doing what you're told to do? Blindly? Like—like an animal?"

Corinthe jerked backward an inch, as though she'd been slapped.

"I'm sorry," Luc said quickly. "I didn't mean—"

"Come on." Corinthe's voice was cold, and, he thought, hurt. "There's no point in arguing. We have to keep going, that's all."

"Where?" As if in answer to his question, the fog retreated and a new path appeared, between the trees: a series of moss-covered stones and tamped-down earth, winding off into the distance.

The whispers grew louder as they walked, and Luc had the uncomfortable feeling that he used to get when he'd first switched schools in sixth grade—when, walking into the cafeteria at lunchtime, there had been a brief moment where everyone stared at him, assessing, giggling behind cupped hands. When Corinthe paused to rest momentarily, he unconsciously reached out for her hand. He was glad she let him take it.

Up ahead, he noticed a shape moving just beyond the curtain of fog. A person? Something else? He couldn't tell. His throat was dry. The voices rose; he could hear tinkling laughter now, and the distant sound of music.

"What is it?" Corinthe asked.

"Come on," Luc whispered, tightening his hold on her hand. His heart rammed in his chest. They moved toward the shape he had seen, toward the voices, and suddenly the fog rose all around them, thicker than ever. It swept into Luc's throat, clotted his nostrils, made him dizzy.

Then it was gone. Luc blinked.

They were standing on Karen's houseboat.

The ground beneath their feet was now polished wood. Music was thumping from the deck, and he was surrounded by all of his friends. There was a keg on one portion of the deck and paper lanterns strung from the railings.

What the hell?

"Dude, that last play was sick," Ty said. He clapped Luc on the back and handed him a beer. The bottle was cold. "The Duke pulled it out of the air again."

"Now let's hope you bring it for SoCal." That was Jake.

Luc stared at Corinthe. She looked as confused as he was. This couldn't be real—must not be real—but he could even feel the mist from the bay.

When a drunk Cindy Strong bumped into him, he felt it, and when he brought the bottle of beer to his lips, he tasted it, too.

He reached out and poked Tyler in the shoulder. He felt real.

"What the hell, man?" Ty laughed, pushing him back good-naturedly.

Had they gone back in time somehow?

They were on Karen's houseboat, and celebrating a *win*. Was this . . . some kind of different reality? Another chance?

"What is this place?" he asked Corinthe. "Did we go back in time?"

Corinthe looked troubled. "Not even the Unseen Ones can control time." She bit her bottom lip, hesitating. "Miranda told me a story once about a Radical who was so powerful that he turned back time to be with his true love. So he could save her." Corinthe looked troubled. "But it was just a story."

A sense of uneasiness slithered down Luc's spine. If she didn't know where they were, what kind of world they were in, how would they ever get out?

Corinthe slipped away from him suddenly, into the thick crowd. Luc tried to follow her, but he kept getting held up—classmates, people he knew, stopped him to congratulate him on the big win.

"This party's sweet, man," Ricky Semola said. He was holding hands with a girl who had a pale, heart-shaped face and long bangs. She smiled up at Luc.

It was the drunk freshman. Who wasn't drunk anymore.

"Thanks," Luc said distractedly. Everything was just a little different, like a familiar picture tilted slightly on an angle. It made his head spin.

"Yeah. Your girl really knows how to throw a rager." Ricky reached out and clinked bottles with Luc. Luc was about to correct him—*she's not my girl, she broke up with me, she cheated on me, didn't you hear?*—but he swallowed the words.

Karen hadn't cheated on him yet. She had cheated on him here, at this very party.

Ricky and the freshman had wandered off into the crowd, arms around each other. Luc noticed that her skirt hung perfectly down to her mid-thighs.

By the time Luc got to the doorway that led downstairs to the galley, Corinthe was nowhere to be seen. He continued downstairs, into the kitchen. From across the room, he saw the sign hanging on the golden rope.

A sick feeling worked his way into his stomach. Not again.

"Hey, Luc, Karen is looking for you." He swung around and saw Lily leaning on the bar. "She said she had a surprise for you tonight." She raised her champagne glass and grinned.

Luc couldn't even respond. This was getting weirder by the second—Lily *hated* him. Winning he could take. But Lily being nice really freaked him out.

He needed to find Corinthe. He ducked under the cord. The door to Karen's room was open. He hesitated, reluctant to relive that painful memory. But what was the worst that could happen? He'd already see Karen and Mike going at it, and at least this time he knew what to expect.

Luc sucked in a breath and stepped into the room. Corinthe stood in the middle of the room, staring at the bed. It was empty. She turned slowly to look at him.

"They're not here," she said.

He didn't realize he'd been holding his breath until he exhaled. "Are there . . . I don't know . . . alternate realities?"

Corinthe stared at him as though he'd just solved a riddle.

"What?" he said.

"There were rumors in Pyralis," she said slowly, "of a world of possibilities, of missed chances. I didn't believe it. Everything is destiny; there are no chances." Corinthe reached out to touch one of the walls. Her hand shook. "But we're here. How can this be real?"

Different worlds. It still seemed too fantastical to believe. But Luc couldn't deny what was happening.

Jas had always believed there was more to the universe than they could see. He remembered when they were sitting on the fire escape and looking up at the stars, and she'd ask him about it. *Think there's life out there somewhere?*

Not really sure, he finally answered. *You?*

She had smiled. *It's everywhere.*

The thought of Jas made him feel sick.

"So . . ." Luc was having a hard time wrapping his head around what Corinthe had just told him. "If it's a world of missed chances . . . that means we *really* didn't win the game, right? This is just some . . . chance that never happened?"

Corinthe nodded. "But I don't understand. . . ." She stopped in front of the gilded mirror, staring at her reflection with an expression of pain.

"Understand what?" Luc asked.

Corinthe hesitated, took a deep breath, then let it out slowly. "How this world can even exist at all. The universe only works one way. It *must* only work one way." She spun around to look at him. "How can other possibilities exist? How can there be more than one outcome if everything that happens was destined to occur?"

"Yeah, it does kinda blow a hole in your fate theory, doesn't it?" Luc said. He stood up. This was all kind of blowing a hole in his mind, too.

"You don't get it." She glared at him. "If things are random—if choice exists—then everything I know, everything I am, would be wrong. My entire existence would mean nothing." Corinthe was practically shaking. "We shouldn't be here," she said, with sudden ferocity. "We have to find a way out."

"And how do you know this wasn't supposed to happen? If you believe in fate, maybe this is it. The way it *should* be." He said it to provoke her, but as soon as the words were out of his mouth, they seemed to take on new meaning. They were standing so close together he could make out individual threads of color in her eyes.

If you believe in fate, maybe this is it.

They stared at each other for a moment more, their bodies leaning ever so slightly toward one another.

"We should . . ." He let his voice trail off.

"Go?" she finished, but she sounded as if she was having a hard time breathing, too.

Her eyes were on his lips again. His pulse stuttered. He wanted to kiss her desperately, just once. He slid his arm around her waist, and when she didn't protest or try to stop him, he brought her closer against him.

Her fingers rested on his shoulders and she looked up at him from under her eyelashes. Her eyes turned violet around the edge of her irises. He slid his hand up her back, along the curve of her neck, to cradle her head. Only an inch apart. Those lips.

She trailed her fingers along his collarbone and he forgot how to exhale. This was crazy. Insane.

Right.

"Luc," Corinthe whispered.

And then, suddenly, he felt a whoosh of air at his back and swung around.

"Mike said you were in here with some girl," Karen spat from the doorway.

Luc backed away from Corinthe instinctively. Karen's cheeks were splotchy and red. Behind her, lounging in the doorway with his arms crossed, was Mike. He shrugged when he met Luc's gaze.

"I can't believe you'd do this to me." Karen's voice was shaking. She took a step into the room, and for one wild second, Luc thought she might swing at him. "*I* went out with *you*, you know. It's not like I couldn't do better."

"You're the one screwing around with Mike, Karen." It felt good to say it out loud, even if it didn't matter anymore.

Karen's mouth opened and closed. She looked at Luc and Corinthe, then to Mike. "I don't know what you're talking about," she said stubbornly.

Corinthe laid a hand on his arm. "Luc," she said quietly. "Does it really matter? Really?"

She was right. None of this was real.

Maybe it never really had been.

Luc's pulse was a hum underneath his skin as he pushed out of the room and off the boat. He could hear Corinthe running after him. The noise from the party faded around them. Everything was silent except for the lapping of the waves, except for the sound of Corinthe's breath.

There was that smell of flowers again.

A breeze lifted the hair around her face and it danced erratically. The air changed, grew cooler, damper. And he realized that the noise of the party really *had* faded; the fog was rolling in. Suddenly, he and Corinthe were once again alone in the mist.

The boat, the party—it was gone. The moment had passed.

The fog began to swirl, becoming so dense he couldn't even see Corinthe. Instinctively, he reached out and grabbed her hand through the thick, cold mist, just as they were wrenched through spinning nothingness like kites on a string.

When the world righted itself again, they found themselves waist deep in cold water.

The mist still hung heavy in the air, but it was different—frozen and salty when he licked his lips. In the distance, a foghorn was blowing.

Boats bobbed against their moorings, and in the

distance, he could see the Golden Gate Bridge. They were at the Marina again.

They were still in San Francisco?

Luc turned, some anxiety needling him, demanding attention. They'd been in this exact spot before. Right before . . . A loud crack filled the silence, and the mast over Luc's head snapped, crashing into the bay only feet from where he stood.

He covered his face against the splash. The next thing he knew, Corinthe was there, so close he could feel her breath on his cheek. Before he could react, a sharp pain seared through his stomach. A wave of pain and nausea made his legs weak and he staggered backward.

He looked down to see the knife handle jutting from his gut.

17

"Oh God, I didn't mean . . . It was just there. . . . I couldn't stop it." Corinthe gripped the knife in her hand. She couldn't believe what she had done.

But this wasn't real. It couldn't be.

He couldn't die. Not like this.

Luc struggled to the shore, collapsing onto the ground. The knife was slick with blood now. Corinthe sank to her knees in front of him. She reached for his face. She was shaking so hard she was nearly convulsing.

"I don't know what to do," she whispered. "This was supposed to happen. But it *didn't*. I—"

Luc groaned. He inhaled a ragged breath and pushed himself to his feet. Corinthe immediately wrapped her arm around his waist to help him stay upright. She could feel his energy flickering, fading in and out. She couldn't stitch from him. He didn't have enough strength to spare.

"This isn't real," he panted. "It can't be. So we just have to keep moving, right?"

She nodded. He leaned into her and together they plunged forward. One foot in front of the other. They made it to the road before his strength finally gave out. There was nowhere to go anyway. He sank to the ground.

Corinthe sat down beside him and slipped her fingers through his again, drawing his head into her lap. His energy was barely detectable, like a flame sputtering in heavy darkness. She was wild with panic—and fear, too: the sickening knowledge that this was what she was meant to do, what the universe had charged her to do.

Luc coughed and shook in her arms. And then, slowly, gently, the fog began to roll in. It swirled around them, stroking its long fingers over his stomach.

"Luc!" she cried. The vision began to fade, and Corinthe felt her limbs trembling. When she thought she'd stabbed him . . . it was as if a piece of herself had died, too.

There was no knife now. No wound.

Corinthe let out a small sob of relief.

"I'm sorry," she whispered. How could she complete her last task when even the *idea* of his death hurt so badly?

He sat up. "It wasn't real," he said. He smiled and touched her face.

It will be. The words were strangling her. Corinthe placed one hand on his chest. As earlier she had been able to draw energy from the tree, now she could feel his

emotions vibrating just below his skin, pressure building, as though he might explode. She tried to stitch just
a little—to work out some of the venom, some of the
despair—even though it made her exhausted.

She could feel his heart hammering. She could sense
his confusion, and his longing, and something else. . . .

How could one person affect the balance so much
when the universe was so big?

Why couldn't Luc live?

What would it hurt?

Never before had she been unable to execute a fate.
His hair had fallen forward into his eyes, and she noticed for the first time that his ears were a perfect seashell
shape, tinged with pink, and that there was a small scar
just below his lower lip.

She kept staring, trying to figure out what it was
about him that made her act so different. She'd met
countless humans during her exile in Humana, had
lived among them for ten years, but she had never
understood one.

Somehow she did understand Luc—wordlessly,
deeply.

And yet, what Luc was doing to save his sister still
didn't make sense to her. His need to rescue Jasmine
was ecstatic and painful, and almost addicting, flowing
through his body and out of his skin, into her touch.

"Your sister," she said automatically, finally pulling
her hand away from his chest. "You love her." It was
more of a statement than a question. The concept of

love was foreign to Corinthe, but she knew it was very, very powerful.

"Of course I do." Luc's brow wrinkled.

A question was building inside her, something she had never thought to ask before. She took a deep breath. "What does love feel like?" she blurted out.

He looked at her then. His eyes darkened, shifted, as though shadows were moving underneath them. She suddenly regretted having asked. The question felt far too intimate.

"I mean, you love your sister," she said hurriedly. "But what does it feel like?"

He ran a hand through his hair and frowned. She wondered if he wouldn't answer, but after a minute's pause, he said, "It's like, you care about someone so much that you'd do anything to keep them safe. That it kills you to think of them getting hurt."

"I love Pyralis," she said, knowing that on some level it was true. It was the thing, the idea she felt closest to in the world.

He shook his head. "It's different. You can love places, but not like you love people. Sometimes it feels totally out of control. Like you don't have a choice. Gets under your skin like this itch you can't scratch and it makes you insane, but in a good way, because you know you can't live without it. Kind of like . . . well . . . kind of like your whole idea of fate, actually. Now that I think about it."

Corinthe shifted uncomfortably. It sounded an awful lot like how she felt when Luc touched her. Maybe this squirmy uncertainty inside her—this desire to feel what Luc felt—was yet another sign she was becoming more human.

"Does it feel the same for everyone? I mean, do you love your sister the same way you love that girl on the boat?" she asked.

His eyes flashed. For a second, he looked angry. Then, to her surprise, he smiled.

"No, it's not the same. I thought . . . Look, I didn't love Karen. I knew we were too different to last. I trusted her, I let her in, and she messed with me. I was pissed. But I can live without Karen. I can't live without my sister. She's all I have. Literally."

"What about your father?" she prodded.

In Pyralis, the Fates just existed with no beginning or end. There were no parents, no families. They called each other sisters, though there was no real relation.

"My father stopped caring a long time ago," Luc said, pushing to his feet abruptly.

Corinthe watched his fingers curl into fists at his side and he clenched his jaw, making the muscles there flex and jump. "Ever since, you know. My mother." He stopped to clear his throat. "He loved her, probably. *I* used to. But now . . . I don't know. Love changes, I guess; people change. Nothing lasts forever." His voice broke.

"But how can you go on, believing that?" she asked. He was right, of course—humans didn't live forever— but also completely wrong. He was so innocent, so fragile in that moment that it made Corinthe's chest ache. The universe was so much wilder and greater than Luc could possibly imagine, and she wished she could convey this to him somehow. That there *were* some things that lasted.

He shook his head. "All that matters is right here, right now. Making sure you have one more day, then one more after that."

For the first time in her life, Corinthe truly understood what being mortal meant. And for her, now, there might not be a tomorrow. The hornets' venom was still working inside her body. She would die if she couldn't reach Pyralis in time.

There was a weight in her stomach, a curdling sense of guilt. Yes, guilt. Because she knew Luc trusted her.

It killed her a little inside to think that she would have to betray him.

They continued forward through the fog. It grew darker, and a wind picked up, so that the mist lashed around their ankles, cold and wet, like weeds. With the wind came whispers, strains of music and laughter, as the sounds of other worlds blew back to them. It was so dark Corinthe couldn't see.

The wind crested to a howl; mist swirled around them like a blizzard. Had they at last reached the Crossroad?

"Luc!" she cried out, suddenly fearful that she had lost him.

Her voice sounded thin in the vast darkness. She reached for him, and he took her hand and squeezed.

"We'll be okay," he said, and she knew he was trying to act brave for her sake. "I won't let anything happen to you."

A gust bigger than all the rest swept through the blackness, forcing them apart. Corinthe felt her fingers—frigid, stiff, and clumsy—slip from Luc's grasp. Inch by inch, they slipped apart as the wind became a tornado, freezing Corinthe's insides, turning her to ice.

"I can't hold on!" she shouted to Luc.

"I've got you!" But he didn't. He tried to grab for an arm, but it was too late: inside she felt frozen, couldn't feel the beat of her own heart. It hurt to move, to breathe, even to think. As his fingers brushed her arm, she watched in horror while her skin began to shatter.

The last thing she heard was Luc shouting her name.

For several seconds, she did not exist. Not really. She had been blown apart, shattered into uncountable pieces. She couldn't feel her body. She was nothingness.

And then, slowly, a pulse came through her and she was able to move. She was shaking, but she was whole. She could feel her arms and legs again. The shattering . . . it had been an illusion, but she'd *felt* it. Like the universe itself, she was losing equilibrium, becoming both Corinthe and *not*-Corinthe at the same time.

One way or another, this was all going to end, and soon. No one got this many chances.

She fought to keep her balance as she took in her surroundings. The ground under her feet was trembling violently, and it was hard to stand. She was on the roof of a concrete building. It appeared to be the very roof-top where she'd first arrived in Humana so many years ago—and where she and Luc had faced off—but she couldn't tell if this was actually the same San Francisco or just another alternate world.

Not until she saw Luc's Giants cap lying in the corner where he'd dropped it.

This *was* San Francisco.

"Luc?" She turned around, searching for him. A low rumble started again, and the entire building shook. Corinthe heard screams and sirens from somewhere down on the street.

Where was Luc?

The roof was starting to splinter and crack. She had to get down to the street before the building collapsed. The red roof-access door was jammed, and it took all of Corinthe's waning strength to pull it open on its bent frame.

Another, harder aftershock rocked the building, and Corinthe slammed into the interior wall so hard it knocked her down several steps. She felt a sharp pain in her ankle as her foot twisted beneath her. Plaster rained down from the ceiling, and smoke started to fill the small space.

Earthquake. Had to be. She'd experienced several of them in San Francisco, but none this severe.

She stood and held on to the iron railing that ran the length of the steps, then put a little weight on her ankle to test it. It held. If she was careful, she could walk on it.

She gritted her teeth and took the steps one by one, hobbling the best she could. Her ankle didn't feel broken, but it hurt worse than the smoke burning her lungs and eyes. Limping and coughing, she pushed herself down the last few steps and shoved the heavy double doors open. She felt as if she'd stepped into one of the nightmares she'd heard humans describe, an awful vision of chaos.

Out on the street, people stumbled out of doors, pushing past her. A child with huge eyes glanced back at her, a tiny trickle of blood running down her temple. The mother jerked her around a corner before Corinthe could react. No one stopped to ask Corinthe if she needed help; most didn't even look at her.

She glanced around. Whole buildings had toppled, leaving piles of concrete and iron in the street. Power wires were down, sparking in puddles of liquid. Plumes of smoke billowed toward the sky, filling the air with a dusklike darkness.

This was her fault. She had disturbed the balance of the universe. All fate was intertwined; the universe was too tightly woven. By pulling on one strand, she had begun to unravel all of the others.

A radio crackled from a car that sat deserted on the street.

Confirmed 7.9.

Extensive devastation.

Multiple casualties.

Bruised people stumbled by, looking dazed. A child bawled in her mother's arms. A man was shouting into a cell phone, and a teenage girl was crying, sitting on the stoop of a house whose roof had collapsed.

The streets were congested, full of abandoned cars and rubble. Fire trucks and police cars wove around the debris, sirens wailing. Down the block, she could see forked tongues of fire licking from the windows of an apartment building.

Blindly, Corinthe began to hobble through the mess. Halfway across the next block, she tripped over something. A leg. It was protruding from underneath a large pile of bricks. There was no shoe on the foot, but Corinthe knew the body was a woman's; she could even make out the pink nail polish underneath the opaque stocking, the dainty toes.

Corinthe's stomach flipped. She thought she was going to be sick. Death had never affected her this way before, another indication that she was becoming more like them. It was wrong. The chaos was all wrong.

She had always been warned that trying to alter fate would have dire consequences.

Was this all her fault—because she hadn't yet finished her task? Because Luc, a human, had been traveling the Crossroad with her?

Her tongue felt thick, and it took enormous effort to swallow. Miranda. She had to get back to the rotunda— she had to find Miranda.

She looked around to try to orient herself. The dust, the howling of the sirens, the smoke—it made everything look foreign. Most of the familiar landmarks were gone—destroyed, buried under rubble. She limped to the next intersection.

Divisadero and Pine: the same place where she had directed the principal to her death. The pharmacy on the corner was missing its sign; half a wall had caved in.

It seemed so long ago that she had performed that task. Now she was back and she felt a spasm of pain, of doubt. Had she done the right thing that day? Had she ever done the right thing?

Who decided?

Corinthe forced the thoughts out of her mind. It was too late to change the past. She could only think of the future now.

She started moving again. She noticed a man advancing toward her. Every few feet, he stopped strangers in the street, gesturing frantically, eyes wild. At first, Corinthe thought he must be asking for money. But as he got closer, she saw that he was holding up a picture. She began to make out what he was saying.

"Please. I'm looking for my children. Have you seen them?"

"Please. Help me find my children."

When he reached Corinthe, he turned to her with the same imploring eyes. "I'm looking for my children. Have you seen them?"

There was a fine line of blood trickling from his forehead, and he was covered in a white dust. Corinthe almost pushed past him, but the panic in his voice made her hesitate and flick her eyes to the small picture: a dark-haired girl and a smiling boy.

"I—I'm sorry," she stuttered.

The man grabbed her arm. "Please. Help me."

Her mouth tasted like metal. *My fault.*

"You're hurt." Her voice cracked. "You're in shock. You need to be treated."

She took his arm and guided him forward; he followed her mutely. A fire truck and two ambulances blocked off the street to her left, and Corinthe led the man toward one of the EMTs, a middle-aged woman with gray hair. The woman was examining a body.

"He's bleeding," Corinthe told her, and the woman looked up. Corinthe felt another squeeze of pain. For a second, she had mistaken the woman for Sylvia, the dead principal.

The principal Corinthe had killed. *My fault, my fault.*

"Thank you," the woman said briskly. "We'll take it from here."

Corinthe nodded. There was nothing else she could do but keep moving.

The route to the rotunda should have only taken a few minutes, but she was hurt, and at the intersection of Richardson and Chestnut the street had collapsed, leaving a gaping hole and a broken gas line, which the police were trying to cordon off. She backtracked to

Lombard and cut across to Lyon. She passed beautiful town houses that had been reduced to splinters of wood and concrete, cars crushed under the weight of trees and lampposts.

Was this the end of Humana?

When she crossed over Bay Street, she had to stop and climb carefully over a toppled tree that lay across the road. The Palace of Fine Arts was barely recognizable. The columns that had once majestically lined the walkway had collapsed and lay in piles across the lawns, one of them half immersed in the lagoon. The roof of the rotunda still perched precariously on broken supports.

Corinthe fought back the surge of terror and broke into a run.

Halfway across the rotunda, the earth trembled and bits of stucco rained down on her head. The supports shifted and the roof sank a few inches closer to her head. A chunk of concrete had smashed into the column with the concealed panel that revealed the secret tunnel. The doorway was standing open, half blocked by fallen rubble; Corinthe could barely squeeze through it.

Miraculously, the power had not gone out yet, and the dim bulbs over her head allowed her to make her way down the narrow staircase. Bricks had fallen loose from the walls, but the steps were intact.

The rooms had not fared so well.

The kitchen was in shambles. Broken dishes littered

the ground, and the table lay on its side. Water overflowed the tub and gushed onto the floor. Steam filled the air and made it thick and hazy.

Corinthe sloshed her way through the debris to her room. It didn't even look the same. The trunk that held her clothes was smashed open, and bits of colorful cloth—her clothes, all her belongings—were visible. The entire wall on the far side had collapsed. The mural she had worked on for weeks was ruined; it lay in tatters on the floor. Corinthe felt a sense of loss so strong it almost carried her off her feet.

Then she heard a low moan from the corner.

"Miranda!" she cried.

Miranda lay pinned under a slab of concrete, her midsection crushed. There was a trickle of blood at the corner of her mouth. Her breathing was labored and short.

Corinthe attempted to heave the rock, but it wouldn't move. Miranda's eyelids fluttered and she opened her eyes. Her lips turned up into a smile.

"You came. I knew you'd find me." She coughed. Air wheezed from between her lips, and a speck of blood dotted her chin.

Corinthe was filled with fear unlike anything she had ever known. It was as though a Crossroad had opened inside of her, filling her with whipping panic. Corinthe reached out and gently wiped Miranda's blood away with her sleeve. "What happened?"

"I came because I couldn't find you. I was worried. I knew your last task was still incomplete. Then the wall—" Miranda coughed again. A spasm of pain passed across her face. "The wall . . ."

"Shhh. Don't try to speak." Another low tremor reverberated through the ground. "I have to get you out of here." Again, she strained to lift the rock, pulled until her lungs felt like they'd burst in her chest. But it was too heavy, and she was far too weak.

Miranda closed her eyes and opened them again. Her breathing was growing fainter.

"It's too late for me, Corinthe," she said.

"Don't say that." Corinthe felt a pressure in her throat. Her fault, all her fault.

Miranda lifted her hand and laid it on top of Corinthe's. It was cold. Miranda had stayed with her in Humana all these years to guide and protect her, to make sure she never stopped believing she'd one day go home again, only to die here, in this splintered, terrible world.

"Have you completed your task yet? Is the boy dead?"

"I'm sorry." Corinthe could barely speak past the knot in her throat. This was what it was to feel, and to lose, too: for a moment, she was gripped by a sense of remorse for all the lives she had taken, all the pain she had helped bring to the world.

"There is still time, Corinthe. You can still fulfill the fate and go home." Miranda squeezed Corinthe's hand and a smile played across her lips. Corinthe thought Miranda had never looked more beautiful.

"I don't know how to find him," Corinthe choked out. "It's too late."

"It's never too late. This is your fate, too. Remember that." Miranda coughed and blood specked her lips. Her grip tightened painfully around Corinthe's fingers. Miranda cried out, her body jerking as though an electric current had run through her.

Then her fingers relaxed.

"Miranda," Corinthe said. Miranda didn't respond. Corinthe felt the pressure in her throat building to a scream. "Miranda!"

Corinthe turned away from the body, fighting the urge to gag. She wanted to cry, as she had seen humans do—to sob, to scream—but nothing would come.

"I'm so sorry," she said. "Forgive me. I'm sorry."

Her Guardian was gone forever. Lucas was lost in another world where the chances of finding him were next to impossible.

It had all been for nothing.

The years of exile, her job as an Executor, the chance to go back to Pyralis.

The walls began to shake again as a low rumble worked its way up to the ceiling. Corinthe stood unsteadily. The ground swayed and she stumbled forward, bracing herself in the doorway. Behind her, another section of the wall collapsed, burying Miranda under a pile of stones.

It was a struggle to remain upright. The stairs seemed so far away. The shelf where Miranda kept her potions rattled fiercely, and bottles slid off one by one, crashing to the ground. The lights overhead flickered and then went out, burying Corinthe in darkness.

Then, for several seconds, everything went still and perfectly silent, except for the gushing of the tub, which was still spitting water.

A thunderous crack sounded, rolling across the ground, up the walls, and into the ceiling. The earth bucked, and an entire section of roof collapsed in a deafening roar, missing her by only feet. Dust blasted her face, and she turned away, coughing.

When she opened her eyes, hazy light filled the room. So much dust sifted down from above it was as though it had begun to snow. Debris was everywhere, and Corinthe saw that a huge hole had opened to the sky above her.

Not since the first day of her exile had Corinthe felt so alone, so lost. She ached all over. Weakness made it hard to stand. She could feel the venom and its sluggish movement through her veins. How long had it been since she had been stung?

Surely she was almost out of time.

She was so tired.

Maybe she would curl up here. Sleep for a bit. She had no fight in her left. But as she sank to her knees, a touch of blue caught her eye. Half buried in the rubble was the painting she loved so dearly—miraculously intact. She grabbed the frame and gingerly stood it on edge, shaking it a few times to dislodge the dirt.

She couldn't believe it had remained undamaged. It was a sign. It had to be.

The children in the painting were still there, holding each other's hands, looking away from the garden.

The sight broke Corinthe's heart.

The simplicity of it. The sense of possibility.

The love.

She knew, suddenly, what she had to do.

18

Luc's skin felt as if it were about to peel off.

He crawled blindly through a world of fire — flames roaring so loudly he could hardly think. The smell of burning singed his nostrils, made him gag. There were no pathways here, no signs pointing to a way out. Just heat and light and smoke and pain, forked tongues of orange and yellow.

And *blue*. His heart leapt. On his left burned a giant flame that was different from the others. A yellow finger of fire burned at its center, but the outer flame was all blue.

The opposite of a normal flame.

Before he could change his mind, Luc flung himself into the flame's center. Searing heat ripped at his skin, and he clenched his teeth tightly to keep from screaming. The pain crested, became unbearable.

And then the light, and the heat, blinked out at once.

He found himself out of the Crossroad and in utter darkness, on ground as frigid and hard as concrete. He shivered. Every breath was painful.

Move, his brain commanded. He had to keep moving, even if he had no idea where he was.

He hoped he wouldn't walk straight off a cliff.

He climbed dizzily to his feet and painstakingly inched his way through the darkness. Terror made him completely disoriented. This was the closest he could imagine to *nothingness*, to an endless void.

His foot hit something—a rock, maybe? As he moved carefully forward, the darkness seemed to become slightly less dense. There were now gradations of shadow, distinctions in the dark—his eyes were adjusting.

Something large loomed ahead of him. He ran his fingers over the surface, recognizing sharp angles and smooth crevices. It was a boulder, judging by the size of it. He navigated around it, keeping one hand firmly on the cold stone to orient himself. On the other side of the boulder, he heard the faint trickling of water.

Tiny lights flickered in the distance. They looked almost like fireflies. And in the sky, twin crescent moons rose over the mountains to his left.

Despair rose thick and high in his chest. He was back—back in the land of Figments and Figures, at the very edge of the universe.

Back where he had started.

And he knew then, knew for positive and for certain, that he no longer had a prayer of saving Jasmine.

Luc couldn't control himself any longer. He spun around, kicked at the first thing he saw, sent a rock skittering into the darkness. He was so angry he wanted to punch something. If Corinthe was right, if this had all been fated, he wished he could burn down the whole universe.

Thinking of Corinthe made him feel even worse. He felt a fierce longing for her; it was here, in this very world, that she had pressed up against him in her sleep.

"Why?" he screamed into the darkness. "Why? Why?"

"Shhh," a low voice said behind him.

Luc whipped around, fumbling for the knife in his pocket. "Who's there?"

A shadow moved separately from the dark around it. "You looking for the pairing?" it asked in a hushed voice.

"The . . . what?" Luc asked.

"The gathering," another voice said.

"I don't know what you're—" Before he could finish, a person seized his arm.

"Don't be afraid," the first person said. A girl, Luc thought, judging from the whispery voice. Her features were dark. Where she touched him, he felt warm. His anger dissipated; he felt weirdly calm. Maybe he could search out Rhys. Maybe there *was* hope.

The shadowy shapes led him down an indistinguishable path. They stopped in front of another huge rock. "Here we are."

"Where . . . ?" Luc started to ask, but once again, his two guides hushed him.

"It's okay. I was really confused my first time, too," said one.

"We missed you," said the other.

Before Luc could ask what they meant, they had rapped three times on the rock face. It slowly slid off to one side, as though it had been set on tracks, and a set of stone stairs was revealed, dimly lit by lanterns.

As the girl passed in front of him, under the light, Luc stopped. The bottom dropped out of his stomach like on the dip of a roller coaster. It wasn't a person at all. It was just a shadowy outline, featureless, faceless.

A Figment.

The girl—the thing—realized Luc was no longer behind her. "Come on," it whispered.

The other person—also a Figment—hovered by his side, as though looking at him curiously.

Luc hesitated. His head was spinning. Figments were supposed to be confined to the Ocean of Shadows. How had these managed to escape?

"What do you mean, you missed me?" Luc said, hedging.

The second Figment put its shadowy, weightless hand on Luc's arm. "You don't remember?" it asked.

"We are yours," the girl Figment said.

"Mine?" Luc's voice cut through the darkness.

"Your shadows," they answered simultaneously, then turned and continued down the stairs.

Luc followed them, stunned and unable to speak. As he trailed his shadows, he felt a sense of relief, or victory, even—the way he'd lose the ball on the field and find his way to it again.

As if reading his mind, one of the Figments broke the silence. "We'll be separated again, after this. . . ." She motioned down the dark passageway, where the faint sound of music drifted.

"But this isn't the end," the other Figment added. Its voice was slightly deeper, more grating, like rocks moving together in a current. "We'll see each other again. In the Crossroad. When we're strong enough to travel . . ."

Soon, the lanterns became more frequent and quick bursts of laughter punctuated the air.

The stairs emptied into a cavernous space. Once again, Luc stopped, amazed. The room was filled with hundreds and hundreds of people—or at least, Luc thought they were people. They moved like people, but their skin was the same reddish color as the sand on the beach and looked thick, almost scaly. None had hair, and it was hard to distinguish males from females.

They had to be the Figures.

Each Figure was dancing with two featureless shadows—Figments—waltzing and spinning, dipping and laughing. The happiness in the room was almost palpable.

You're looking for the pairing? The Figments' words came back to him.

Luc looked around at the cavelike space, ornately decked out with furniture from the human world—some of it ancient and crumbling, some of it pristine—like Rhys's raft had been.

Just before the shadows next to him slipped into the crowd, Luc called for them to wait. But when they both turned, he realized he was lost for words.

"Like he said, Luc. This isn't the end." The girl reached out to squeeze his arm. They nodded reassuringly before disappearing into the throng of Figments and Figures. Luc was left alone, mesmerized.

As he moved out of the doorway, into the whirling mass of strange bodies, he saw something catch the light of the lantern: Corinthe's crystal earrings, dangling from the ear of one of the dancers.

Rhys!

As Luc got closer, Rhys tipped back his head and downed the contents of a vial. He wiped his mouth with the back of his hand and turned toward Luc. His eye covering hung loose, and Luc saw a violent gash where the eye should have been.

"Ah, you came back," Rhys rasped. His long hair partly concealed his face. "Did you find your sister?" He swayed lightly, and Luc smelled sweat and herbs and something musty-sweet, like tobacco.

"No," Luc said shortly. "What's going on? What is this place?"

Rhys grinned and raised a glass. It occurred to Luc that the man was slightly drunk. "It's a celebration, my friend. Once a year, at the end of the moons' cycle, I arrange this secret get-together for those who wish to be whole again."

"I thought the Figures were afraid of the Figments,"

Luc said. But even as he said it, he knew it couldn't be true. They didn't look afraid. They looked . . . joyful. Free. The Figures and Figments laughed and touched and danced without pausing for breath. It was intimate in a way that made him want to look away, but at the same time, he was fascinated.

"The old generation were the ones to battle, the ones who banned the Figments. The young Figures only want to be whole again. They don't have the fear of their fore-fathers." Rhys shook his head. "They know only the feeling of division."

Luc watched two Figments twirling on the arm of their Figure in the very center of the room. He felt an ache deep in his chest. Jasmine would love this place: the energy, the excitement. Dancing with shadows.

He was reminded of the outdoor concert he'd attended with Jas a few years ago. She hadn't stopped dancing all night; her hair had been whipping around so fast, she joked she could use it as a weapon. The air smelled like cigarettes and patchouli and sunscreen, and he remembered thinking that he needed to memorize everything: the look and the smell, the way she was dancing, how she'd fallen asleep on the train back to the apartment with her head resting on his shoulder. It was as if he already knew that things would start to fall apart. That she would grow up and get stubborn and wild and moody, that he wouldn't be able to protect her.

"Don't you see?" Rhys said in a low voice. "They *must* have their Others. Their shadow selves. Isn't that what it's all about—finding the one who makes you feel whole again?"

As Luc watched the Figure spin faster, he found that it seemed to merge with its Figments so that they were indistinguishable, moving completely in tandem. The music was wild, full of joy and longing. All around him, Figures and Figments converged, melted into each other, became one. Even Rhys was soon swept away by his Figments, drawn into the middle of the floor, where they'd had made room for him.

The music changed and a thumping beat began to vibrate through the floor. The tempo started out slow, then picked up speed.

The Figures and Figments moved with it, as if they all shared the same pulse. They lifted their hands in the air. They shouted, cries of happiness and freedom. Rhys passed in and out of view. He looked so happy. So joyful.

And still the dance went on—faster, more frenzied—nameless arms reaching out and pulling Luc into the mass of undulating bodies and shadows.

Luc's own heartbeat pounded frantically in his chest as he was swept up in the crowd. He swayed with the others, letting their movements guide him. There was a pressure building in his chest, something he couldn't name or explain. And then, as the music crescendoed, as the shouts of joy crested over him like a physical force, it brought with it a single word, blazing through him, impossible to ignore.

Corinthe.

When his mother died, she had taken part of him with her. He had never expected to feel whole again.

But he did. He had. A spark, long buried, had jumped to life when he met Corinthe.

He understood her. They were so similar. Both holding tight to responsibilities that were too big, too heavy for them. Trying so hard to do the right thing, struggling to find a place where they fit in.

A realization struck him as swiftly as a lightning bolt: Corinthe made him feel whole again. Around her, everything made sense. He felt the awareness in his whole body, down into his fingertips.

He loved her.

She was his Other.

He didn't know whether to feel relieved or heartbroken. She was the one—he knew that now—and he might never see her again. Gripped by twin feelings of terror and awe, he pushed his way back out of the crowd, then through the entranceway and back up through the tunnel. He needed air.

Once outside, he stood heaving, his head still thumping from the smoke and music below. At first he didn't even notice that Rhys had reappeared at his side.

Rhys leaned in close. "Need something for your head?"

Luc could smell his breath. It was clear Rhys was drunk on something. He opened his coat and reached into the inner lining to retrieve another of his vials. As he did so, the various contents of his coat caught the moonlight. One object in particular spilled out and swung from a chain attached to his waist. It reminded Luc of an antique watch, but the shape was different. Whatever it was, it looked somehow, impossibly, *familiar.*

"What is that?" Luc demanded with sudden urgency.

Rhys shrugged and grabbed the swinging object in his hand. "The compass? Something I made a long time ago," he slurred. "It was part of a pair. Worthless, I guess. It was supposed to mean something, but she lost hers—" He broke off.

"She, who?" Luc said, taking the object into his hands and turning it over.

"Miranda," Rhys answered, his voice slurry and heavy with sadness. "Love is bigger than any of us, my boy. It follows its own rules. For love I have lost everything. Even my eyes."

"Love made you blind?" Luc asked with uncertainty.

"Not *blind,* you fool." Rhys suddenly swung around and grabbed Luc's shoulder. His grip was hard and firm. It was as if he were looking straight into Luc's soul. "I turned back time," he whispered. "Not even the Unseen Ones could stop me. And it was worth it. Even though I lost her, too. . . ." His voice trailed off, and Luc watched him pull another vial from his coat and bring it unsteadily to his lips.

"You . . . you were the one?" Luc's heart was pounding against his rib cage. Was *Rhys* the Radical Corinthe had told him about? Luc hadn't understood what she'd meant by a Radical—it sounded like the universe's version of an anarchist. Now he realized that maybe his assessment hadn't been so far off.

Rhys swiped his sleeve across his mouth. "Time . . . space . . . they flow like water. Only love is eternal. Remember that." Rhys tried to return the locket to his pocket, but it popped open as he fumbled with it. Luc stiffened; he recognized the tune that suddenly floated on the air. It was the same tune that Corinthe's locket played. The lockets were almost identical.

Only there was no ballerina inside.

It was an archer. His bow was pulled back, strung with an arrow that pointed up toward the heavens. It spun slowly to a halt, and Rhys looked up at a point in the sky.

"Where does the compass point?" Luc asked.

"To the thing I want most. A dead star." Rhys stumbled forward, determined, as if he might walk up an invisible staircase to that phantom star in the sky. But he tripped over his own feet and pitched forward, straight into Luc.

"Easy," Luc said, slipping a shoulder under Rhys's arm. Without thinking, his free hand unclasped the chain on Rhys's waist and the compass swung free. He slipped it into his own pocket in one fluid motion. "Let's take you back inside."

Luc supported Rhys back inside. Rhys was moving clumsily, tottering from side to side, singing along with the music and trying to get Luc to dance. Luc finally managed to wrestle him into an oversized chair just outside the ring of dancers. As he started to leave, Rhys reached out and grabbed Luc's arm. The candlelight lit up the bloodshot whites of Rhys's eyes.

"People leave us all the time, but it don't mean they didn't love us," he said. "You gotta hold on to that no matter what."

In the middle of the celebration, Luc thought about his mother, as she used to be, for the first time in years.

"Forgive," Rhys whispered, even as his eyes were fluttering closed and his head nodding to his chest.

And Luc knew that maybe, someday, he could.

19

The sky was lit an unnatural, smoky color. Gray wisps drifted across the open space over Corinthe's head. She wiped a thick coating of dust from her face with the hem of her shirt.

Miranda was gone. If Corinthe stayed here, underground, she would die with her.

Sirens still screamed all around her, mixing with frantic shouts. As she lay there, staring up at the sky through the broken-apart ceiling, a soft crying sound filtered through to her over the din of sirens and yelling—almost like the noise of a tiny kitten. She tried to ignore it, but it tugged at her insides, compelled her to her feet. She remembered that once, years ago, she had found a stray cat and wanted to keep it; Miranda had forbid her to do so, telling her that pets, obligations, *affections*, were too human and thus unbecoming of a Fallen Fate. Corinthe hadn't been able to explain that animals connected her to her old world, to a place where energy flowed between beings, where she had felt safe and necessary.

Corinthe hadn't thought of that stray kitten, and Miranda's response, in years. She felt a pulse of sadness. She wondered whether the kitten had lived.

Carefully, she listened again for the sound of crying, cocked her head to isolate the noise. It was coming from the lagoon. Something inside her chest tugged, pulling her toward the sound. She clawed her way out of the rubble. At the edge of the water, half hidden under an uprooted eucalyptus tree, was a very young girl, maybe four or five. Tears had made tracks down her dirty face, and though she had her thumb jammed into her mouth, she continued to cry. When she saw Corinthe, she dropped her hand and lifted both arms to be picked up.

Corinthe didn't hesitate. She reached out and gently scooped up the girl, who wrapped her arms around Corinthe's neck. She was surprisingly heavy and smelled like something familiar, from Humana. Strawberries.

Suddenly, Corinthe had a wave of memories: summertime farmer's markets, passing stalls filled with fruit the color of rubies . . .

Soap and clean sheets . . .

The smell of Luc's shirt . . .

Corinthe forced the images out of her head. "Where's your mommy?" she asked.

The girl shook her head, pointing a stubby finger

back toward the fallen rotunda. Corinthe looked over her shoulder at the pile of broken columns against the backdrop of a burning city. How could anyone survive that destruction?

She couldn't leave the girl alone. Corinthe remembered when she'd been exiled, how scared and alone she had felt before Miranda found her. She knew it shouldn't matter what happened to one random little girl—she knew it wasn't her business—but it *did* matter. At the moment, it mattered more than anything else.

"Let's go find her," Corinthe said.

They turned away from the water, and gradually, the girl's sobs turned to sniffles. The girl's weight was almost too much for Corinthe—she was so weak—but she refused to put her down. As they started across the lawn, which was torn apart now, gaping with fresh wounds in the earth, she felt a tickle against her cheek. The girl was brushing her fingers through Corinthe's tangled hair.

"Pretty," she said softly.

Corinthe managed to smile. "Thank you," she said. She felt a prickling behind her eyes and blinked rapidly.

Now what? In the distance, the road looked mostly empty of people—overturned, abandoned cars emitted smoke in the street, but most of the damage, and most of the medical help, would be in more populous places.

Which way should she go?

Another aftershock rumbled through the ground. Corinthe ducked, shielding the girl with her body. Bits of floating debris stung her back and arms.

When the noise subsided, Corinthe pushed back to her feet and hefted the girl, now wailing again, to her chest. Then she heard a woman shouting behind her.

Corinthe turned around.

The girl lifted her head and began to cry. The woman ran toward them, arms outstretched, stumbling over the uneven ground. When she reached Corinthe's side, the girl launched herself out of Corinthe's arms and into her mother's.

The woman wept, clinging to her daughter, murmuring, "It's okay. Mommy's here. It's okay." Then she looked at Corinthe. "God bless you," she sobbed, and she threw one arm around Corinthe, drawing her in.

Corinthe froze.

She felt the woman's gratitude. No one had ever hugged her like that before.

"Thank you," the woman said as she pulled away. She reached up and tugged on something around her neck, then pressed it into Corinthe's hand. "Thank you."

The woman made her way toward the street, the child still clinging to her, sobbing into her shoulder. Corinthe looked down at the object the woman had given her. A St. Jude pendant rested in her bloodied palm.

The patron saint of lost causes.

She held it up by its silver chain, watched it twirl like the tiny ballerina in her music box. An ache started deep inside her and took away her breath. The pendant started to tremble.

All she'd ever wanted was to return home to Pyralis.

That had been the reason for everything: the single driving force behind all of her actions. Every time a horn blared, tires screeched, or music blasted from a car stereo, she had longed for the serenity, the quiet, of the twilight world.

She had never wanted to be human—had feared it more than anything.

She had never *felt* human. She had never felt anything at all.

Until Luc.

He had made her question everything; he had made her see the world differently. He was stubborn and opinionated and selfless and loyal. She wanted to see him again, to tell him he was right, ask him to tell her more about his family, his friends, his dreams. She wanted to show him she understood, now, why he had to save his sister. That she knew what it was like to care that much for someone else.

She tried to swallow, but it felt like something had wedged in her throat. Pressure built inside her chest. She felt like she would explode. She opened up her mouth to scream, but nothing came out.

She felt her legs shake. She fell to her hands and knees. The pendant landed a foot away in the dirt. She gasped for air, felt her lungs burning. Then something inside her broke, and a sob burst from her throat.

A gut-wrenching, half-strangled noise.

She'd never cried before.

Tears ran down her cheeks and made strange patterns

in the dirt. She stared, horrified and fascinated, even as sobs continued to consume her, as her chest heaved and pain clawed through her chest. She wondered if this was death. She had expected pain, but this was so much more. It went on and on, didn't subside, just battered her until she felt nothing else, as though a deadly current had been unleashed inside of her.

She pushed to her feet, half blind, desperate. Without knowing what she was doing or where she was going, she stumbled toward the lagoon. Tears blurred her vision, but she could still see that thousands of fireflies were swarming around the choppy surface of the water.

She swallowed back a sob. Why didn't they fall? They must complete the cycle; they must return to Pyralis.

Corinthe had waded into the water. Her thoughts had somehow become fixed on the idea that she could help, that she could restore this tiny bit of balance. When the water was waist high, she inhaled and submerged herself. Her arms and legs burned, but she ignored the screaming pain in her muscles as she kicked out and swam to the center of the lagoon.

She surfaced, spitting water. "Go!" she shouted. "Go before you're lost!"

She swung her arm, lifting a spray of water toward the hovering mist of fireflies. But they had obviously lost their way and wouldn't become submerged.

Tears stung her eyes. All of those fates would be lost forever. Would the whole world end, now that everything was chance and choice? Would everything fall into ruin?

Corinthe thought of Luc's warm eyes, the way he said
If you believe in fate. . . .

Was it chance that she had fallen in love with him?

Did it matter?

Corinthe drew in a mouthful of water, then spit it out,
coughing. The surface of the small lagoon was choppier
than it had been only a few minutes earlier. A vibration traveled across the surface, growing louder, until it
swelled to a roar. The currents surged, tugged her in different directions. She took another mouthful of muddy
water and spit it out, retching.

A wave crashed over her head, burying her in sound
and tumult. For several panicked seconds, she was
turned around. She surfaced to suck in air just in time to
get another mouthful of water.

She went under again.

Her lungs burned and her legs felt like deadweight.
She clawed for the surface, could barely breathe in before
she was once again pummeled by a hard wall of water.

Corinthe let go. There was nothing left inside her,
not a single ounce of strength to call on. She heard faint
strains of music drifting softly on the current, felt something like wind on her skin. . . . Her music box was playing. . . .

Then she heard nothing but silence.

20

Miranda lay in stillness after Corinthe left; even the beating of her heart was muffled. She didn't breathe. She didn't move.

Then, at last, she inhaled deeply, a gasp that was also a laugh.

She was hurt. It had not all been a deception. But she had known, too, that she could use the injury to convince Corinthe that she was to blame for all the destruction, that she must kill Luc or bear the guilt of Miranda's death.

Her shelves had been broken and most of her bottles shattered, spilling her precious tinctures and potions. But she was able to salvage some crushed poppy, which would help her pain, and slowly she extricated herself from the rubble. Her powers were weakened; she had to do it the human way: by climbing. She had to stack the rubble, piece by painstaking piece, before using it as a springboard.

Thankfully, not all her powers were gone.

She made it to the lagoon just in time to see Corinthe go under. So. Corinthe was at last going to return to Pyralis.

This was it: the moment she'd been waiting for. The chance to show the Tribunal that the destruction of Pyralis could be orchestrated—that they should have listened to her all along.

They would bow to her now, look to her for leadership and counsel. *She* would control the Radicals. Together, they might grow even more powerful than the Unseen Ones.

The irony, the part that was poetic, was that she would use one of their own to do this. A Fallen Fate, the *first* Fallen Fate, would be the key to their demise. Ten years in Humana had changed Corinthe, and Miranda had been the one shaping her. She had trained her, subtly and slowly, for choice—for one choice, at least.

She had waited for ten years for the perfect opportunity, and when she received the marble from the Messenger, she had known: the fate within it had been Corinthe's. *She* was destined to die by the boy's hand. But the marble was cloudy and hard to interpret; and Corinthe had readily believed in a different meaning. She wanted to believe. She wanted to believe that she would at last go home.

Miranda dove into the lagoon. The trail left by Corinthe was faint, but Miranda followed it down into the swirling mass of color at the bottom of the pond. Faint strains of music filtered through the water, a tune familiar enough to cause a moment of pain in her heart.

That was the past.

The future now depended on one girl. Would Corinthe have the strength to do it? She would save herself; but she would also bring about the destruction of Pyralis.

Miranda kicked and propelled herself forward. The farther she swam, the more the pain eased in her head and limbs. Above, a dull purple light glistened, and she swam toward the surface. The pressure on her limbs had eased. She felt strong again.

Surely her plan could not fail. Not after everything she'd done to make it happen.

Miranda broke through the surface just as Corinthe was sloshing—shivering, thin, and pathetic, like a wet dog—to the shore. Hazy purple light filled the sky. Tiny fireflies blinked over the water. Miranda dove back under and swam several yards farther, to be sure Corinthe did not see her.

Once Miranda could stand, she stepped out of the river, kicking off her waterlogged sandals. Even the stones here were soft, as though they were made of velvet. Everything in Pyralis felt pliable, as if waiting to be molded into something else, something better.

Her fingers itched to unleash a storm, winds so strong they could swallow up the beauty of this place, but she knew it wouldn't work. She'd tried before, when she was younger, stronger.

Only the Fates had power here: Corinthe and her sisters, the forever-children. Only they could act in this twilight world.

So she had waited, and waited, and waited, until patience became like a taste curled under her tongue, bitter and ever familiar.

Miranda glanced at the sky and smiled. The twilight was fading already. Her plan was working, and the time had finally come for her to exact revenge on the Unseen Ones.

There was just one thing left to do to ensure that Pyralis would be destroyed forever.

21

The blackness in her mind, the fog, began to break apart when Corinthe heard the soft strains of music again. The familiar melody calmed her. A gentle current lifted her body. When her head broke the surface, she inhaled deeply. The air was fresh and carried with it the scent of flowers.

The scent of home.

Her mind felt clear, unclouded. Refreshed. When you truly believed in what you were doing, it came naturally. The burning sensation in her limbs receded slightly. She sank her hands into the soft sand of the river's bottom and slowly dragged herself to shore.

At the edge of the water, she paused and looked down at her reflection. Her head was haloed with soft purple light from the sky above her, and her skin practically glowed.

Her breath hitched in her throat.

Home.

The word whispered across her mind, enveloping her in warmth.

She almost couldn't believe it—she hadn't fulfilled the final act, and yet she was here. Not transformed, though—she was still in her semihuman form. But already, the healing winds of Pyralis were working. They sang through her blood, a decade full of pain, an ache that had lodged itself in her bones, in her teeth, behind her eyes. It was so close, so close . . . If she did what was expected of her, she'd be a Fate again, so soon she could taste it. That was what Miranda had promised, what the marble had indicated: her own knife. The rising sun in the background as the knife flashed in the air before coming down. One life lost, one fate fulfilled. And yet . . .

She gasped. It felt as if she had been holding her breath forever; only now was the weight in her chest truly eased. The sense of relief, the release from pain, was like joy. The scrape on her cheek had faded, and her tangled hair softened when a light breeze teased it into a loose braid. She looked younger, healthier again. She could feel the hornets' poison loosening its grip on her. . . . She would soon be strong again. Capable of fulfilling her task once and for all, restoring the balance of things, regaining her proper place. She looked *almost* like a child. Innocent.

But she wasn't innocent anymore.

Something had changed inside her.

She glanced at the unnatural hue of the sky. It was

too light. The vast purple sky was webbed with red, as if dawn were breaking.

Corinthe felt fear lodge in her chest. She had not yet fulfilled her task. She had altered the flow of the universe.

She had already altered the fate of one boy.

The universe, she had learned, contained ripples and grains of doubt. Just like the marbles, destiny wasn't flat and one-directional. It was round and could be seen from infinite different angles, full of shifting, swirling gradations. Every rule seemed to have its exceptions.

And this was one of them.

Because she had made her choice.

Beyond the stone walls that surrounded the Great Gardens was the flower that could save a life, though it would kill whoever plucked it.

Corinthe no longer had any regret or doubt. Just a sadness swelling inside her, making her feel lightheaded, weightless, as though she were disappearing. The decision felt as intimate and essential as her own name.

The balance of the universe still had to be set right—which meant someone had to die.

She turned away from the river, pulled by an invisible force inside her. A force that had nothing to do with the power of this place; a force that was all her own. It amazed her how simple it all was, really.

Pyralis was filled with endless walks of flowers—great, tangled stretches of vivid green fields, bursts of wildflowers, forests dappled in twilight. This world was an island surrounded on all sides by the river, and the Great Gardens were at its center, walled off, forbidden. There was a spot, though, a gap in one portion of the wall, where a Fate might just wiggle through. Alessandra, one of Corinthe's sister-Fates, had found it one day and showed Corinthe. Together, they had slipped beneath the wall, but Alessandra had grown scared when they came face to face with the giant statues in the Gardens, and Corinthe had had to lead her back out.

It was said that the statues, the Seven Sisters, had once been real beings who had displeased the Unseen Ones in some way. Corinthe had never given it a thought until now. For the first time, she wondered what their great sin had been. What had they done to deserve being locked in that stony, monstrous state?

Maybe they simply wanted something they couldn't have. Something not destined but found. Like Luc. Luc, who had risked everything to find a flower that would save his sister.

Risked everything for love.

As she made her way to the Gardens, through a field spotted with flowers in colors she had not seen, except in her imagination, for ten years, she found it difficult to breathe through the thickness in her throat. How she had missed all this. Everything was so familiar, and also so strange. The air was quiet, buzzing only with the soft hum of the fireflies and the sighing of the wind. No laughter, no voices, no car horns and screeching wheels and doors slamming and . . .

Life. No life.

Not a single animal rustled the grass; no Fates, either. They must have been farther down the river, bent over their tasks, perhaps trying to correct the balance she had disrupted.

Even now, she could see that the sky above her was lightening quickly. The violet had faded to a dull gray. There was a fine line of gold at the horizon, and Corinthe suddenly remembered her first sunrise: crouching on the roof, watching the explosion of light and the noise that seemed to come with it as Humana shook itself awake.

She thought of Luc. She wondered what it would have been like to watch a sunrise next to him. To wind her fingers with his and walk down Marina Boulevard together. But there were some things that just couldn't be, no matter how you looked at them.

The chaos had started to invade Pyralis. Day was coming, bringing not just the heat and the light but the passage of time. And in a place of timelessness, a place of eternity, time was a cancer. It would eat away at the edges of this world until the Gardens wilted and died. Until Pyralis disappeared completely.

Tall grasses whispered against her skin, sending shocks of life through her, a constant, pulsing reminder that everything was connected, that everyone had a place, that nothing ever truly ended. Here, she didn't even have to stitch; the life flowed through her and she swam inside it, as though moving through the river.

She made her way deeper into the island, into the lushness, following a well-worn path that led straight to the main entrance of the Great Gardens. Straight to the soul of Pyralis. She felt buoyed by certainty, almost floating.

She passed the stone maps of the universe, ever shifting, and treaded lightly across the plains of white tea flowers she and Alessandra used to play in. Corinthe stopped for a minute, almost certain that she heard Alessandra calling her name. She spun around. No one was there.

The path left the tea field behind, and she passed through a thicket of overgrowth. She could feel that she was getting close. And then the path arrived at a towering iron gate, permanently locked. It connected the walls of the garden. Impenetrable. Here she could feel the pulse of the place surging through her veins, making her almost delirious. She ran her fingers over the lacy ferns that crowded the perimeter of the main gate. Then she found the place where a fiery red patch of grass grew among the ferns. She followed a path of stones that led into thick growth, going by a hundred-year-old memory, an intuitive language that allowed her to feel her way, always and forever, through Pyralis, like a bird wheeling south in winter.

The ground seemed to rise up beneath her feet and lead her deeper into the ever-thickening foliage around the edges of the stone wall, and she became so entranced by the healing, seductive energy that flowed through her here that she almost didn't see it at first: the gap.

She felt a pang in her throat. This was it: the secret entrance Alessandra had discovered all those years ago.

The stone wall was overgrown with vines and tall grass, but this tiny portion had been somehow disrupted, dug up. Crumbs of stone and dust lay mingled with the verdant mud at the base of the wall.

A strange feeling came over Corinthe. Why hadn't any of the other Fates ever discovered this break in the wall? Why did the break exist at all? Could it be that the Unseen Ones had known of it forever . . . that its presence was a temptation, a test of faith to see who would obey the rules and who would break them?

Or was it possible that this, like so many other things Corinthe had encountered in the last few days, was an anomaly, an accident? Like the faulty marbles, like ripples in the river. Perhaps the great plan was made of water and not stone: it changed, flowed, and adjusted.

Corinthe touched the broken section of the wall—she knew which stones were loosest, and began to move them aside. Then she crouched down to crawl through the narrow hole.

The Gardens contained every flower, every known plant in the universe, and for a moment Corinthe was almost overwhelmed by the smell on the other side of the wall: a hot, heady, intoxicating scent of growth crowded on endless growth. A narrow rock path spiraled through the garden, down to its very center, and Corinthe followed it, her heart beating fast. She almost feared that each footstep, however quiet, might waken the Seven Sisters, send them running after her.

At last the path ended, and Corinthe found herself

standing at the edge of a great grass amphitheater. At its very center grew a single purple bloom.

The Flower of Life.

The petals, exactly eight, were each as long as her forearm, extending from a pure white center. For a second, she couldn't move. She almost felt as if she could cry again. She was here, at last, after all of her years of exile, all of her tasks, all of her trouble. This flower would save her, in its own way.

Again, the simplicity of it all struck her as somehow funny. Easy. Painless.

With the pain in her legs gone, all she could feel was the beating of her own heart. She was kneeling in front of the flower before she could register that she had moved. She was filled with a feeling bigger than joy or sorrow—an emotion so strong it renewed her strength and purpose.

She reached out and wrapped her fingers around the stem, right below the petals: the only flower that would ever grow, the only thing that could save her, here, underneath her fingers. She gasped. The flower's pulse was so strong it almost knocked her over. She could feel her hand burning.

She would die, but it would be worth it. Because Luc would save his sister. It would be Corinthe's gift, to thank him for what he had given her.

She had finally found something more than fate to believe in.

22

The sounds of the partiers had long ago receded as the cave faded into darkness. Luc ran. He ran for what felt like hours, though the world around him remained dark and freezing. He ran blind and yet he didn't stumble, not even once . . . and despite his guilt, the path in his mind was so clear, so certain. His legs moved without any effort, and as he ran, he felt all the exhaustion and fear of the recent past sliding down his back and away. He grew stronger, fiercer, faster. It was more intense than any sprint he'd made across the soccer field.

He felt, for the first time in a long time, free.

As he ran, he thought about Jasmine. The compass grew warm in his hands. He would find a way to return it to Rhys. He shouldn't have stolen it, but he knew, intuitively, that this would lead him to Jas.

Jasmine. When she was five, she would demand horsey rides from him for hours at a time.

When she was eight, she'd wanted to see a real live monkey at the zoo and would not stop asking until he took her to see one.

And when she was fourteen, he had finally told her the truth about their mom.

Jasmine was all he had.

He *would* find her.

Luc dove into the frigid river—the one that flowed in two directions at once. The river of darkness. He knew what to expect, but the feeling of drowning consumed him and, for a second, took his breath away.

But he knew how to do this. *Don't fight it. Just . . . feel your way. Listen.* And so he listened, and inside his palm, the archer spun and spun and . . . finally stopped spinning. The water faded to air that was thick and humid.

Sounds trickled into his awareness. The low drone of bees. A soft gurgling he couldn't identify.

He blinked the dizzying fog from his vision when he felt solid ground under his feet. He stood in a lush green forest, threaded with mist. Enormous trees towered above him, forming a canopy that barely allowed light to penetrate. In front of him was a clearing filled with huge flowers—just like the image Corinthe had shown him.

His mouth went dry. It had happened so fast this time.

He was here. In the Forest of the Blood Nymphs. This had to be it.

"Jas?" He called out his sister's name, and as though

in response, he heard a strange whine coming from above him—like the whine of a thousand mosquitoes. Goose bumps broke out over his arms. This world was all wrong. It was filled with growth, but it felt off, like death and decay.

He moved into the clearing, watching carefully for signs of movement, for predators that might be lurking behind the thick foliage. Nothing.

And then his heart stopped.

He almost didn't recognize her. Her eyelids were translucent. The roots of her hair had turned blue, and her face looked tight, drawn, like that of a much older woman. Thick veins ran over her face and down her neck, covering her shoulders like spidery tattoos.

"Jas?" he whispered.

She didn't answer. Didn't even stir. Luc felt the pressure of a panic unlike any he had ever known. This was worse than seeing in her in the hospital—worse than the drive there, half blind, shoeless, not sure whether he would find her alive or dead.

"Hold on, Jas. I'm going to get you out of here, okay? Just hang on." He didn't think she could hear him, but speaking made him feel better. He pulled hard on the vines that encased her, but they almost seemed alive— they resisted him, tightening around her instantly.

He spotted a vine, thicker than the rest, that had pierced the skin of her wrist just below her jasmine tattoo. Without hesitation, Luc pulled the knife from his back pocket and slashed through it.

A horrible screeching filled the clearing. The remaining vines released her at once, and the flower began thrashing, as though it had been injured. The treetops exploded with movement and sound.

Jasmine slumped forward. He wrapped an arm around her waist, steadying her. She was unconscious, but he could feel a faint pulse in her neck. He quickly slid the knife into his belt and hefted her in his arms as though she were a child.

Somehow, he had to get Jas to the Gardens, to the flower that could save her life. Rhys hadn't told him what to do if he managed to find his sister.

Suddenly, two creatures dropped lightly out of the trees. He stopped. Turned. Two more creatures landed soundlessly behind him.

They had to be Blood Nymphs. Their bodies were translucent, and they had flat, inhuman eyes. Luc could see the veins running with different colors under their skin, and he felt his stomach lurch.

He tried to sidestep one of them and it let out a shrill whine. The other three joined in, and soon the canopy above them was filled with the sound. Luc looked up. There were hundreds of them, massed in the trees, skittering over the branches like overgrown insects.

Jas stirred in his arms and groaned.

"You can't have her." Luc's voice, miraculously, didn't falter. He hitched her higher onto his shoulder with one arm and with the other fumbled to extract his knife from his belt.

A nymph with pale yellow skin hissed at him, revealing sharp teeth. Luc slashed through the air and the nymph drew back, but only for a second. The whine above them was like a stake driving cold fear into his back.

And then the trees began to move and sway. He noticed one tree that did not look like the others—its leaves looked like shards of sky, and it didn't move like the rest.

Could it be a Crossroad?

He backed toward it as vines began to unwind from the tree trunks, slithering across the ground toward him. One of them began snaking around his ankle, and he reached down instinctively and slashed at it. The vine withdrew, spitting a thick black liquid into the grass, and immediately the other vines began to crowd him, a circle of twisting, ropy snakes.

And it gave him an idea.

As the vines writhed upward, about to form a cage around him, Luc pricked his finger with the knife.

Instantly, a hush fell over the nymphs—they were fixated on the tiny drop of blood on his finger.

He could practically feel their hunger. Their eyes dilated.

And then they lunged for him.

Luc, hauling Jasmine over his shoulder, stabbed the knife into the trunk of the tree behind him—the one with the blue leaves. He stepped onto the knife, which formed a kind of rung, and heaved Jasmine over a high branch. Just at that moment, the Nymphs dove straight into the cage of vines.

They were trapped.

The Nymphs' squeals and whines grew wild.

Luc had climbed over the higher branch and removed the knife from the trunk. Then he grabbed Jas's limp body and climbed even higher, into the blue leaves. As he did, a feeling of familiar dizziness overcame him.

As the trees hissed and the trapped Blood Nymphs screamed, Luc's fingers closed around the compass.

He thought about the Flower of Life, his only hope. He pictured the vivid bloom, the slender purple blossoms, the white center.

It wasn't working.

And then he thought of Corinthe. He saw her lips in her head, her vivid eyes, the way they went from stormy gray to the subtle softness of violet. He felt her soft hand in his, the tangle of her hair on his cheek.

He felt a sudden explosion of light, a bright burst in his mind.

Still he held Jasmine tightly in his arms.

And then the light went out, and they were on an island in the middle of the sky.

Luc could hardly breathe. It wasn't exactly night — closer to dawn — but they were surrounded by more stars than he had ever seen when he and Jas snuck up onto the roof and made a game of spotting constellations.

"Jas, look," he whispered, but his sister didn't stir.

He knew he had to hurry, but instinctively, he sought out the familiar constellations — Andromeda, Pegasus, Orion. For companionship. For luck. They were all there, just like in his world, but none were in the correct order, as though a great hand had reached up into the sky and rearranged the puzzle pieces, and for the first time since he was a very little kid, Luc almost felt the urge to cry.

"Which one is the flying horse, again?" Jasmine asked.

Luc pointed out Pegasus, ran his fingers over each star, and drew a picture for her in the sky.

"That looks nothing like a horse," she scoffed. "The only thing that even looks close is the Big Dipper. I mean, this one is supposed to be a bear. Seriously?" She pointed a finger at the constellation in the library book they'd checked out earlier.

"You have to fill in the blanks with your imagination. See how they show you a real bear here, and then where each of the stars falls inside it?" He traced the outline on the page.

"It still makes no sense," she said. And then, after a pause: "Show me another one."

Luc went through the book, page by page, illuminating the drawings with a flashlight, pointing to the corresponding stars in the sky. They stayed on the fire escape until dawn. Jasmine had nodded off earlier, but Luc tucked his sweatshirt around her and let her sleep. Then he sat there in the quiet, staring up at the stars.

Luc inhaled. Strangely, he no longer felt afraid. He felt peaceful, certain.

He would save Jasmine.

Maybe Corinthe was right after all. Maybe it had all been fated this way.

Tiny fireflies darted around over his head—and yet they were not just fireflies, and seemed to be filled with light far too bright for their tiny bodies. Flowers in colors Luc had never seen, never even imagined before, bloomed everywhere. Their aroma made the air feel thick against his skin.

He heard the faint echo of girls laughing, and it seemed to come from nowhere and everywhere at once. He heard, too, the sound of rushing water. He shouldered through a wall of lush, unfamiliar plants, and found himself standing at the top of a majestic waterfall that seemed to flow directly off the edge of the world.

Hundreds of tiny silver marbles bobbed in the waves.

This was it—the place Corinthe talked about.

Pyralis Terra.

His chest hitched. "We did it," he said to Jasmine. Her breathing was shallow, barely audible. "Just hang on, okay? For me. Almost there now." His voice broke and he cleared his throat.

At the edge of the stream, he laid Jasmine down gently on a soft patch of moss. He hated to leave her, but they were running out of time; she was so pale, and her lips were almost purple. He had to find the flower quickly, and he could move faster if he was unencumbered.

He reached out and smoothed a lock of dark blue hair away from her face. For a second, his throat tightened up. He remembered how she used to fall asleep on his shoulder on the car rides back from San Jose, when they went to visit their grandparents.

"I'll be right back," he said, even though he knew she couldn't hear him. "I promise."

Then he straightened up. He was close—so close. He just needed to find the flower.

A makeshift path of white rocks was studded in the ground, and he followed it. It was as though he *knew*, instinctively, where he needed to go. Everything about this world felt intuitive, fluid, as though he'd been here before, or seen it in a dream.

He pushed deeper into the crowded growth. Enormous ferns brushed his shoulders, like the touch of gentle hands. He accidentally nudged a pink, bell-shaped flower, and the air filled with a heady, sweet scent that made his head swim—like the pine tree on Christmas morning.

He felt almost drunk and had to force himself to concentrate.

The path ended abruptly at a gated entrance between a pair of enormous stone walls. Seven huge statues confronted him, three on one side of the walkway, four on the other, towering above him like sentries. They had to be over ten feet tall, and all had women's bodies, but their faces were completely blank except for half-crescent slashes to indicate mouths.

Despite the fact that they had no eyes, Luc got the sudden impression that they were watching him, and he shivered as he passed under their shadow. Beyond the gate, he saw a riot of blooms; this must be where the flower grew. He pushed hard on the gate, but it wouldn't budge. He shoved harder, leaned all his weight against the heavy iron fretwork, and still it held strong, although he couldn't see any signs of a lock. He stuck an arm through the gap in the bars but lost hope of slipping through the gate—he was far too broad, even turned sideways.

If he couldn't open the gate, he would just have to climb it. Luc jumped and grabbed hold of one of the iron bars.

Then it began to shake.

No. The ground began to shake.

There was a heavy grating sound, and for one wild second, he thought he'd found a way to make the gate open. Then he saw an enormous shadow passing over him, and all the hairs on his neck stood up.

Luc dropped back to the ground. He turned. His heart stopped.

The statues had moved.

The statues were *alive*.

Their stone mouths had opened to reveal two rows of sharp, blackened fangs. Luc took a step back and stumbled, fell, scrambled backward like a crab until the gate stopped him, then pushed up to his feet.

One by one, the statues dropped to their hands and knees, snarling and snapping their stone teeth. And as they did, they changed; rounded stone fists became hands with terrible claws, digging through the earth. Luc felt the vibrations through his feet, all the way to his head. Three of the statues crowded him, so close he could have reached out and touched one of their blunt, blind faces—faces that knew, somehow, exactly where he was.

By smell.

By taste.

Luc was helpless. He had nowhere else to go. In his panic, in his terror, he couldn't even think of trying to climb over the wall. He was rooted, frozen, watching them advance, inhaling the foul smell of wet stone and turned earth. The shadow of the monsters swept over him, blotting out the stars.

He edged a few inches to the right. Big mistake. Immediately, the monsters launched forward.

"Wait!" he shouted. "Wait!"

It was instinctive, desperate, but suddenly, they obeyed. The enormous stone beasts stopped advancing, but they moved, restless, pawing the ground with feet the size of tree trunks. One careless swipe would be enough to crack his skull.

"Okay, listen." He didn't know what he was saying. He was terrified, babbling, playing for time. He thought of Jasmine lying near the flowing water. He had promised that he would never let anything happen to her. It could not end this way. "Look, I don't know if you can hear me, all right? I don't know if you understand." Those blind faces. Christ. What was he doing? Still the words kept coming: "My sister is dying, and I need a flower inside this gate to save her."

The monsters had come no closer. Even though they were without eyes, he had the sense that they were watching him closely.

"I've been all over the universe, through worlds that make no sense to me, but I finally found her." His voice cracked. Which girl was he talking about now, Jasmine or Corinthe? "I can't lose her."

The monsters threw back their heads simultaneously and roared, a noise so loud and furious it drove Luc to his knees. It whirled through his head, bringing images, hard and fast, like a driving dark rain, freezing his center: his mother's face, Jasmine arranging graham crackers on the floor, the cramped San Francisco apartment with its smell of beer and old beef.

Was this how it ended, then? Drowning in dark memories?

It seemed as though everything might shatter, including him.

Then he thought of Corinthe. He saw Corinthe's fingers, her seashell nails, remembered how he had pressed himself against her in the Land of the Two Suns, breathing into her hair. And it was as though a little bit of light broke through in his mind, a small bit of quiet in the storm of noise.

And suddenly, just when he thought he couldn't take a single second more, everything grew still.

Luc pulled his hands away from his ears. The silence was beautiful, liquid and deep. The monsters were perfectly still again, inert, their stone heads bowed toward the ground, as though in consent. Still careful, moving very slowly, Luc stepped past the two statues in the front of the gate and pushed the heavy iron bars. They swung open with little effort.

And then he stood inside the gates. Inside the Great Gardens. He looked behind him and saw that the monsters had returned to their original arrangement, once more lining the pathway to the gate. One of them had deep twin tracks carved into its blank face now, as though by water, or tears.

"Thank you," he said.

He went forward. Time was running out. There was only one pathway leading into the Gardens, so Luc followed it at a jog. Flowers blurred past him. He remembered what the Flower of Life looked like, but how would he ever find it in this vast space?

He came to a fork in the path and stopped. Both ways looked identical.

Shit. Luc could almost feel time spilling away from him, ticking Jasmine's life away with it,

Then he remembered: Rhys's locket. Would the archer work here, too?

Luc pulled it out and flicked open the clasp. The archer popped up and began to spin. Tinny music filled the air. It reminded him of Corinthe's locket and the song it played. Thinking of Corinthe made his heart squeeze tight as a fist. He refused to believe that she was really gone.

The music and the archer stopped at once. The archer stood poised on one foot, his arrow pointing down the path on the right. Luc took off at a sprint.

After a minute, the pathway ended abruptly at the top of a natural amphitheater, a huge indent in the earth, like a giant's soup bowl.

Growing right at the center of it was the flower he had crossed the universe to find.

And kneeling in front of it, with her back to him, was Corinthe.

His heart leapt. She was here and alive. It had to mean something that they both found their way here, to Pyralis.

He wanted to call out to her, but emotion made his throat tight. Corinthe was here. For the first time in what felt like forever, he had hope. He jogged down the hill toward her, taking in everything: the wild length of her hair, the soft curve of her shoulder and lower back. She almost looked like she was praying.

I love you, Corinthe. He said it in his head. He would say it to her now. *I love you.*

Just then, she reached out to pluck the flower from its stem. Her fingers wrapped around its thick stem.

He froze. Her name died on his tongue, leaving a bitter, smoky taste.

She was taking the flower for herself.

He had trusted her.

Corinthe had used him all along.

A hot fury rose inside of him, melting through the ice, through the blackness.

He had a sudden flash of a memory, of a phantom knife blade sinking into his stomach.

His stomach was burning as though he'd been stabbed again. Luc raised the knife in front of him. When he spoke, his voice sounded distant, as though it belonged to someone else. Someone he didn't know.

"Put it down," he said. His voice was alien, a growl.

Corinthe spun around with a smile so bright he actually believed for a moment that she was happy to see him. "Luc! I knew you would find me. . . ."

"Get away from the flower." His jaw clenched so tight his teeth ached, but he didn't care.

Her smile faltered. She stood up. "It was meant for you—for Jasmine—all along."

The color of her eyes changed, shifted from deep purple to a soft lavender. She reached out and tentatively put her hand on his arm. His pulse stuttered under her touch.

"That's not true. She's lying."

Luc spun around. It was the woman from the Land of the Two Suns, the one who had told him where he could find his sister. Her long black hair twisted into a single braid that hung over one bared shoulder.

"Miranda?" Corinthe burst out.

The woman ignored Corinthe. Luc took a step back as the woman advanced on them. There was something about her eyes that was off—wrong. Too much pupil; no color at all. "She never intended to give you the flower. She planned to kill you as soon as you got her here. She used you."

"That's not true!" Corinthe cried. "What are you doing here? How did you get here? I thought you were—"

"Dead?" The woman spread her hands. "Evidently not."

"Who are you?" Luc demanded.

"She's my Guardian," Corinthe answered instead. Her voice was thick with emotion. "She—she taught me."

The woman, Miranda, narrowed her eyes. "Apparently I didn't teach you well enough. Your last task was to do what, Corinthe?"

He felt Corinthe stiffen next to him. He wondered whether she would admit it—that she had meant to kill him all along—but she only shook her head.

Miranda began circling them like a predator. There was something feline about her eyes. "In order to return to your life as a Fate, to return *home to your sisters*, you had one simple task to execute. There is still time, Corinthe. Kill him now, before it's too late, and you can stay here in Pyralis, where you belong."

Corinthe hesitated. He remembered that she had told him it hurt to live anywhere else, that being away from Pyralis was a physical ache, constant torture. He watched Corinthe warily, his grip firm on the knife.

The beauty of Pyralis faded under the harsh glow of a rising sun. He felt as if he were standing in a photograph: everything was too bright.

Still Miranda was speaking. Now her voice was a whisper, like the hiss of a snake through the grass. "You will destroy Pyralis, Corinthe. You will destroy everything you love. Is that what you want? The only way to stop it is to kill him." Miranda stepped closer and smoothed the hair away from Corinthe's forehead, like Luc's mother used to do to Jasmine. "This is the way it has to be," she said softly.

Corinthe's heartbeat was rapid, as though she'd been running. She was staring at Miranda as though hypnotized.

"I don't love it," she whispered.

Miranda frowned. "What?"

"You said I would destroy everything I loved. But I don't love Pyralis. Not anymore." Corinthe shook her head, as though rousing herself from a dream. "Him. I love him." She turned to Luc. The breath he had been about to exhale froze in his lungs. He waited. She stepped away from Miranda, closer to him. Her eyes were shining. "I love you."

She smiled so brightly he could barely think. He could barely think, see, move. He knew. He believed her.

"I love you, too," he said, and reached for her.

The sun burst free of the horizon.

A shriek of rage split the silence. Miranda lunged for Luc; Corinthe screamed something. Miranda was on top of him, stronger than he could have imagined, teeth bared: an animal. She tried to wrest the knife from his grasp; he put an elbow into her side and felt her release her grip. Sweat dripped into his eyes and Corinthe was still screaming and he stumbled backward, gasping, clutching the blade.

And then Miranda lunged for him again, came charging toward him, howling, transformed into something not human, and instinctively Luc swung the knife.

Just as Corinthe threw herself between them.

Another cry shattered the quiet.

Time stopped.

Sound stopped.

Corinthe was pressed against him, leaning into him, her lips only an inch from his. So beautiful.

Then she gasped and time started again and she fell,

holding the handle of the knife that protruded from her stomach.

"Corinthe! Oh my God! Corinthe!" Luc caught her and gently eased her to the ground. And the sun sank with them; it retreated toward the horizon, leaving only shadows and violet light in its wake.

"What do I do?" he asked desperately. Luc looked up to Miranda, hoping for some kind of help. But she was frozen, white, motionless.

"Idiot," she said. She sounded almost disgusted. "It should have been you."

"You did this to her!" he yelled at Miranda. "*Do* something!"

Miranda didn't even look at him. "She made her choice," she said. Then she turned and began walking away.

"Please!" he called after her, even though he knew it was no use. His fingers were shaking. There was so much blood. It was everywhere.

"Look at me," he said gently, leaning down to whisper in her ear. "Corinthe, I need you to look at me." Her chest was rising and falling in shallow movements, and her skin had taken on an unnaturally pale hue.

Her eyelashes fluttered open and she looked up at him.

"I couldn't let you kill her," she whispered. "It's not who you are."

He couldn't think. His pulse thundered in his ears. Panic squeezed the breath from his lungs. "Corinthe, what can I do?"

"There is nothing left to do. It's too late for me," Corinthe whispered. She smiled, just barely, and lifted her hand, reaching for the flower. She snapped its stem in half. "The flower gives life, but is deadly to whoever picks it. It doesn't matter for me. I'm already dying. It's all in balance. Life and death." Corinthe's eyes were the same violet color as the sky. "Now you can use it to save your sister."

"No," he said. His tongue was thick with emotion; he could hardly speak. "Corinthe, stay with me."

She shook her head. "No, Luc. I finally understand. . . ." Her body trembled with a flash of pain as he watched helplessly.

He was crying without knowing it, choking. "Shhh. Don't try to talk." He felt as if he was going to be sick. He stroked the hair away from her forehead, completely helpless. "I'm not going to let you go. This isn't how it ends, okay?"

She shook her head. That faint smile passed across her face again. "Luc, it was all wrong. Don't you see? The last task, the last marble. The knife. The rising sun. She made me believe one thing, but it was a trick. I misunderstood everything. I had it backward the whole time. *I* was the one to die, and you were the one to live. *This* is what was always meant to be. I feel it. I know it's true." Corinthe threaded her fingers through his. She smiled and looked up at the sky. "Look."

The sun was gone now. The twilight had been restored in moments, like a giant sweep of soft velvet. Millions of stars had appeared, more stars than he had ever seen or even imagined.

It was breathtaking.

A smile passed quickly over her face; then she seized up, as though in sudden pain. "It was always my destiny to die," she said. "This *is* how it was supposed to end. And I can go now, knowing that it's right. I want it, Luc. I want my fate. I want you to live. I love you," she said again.

"No," he said. His tongue was thick with emotion; he could hardly speak. "Corinthe, stay with me, please. I'm going to make you better."

"No," she murmured. She squeezed his hand weakly before her fingers slipped free of his.

"I love you, Luc," she whispered once more.

"I love you, too," he said.

He leaned down and their lips met.

And for the first time in all the length of the universe, they kissed.

She tasted like wildflowers, like sunshine and honey, like the air before a storm. He wanted to kiss his breath into her lungs, kiss his blood into her veins, kiss his heartbeat into her chest. And in his head he saw little explosions, stars being formed and re-formed, worlds where time ran in deep, endless pools.

"Thank you," she said. She pulled away, and closed her eyes again. "You made me . . . happy."

He laid his forehead against hers. "Please stay with me, Corinthe. Be with me. Choose me. I need you."

Her smile this time was the barest flicker, like a candle trying to stand up to the storm.

"I did choose you, Luc. Luc . . . I . . ." For a second a tremor went through her, and she inhaled, as though she wanted to speak.

But she didn't speak.

She didn't move, or breathe.

Luc felt as though a giant weight were crushing him from all sides. Tears blurred his vision. A low, animal sound worked its way out of his throat.

It wasn't fair.

He had finally found love, and then he had lost it.

And somehow, all of it had been fated: Corinthe's choice, his love for her, her sacrifice for him. Somehow, there was supposed to be meaning in all of it.

He pressed a lingering kiss to Corinthe's lips and cradled her body against his. "I love you," he whispered urgently. "You are my Other."

A distant memory ticked his mind.

A voice whispered through his subconscious.

There might be a way.

"That story Miranda told you—about a Radical who turned back time—it wasn't just a story." His throat was so raw it hurt to speak. He knew she couldn't hear him, but he pressed his lips to her ear anyway. "Rhys told me there was a way. I'll have him do it again. I'll find him and he'll rewind time and everything will be okay. I'll go back and save you."

Luc looked down at Corinthe's face, traced his fingers

over the curve of her chin. He couldn't lose her. Not like this.

He pressed one last kiss against Corinthe's lips and gently eased her off his lap.

"I promise I'll find a way, Corinthe. I won't stop. Not for anything. Not ever."

23

Luc stood over Jasmine, watching the covers rise and fall with her breath.

Her dark hair spilled over the faded green pillowcase. Her eyelids fluttered as though she was dreaming; she was still pale, but her lips were losing the last of their blue tint. The flower's nectar had worked exactly as Corinthe had said it would: it had cured the poison in Jasmine's blood.

When he'd returned to San Francisco with Jas through a Crossroad, they'd emerged near the rotunda to find the city recovering from a massive quake. As he struggled with Jas, who was still too weak to walk back to their apartment, he saw signs of devastation everywhere: crumbled buildings, flipped cars, and streets with gaping crevices, like grins.

And though it felt like days—weeks, even—that he'd been gone, a flashing daily lotto sign indicated that only a day had elapsed.

How was it possible that only one day had passed in this world, when he and Corinthe had gone through so much?

What was it that Rhys had said about time? That it was fluid. That it flowed like water.

Thinking of Corinthe brought a familiar ache. She should be here with him. She would be someday; he'd promised her.

"How's she doing?" a hushed voice asked from behind him.

Luc turned and moved out of the room, careful to close the door quietly behind him.

"Better," he assured his dad. "She ate a little bit of soup when she woke up this last time."

His dad smiled, but it looked forced, and it did nothing to hide the shaking in his hands or the sweat that beaded on his face and neck. He looked sickly. Since realizing that his kids were nowhere to be found during the earthquake yesterday, he had stopped drinking. Now, twenty-four hours later, the withdrawal symptoms were catching up.

"Let's get you some water," Luc said as he ushered his dad down the short hallway to the kitchen. It still felt like a dream. To see his father trying to get clean and sober and acting like . . . well, acting like a father was an incredible relief.

The kitchen smelled like soup and garlic bread. Luc couldn't remember the last time their dad had fixed anything besides a frozen burrito, but that was before.

Before Luc had brought a half-dead Jasmine back to their apartment.

Before Dad had come home and sworn things would be different from now on.

Before Jasmine had begun to heal and Luc had finally fallen into a deep and dream-filled sleep in which he saw Corinthe, smiling, leaning over to kiss him—and then snatched away suddenly by a wind.

He needed to find Rhys again. He had sworn he would. Now that he knew Jas was safe, it was time.

"I need to go out for a while," Luc said. "If she wakes up, just make sure she eats some more soup. And she has to drink lots of water, too. I won't be long."

"I know what to do, Luc." His father stared down at his hands. They were shaking. "I know . . . I know I haven't been the best father to you, but I swear . . . I can do better."

"It's okay, Dad." The last word felt foreign on Luc's tongue, but in a good way. *Dad.* How long had it been since he'd said that?

"Do what you need to. I'll be here in case Jas needs anything." A spasm of pain passed across his father's face.

"Thanks," Luc said. He wanted to say something more, something deeper, but the words didn't come. Maybe someday they would.

Luc left the apartment and made his way down the stairs. Miraculously, their building had suffered very little damage, aside from some bare patches on the ceiling where the plaster had crumbled.

A few blocks over, the buildings hadn't fared so well. In the forty-eight hours since he and Jas had been back, heavy equipment had cleared the streets of the largest debris: sections of brick walls, massive chunks of concrete, tangled twists of metal that had once provided structural support. Glassless windows gaped at him, boarded-up storefronts lined the streets, and a thick layer of dirt covered everything. Luc's boots crunched on broken glass as he walked past Fiend. Jasmine would be devastated that her favorite coffee shop was just a pile of rubble now.

Could Luc fix this, too, if he succeeded in going back in time?

He clutched the archer locket in his pocket as he walked. He didn't want to think about what would happen if he became lost in the Crossroad, with no one to help him. He just had to focus—then he would return to the Land of the Two Suns directly. At least, he hoped so.

Luc passed by the building twice before he realized it was the right one. This was where Corinthe had chased him after she'd attacked him on the beach—this was where everything had begun.

But now, the brick façade had fallen. Only a corner of the front door was visible. There was a NO TRESPASSING sign hanging from a broken piece of metal just above a shattered window.

Luc's throat tightened. He had to get up on the roof—no matter what.

He climbed the pile of debris carefully, slipping a little

on the splintered plaster, and looked once over his shoulder before slipping through the glassless window. He thumped clumsily to the floor inside, but no one called out to stop him.

The hall was patchy with light where the sun penetrated the half-collapsed walls. The stairwell had survived, thankfully, but Luc took the stairs carefully, testing his weight. They groaned loudly, but they held.

Finally, he reached the roof-access door and paused for a moment to catch his breath. But just for a moment. He was ready.

He pushed open the door and once again stood on the roof that had changed everything.

A cool breeze was sweeping off the bay. It felt good, like a murmur of reassurance. His gaze moved to the spot where he had stood and tried to reason with Corinthe.

Corinthe. Those violet eyes, the smell of flowers on her skin . . .

It was all for Corinthe.

He moved across the roof. But when he reached the spot where he had jumped, his stomach dropped to his feet. There was no laundry standing motionless despite the wind—just the fire escape, dangling at a strange angle from the roof and clanging against the side of the building every time the breeze picked up.

He scanned the area, trying to locate any weirdness, any anomaly that would indicate a Crossroad.

But everything looked normal. Damaged, but normal.

Could the quake have closed the Crossroad somehow?

Luc's palms were sweating.

Impossible.

He reached into his pocket and pulled out the locket he had taken from Rhys. The archer sprang up when he flipped the release and began spinning in circles. Tinny music filled the air.

Luc waited, but the archer only kept spinning.

Luc circled the roof, holding the archer above his head like a beacon, and still it kept spinning. A sick feeling started in his stomach. It clawed its way up into his throat.

It had to be there.

Maybe he had the wrong building. His memory from that night wasn't a hundred percent clear. Corinthe had been chasing him with a knife, for Christ's sake. It was possible he'd gotten it wrong. He closed his fist around the locket, feeling the cool metal in the palm of his hand before tucking it back into his pocket.

Just need to go back down and retrace my steps. That's all.

But when he turned to go, something orange, buried in a bit of debris, caught his eye. He knelt and pushed bits of concrete out of the way. There, in almost the same spot it had fallen days earlier, was his Giants cap.

This *was* the right roof.

Luc straightened up slowly, filled with a sudden sense of hopelessness.

The sun had sunk below the horizon, and brilliant streaks of color painted the sky in bold strokes. The air had a violet haze to it. It reminded him of Pyralis.

Of Corinthe's eyes when she had said that she loved him.

He had made a promise to her. And no matter what, he would keep it.

There were other Crossroads in his world. There had to be. He had emerged with Jasmine near the rotunda. Didn't that prove it?

Crossroads everywhere . . .

He only needed to find one.

"I'm coming, Corinthe," he whispered into the wind.

And for just a moment, he could almost swear he heard the wind whispering back.

Acknowledgments

First I would like to thank Lexa Hillyer and Paper Lantern Lit for this amazing opportunity. Writing *Fates* was so much fun, and I learned so much over the past year.

I'd also like to thank my editor at Delacorte Press, Wendy Loggia, for taking a good book and helping me turn it into a great book. No matter how many times I read back over the pages, I'm still amazed at how awesome they turned out.

My agent, Mandy Hubbard, made my writing dream a reality, and without her dedication and support, I wouldn't be where I am. So thank you, Mandy!

And finally, to my family, who put up with dirty dishes and too many peanut butter sandwiches, so I could finish writing this book: I love you guys.

CAN YOUR FATE
BE CHANGED?

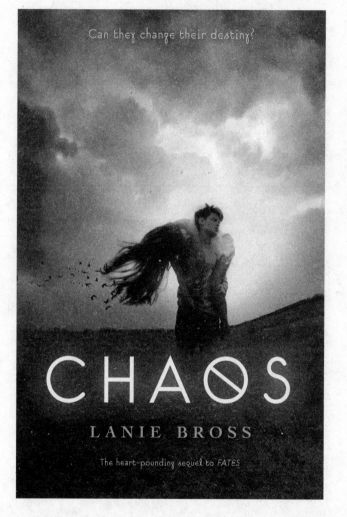

Can they change their destiny?

CHAOS

LANIE BROSS

The heart-pounding sequel to *FATES*

Corinthe's, Luc's, and Jasmine's stories
continue in the sequel to *FATES*.

1

"Close your eyes. Tell me what you see."

Luc scowled and crossed his arms. "How can we see anything with our eyes closed?"

"Just try."

Jasmine slipped her hand into her mother's and squeezed her eyes shut dutifully. It wasn't often that Mom took them out of the house anymore, and the trip to the Botanical Garden had been so spur-of-the-moment, so unexpected, that Mom had even forgotten to put Jasmine's shoes on. Jasmine was halfway to the car in socks before Luc had run after her, holding a pair of sneakers.

"Good girl." A soft hand rested on top of Jasmine's head, and fingers stroked her long dark hair. "Now take a deep breath. What do you see?"

Jasmine inhaled a breath as big as her lungs would

allow. A color came to her. Yellow. "Lemon?" she asked hesitantly.

"Yes. And what else?"

Luc snorted but Jasmine ignored him. He was going to ruin it. It felt so good to have Mom close, to feel her delicate fingers running through her hair again. She wanted to make her happy more than anything in the world.

"Strawberry," she said. "I see a strawberry."

Mom crouched down beside her. "That's good. What else?"

Jasmine took another deep breath and concentrated with every ounce of her being. She squeezed her eyes so tight, she saw little bursts of color. Bursts like fat fists. Fat fists like bright blooms. The heady aroma wrapped around Jasmine, filling her lungs, her veins with the throbbing scent.

"What do you see, Jas?" her mother prompted.

"I see . . . the flowers Daddy brought you for your birthday, only . . . brighter."

Her mother's delighted laughter sounded like music. "You can open your eyes now."

She did, feeling a rush of triumph. She had done it. She had made her mom laugh.

But when she opened her eyes, her mom was gone. Luc was gone. She was alone in a lush forest where the trees seemed to be whispering to each other. If she listened hard enough, she could make out what they said, except for an annoying whine coming from overhead.

"Mom?" The sharp bite of panic put an edge in her voice.

An ache started in her stomach, like she hadn't eaten for a week, and she doubled over from the pain.

Blood pounded in her ears, drowning out all other sounds.

Then a voice called to her out of the fog. Luc? She tried calling out, but her mouth wouldn't form words.

The whining returned, louder and filled with rage. It filled her head, pushed to get out until she thought her body would explode. In a moment of clarity, she knew what was happening.

She was dying.

"Jas, I'm coming. . . ." It was Luc.

But before he reached her, she fell.

Jasmine jolted awake, gasping for air. It took her a second to recognize that she was in her own bed, her own room. The heavy perfume that had haunted her dream clung to her sheets and her hair.

Outside her window, the sun had begun to rise, and the sky was alight with streaks of red and orange. Cracks in the plaster ceiling revealed intricate patterns, spidering outward into a twisted mass, like tree limbs in winter. Someone had made coffee and the aroma made her feel nauseated.

Jasmine sat up slowly, waiting for the usual fuzzy-headedness that followed getting high, but there was none. In fact, things were sharper than they'd ever been.

Except for her memory. Her memory was a blank. Had she partied too hard?

Carefully, she pushed the blanket aside and swung her legs over the side of the bed. Her muscles ached as she stretched her arms overhead. Jas waited for the room to tilt, for the bile to rise in her throat. But it didn't happen. She scanned her desk for her phone, but it was nowhere in sight. The clock on her nightstand read 8:42 a.m.

What the hell had happened? How had she ended up back in bed? What had she taken last night? She was hangover-free, at least. She felt clear, alert.

So why couldn't she remember?

Jasmine slipped on a pair of jeans that were slung over the chair. She looked at herself in the mirror on the back of her closet door. Her hair was a wild dark mess splayed out in a million directions, but her skin looked oddly glowing, as though she were standing in a patch of sunlight.

She shook her head. It was as if a curtain had been pulled over her memory. She could catch only glimpses, snippets of images, when the curtain fluttered.

T.J.

She was meeting him at the marina, but why?

Jasmine grabbed her favorite threadbare black sweater on her way out of the room. It was June in San Francisco and she was freezing. Maybe she'd been sick. Fever or flu or something. It would explain the whacked-out dreams she'd had.

Jasmine walked into the kitchen and found Luc sitting at their tiny table, absently looking out the window. There was an untouched piece of toast in front of him. Coffee was brewing, but it barely masked the scent of stale cigarette smoke.

"Hey," she said. He looked up, relief evident on his face.

"How are you feeling?" He pulled out the chair next to him and motioned for her to sit.

Uh-oh. Luc was in *serious mode.* His eyes were bloodshot and there were dark circles beneath them. It reminded her too much of when she'd woken up in the hospital after her overdose.

Oh God, had it happened again? Why couldn't she remember anything? Everything was a haze, and her last clear recollection was of Friday night. She'd gone to meet T.J. to break it off with him.

"Am I in trouble?" Her voice was hoarse, like it hadn't been used in awhile.

"What? No. Not at all." He shifted in the cracked plastic chair and looked at her. "I'm just . . . glad you're okay."

"What happened last night? I went to the marina, but after that . . ."

Luc shook his head. It put her on edge when he was quiet like this—like there was bad news he was trying to break to her. Like when he had to explain to her that their mom had died.

Wait. Had someone died?

Jasmine looked around the apartment. Dad wasn't on the couch, where he could usually be found sleeping off a hangover. Dread pooled in her stomach.

"Dad?" The word squeezed out through her tight throat. "Did something happen to Dad?"

"No, he's okay," Luc said. "He checked into some residential detox program."

"He *what*?"

"He decided he wanted to get sober," Luc said, poking at the toast. "After you came home he said he wanted to get sober for us."

Jas couldn't understand how casually her brother was treating the news. Their dad was not the kind of man who asked for help, who admitted to an addiction.

"Which hospital? I need to see this for myself." She stood up and immediately felt dizzy, like the floor was dropping out from under her. She placed a hand on the table to steady herself.

"Whoa," Luc said, standing to ease her back into the chair. "We're not going anywhere. Not yet, at least. The roads are still a mess and you've been gone for two days—"

"Two days? It's *Saturday*," she interrupted. "What are you talking about? And why are the roads a mess?"

"Jas, it's Sunday," Luc said. "And there was an earthquake . . ."

"That's impossible," she insisted. Nothing felt familiar. The single bulb over their heads flickered; she felt a sting of pain as if the light shot straight through her brain. This was worse than a hangover, she was sure. She rubbed her throbbing temple and tried to focus.

Why couldn't she remember what had happened after the marina? If she went to see T.J., it was possible she took something—but she hadn't *wanted* to take anything after the overdose. Not ever again.

"What happened to me, Luc? It wasn't drugs again, was it?" She had to be sure.

"No." He scrubbed his fingers through his hair, exhaled deeply. "I found you at the rotunda. There was this woman, Miranda . . ." He cut himself off. "You know what? It's not really important. The important thing is that you're home and that you're careful from now on."

"How can I be careful if I don't know what happened?"

"Jas, so much has happened in the last couple of days." He closed his eyes and took a ragged breath in. "Can we talk about this later?"

The last thing she wanted to do was talk about it later. He was keeping something from her and she wanted answers—now. But she could tell that Luc was upset. He'd done so much for her over the years, taken care of her when their dad hadn't. If he needed time, she would give it to him.

"Fine," she said as she leaned back in the chair. "But I need to get out of this apartment."

Luc had been more overprotective than ever, and it had taken a whole lot of convincing for him to stay home. He looked exhausted anyway, and Jasmine needed to be alone to think. She walked to the end of the street, where a large dump truck sat rumbling. Jasmine could smell the diesel in the air as men in yellow hardhats moved around the street, patching gaps in the sidewalk. A lamppost sagged close to the ground, and the fence of a parking lot bowed out toward the street.

California Pacific Medical Center was in walking distance, but she moved slowly, still recovering from the headache. She wondered about her dad's sudden change of heart. Why check himself into a program now? She could barely remember that warm, caring father — the one who threw her up in the air and called her his princess. Maybe deep down, she had always hoped he'd come back.

Jasmine passed a small café and could almost smell the roasted beans and buttery pastries. Her stomach churned, but she couldn't be sure if it was the smell of food or her own nerves. What if her dad wasn't really there? Or worse, what if he was sicker than Luc had suggested?

A deep pain returned to her temples, and Jasmine rubbed at the spots with her fingers. The light and noise drove tiny knives into her skull. The sounds of construction surrounded her — men drilling into the concrete and dump trucks collecting debris. It was too much. Every sound built on another until it reached a crescendo.

Jas walked faster, and she caught her breath when the hospital entrance came into sight. She had been brought here when she overdosed, and hoped to never come back. And now, here she was.

She needed to sit down for a minute, to tune everything out.

The doors whooshed open and Jasmine walked to the reception desk, leaning on it as she regained her senses. The smell of chemicals made her stomach flip.

"Are you okay?" the woman at the desk asked. She looked concerned.

"Yes—yes, of course," Jasmine stammered. "I'm here to see a patient. Jack Simmons?"

The woman nodded, then tapped on her keyboard. Jasmine looked around and realized how chaotic it was. Nurses and doctors hurried up and down the hallways, and the waiting room was overrun with people. A man was being treated in the hallway, a nurse in green scrubs wrapping a white bandage around his head. A doctor in a lab coat pushed along a woman in a wheelchair, barely missing Jasmine's foot.

Jas swallowed uncomfortably.

"Room one twenty-nine," the woman behind the desk said. "Down the hall, take the first right, and then push through the double doors and take a left."

"Thank you," Jasmine said. She willed her feet to move down the hallway. The deeper she went into the hospital, the stronger the smell of disinfectant was. It clawed at her throat, and she had to cover her mouth and put her head down.

The gray tiles under her feet didn't change as she walked, so she turned left and started to count them. When she got to twenty-two, she looked up and saw that she was only steps away from the room number the woman at the front desk had given her.

One twenty-nine.

Jasmine stood at the doorway. A soft *beep-beep* came from a machine at her father's bedside. The overwhelming scent of antiseptic filled her lungs.

This was a mistake. She turned and almost ran into a nurse.

"Hello. Are you a relative?" the nurse asked.

"His daughter," Jasmine managed to get out around her constricted throat. "Is he okay?"

"He's suffering from severe alcohol withdrawal. It's a good thing he checked himself into our detoxification program when he did."

"And how long will he be here?" She avoided looking in her father's direction. He looked small and sickly against the white sheets of the hospital bed.

"He'll need to meet with a mental-health professional. Then he'll begin a weeklong inpatient stay." The woman placed her tray down and checked his monitor. "He was given a sedative to help with the withdrawal symptoms for now, but you can say hello if you'd like."

"No, no, it's fine," Jas said, backing away from the bed.

"But there are no visitors allowed during the program. . . ."

"You said it was a week long?" Jas asked. "I can wait until he's out." She'd gone a week without seeing her dad before. At least he was here instead of passed out at O'Rourke's pub. She didn't want to say hello; she wanted to run away as fast as possible. The lights overhead made dots dance in her vision, and the sickly-sweet scent of hand sanitizer coated her tongue. She needed to get out, now.

She turned and ran.

At the end of the hall, she saw a bright red Exit sign and focused on it.

The doors exploded open under her hands.

Outside, she hesitated for just a second before turning left and running faster. Her only thought was to put distance between herself and the hospital as quickly as possible. She ran down Sacramento, turned right onto Fillmore, and then left, where a tilted sign indicated she was now on Clay Street.

She slowed to a walk, amazed that she didn't even feel winded. Luc always made fun of her for being a sloth, just because she didn't see the point of running up and down a field and kicking a ball into a net. And it was true she did fake illnesses a lot to get out of gym class. One time she'd even claimed she was coming down with whooping cough.

Since when could she run so fast?

She felt strangely alive, buzzing. Beneath the squealing of tires and occasional blaring of alarms and car horns, it was as though the air itself was speaking to her. She felt *connected* to everything—to the people lighting a fire in the alleyway as she passed by, to an old lady walking across the street, to the old lady's small dog. She could *feel* them, could feel what they were feeling. *Hunger. Loneliness. Curiosity.* She could suddenly sense all of it around her, as though the whole world's volume had been turned up.

Just across the street Jas saw Alta Plaza Park, which had not been damaged too badly by the earthquake. A longing rose up, fierce and fast, to run her fingers through the grass and inhale the moisture of the ground.

The wind whispered through the trees and she imagined it was saying *Jasmine*. She was halfway across the street before she even realized she had moved.

"You're supposed to block the ball, you shithead!" a voice shouted. The loud, familiar shout was followed by laughter.

Tyler, Justin, and Devon, all in their soccer uniforms, were kicking a soccer ball around the field just next to the trees. Jas ducked into the grove of trees. The last thing she wanted to do was explain to those guys what she was doing on this side of town on a Sunday.

She didn't trust them enough not to spread it around school that her dad was in the hospital, either.

She sat down and closed her eyes. The sounds she heard brought colors to mind—the bright blue *shush* of the ball through the grass, yellow explosions of voices, the deep purple of the wind. It made her feel a little dizzy.

She must have hit her head on something, *really* hard.

She didn't know how long she'd been sitting there, motionless, when she realized that Tyler and the others had gone. She peeked out from the trees and saw them, distantly, at the other side of the park, getting into a car she recognized as Tyler's.

She stood up, leaning against the trunk of a tree for support. There was a faint pulsing under her fingers, through the rough bark. The air shifted. She felt as if the tree was a hand, warm and inviting; she could feel its sap like blood. A high-pitched whine started in her head, just like in her dream, and it made her pulse leap. When she inhaled, there were new aromas, exotic ones that had no place in the middle of San Francisco.

She could hear everything: not just the wind through the leaves, but the clouds floating overhead, the trees inhaling and exhaling.

And . . . footsteps.

Two people were with her in the grove talking in hushed tones. A boy and a girl.

"I don't see him anywhere," the girl said.

"He is expendable. She's the one we're after." The boy sounded cold and determined.

Their whispers were as clear as if they were talking directly to Jasmine.

Jasmine felt uneasy, filled with a buzzing electricity that came from the air, from the wind, from the trees. She crouched in the cluster of trees, listening. She heard the wisp of metal against denim, knew instinctively that one had just pulled out a knife.

"There she is!" the girl shouted, pointing in Jasmine's direction.

A shock of red hair flashed between the branches as the girl fought her way toward Jasmine. The boy, a dark figure dressed in camo pants and a black hooded sweatshirt pulled low over his face, threw himself at the thick curtain of leaves between them, slicing through them with his blade.

The tree screamed—or maybe the screaming was just in her head. Jasmine felt hurt as though it were her own body that had been cut. She moved in the opposite direction. Her skin screamed in pain as she backed up against the trunk. The whine got louder, but the boy didn't appear to hear it at all.

He lunged again, and the noise grew deafening. Bloodlust ran through her veins like a fever. Without thinking, she grabbed the boy's wrist and twisted it forcefully, sending the knife to the ground. His eyes grew wide and he tried to get away, but he couldn't. Jasmine was stronger, and yet she felt completely wild—she had no control over this strength, no idea where it came from.

Her fingers slid around his throat and she started to squeeze.

The hood of his sweatshirt fell back.

A calm deadliness settled over the grove.

The scent of blood filled the small grove. Instinct took over.

The sharp points of her teeth felt unfamiliar against her tongue.

"Jas!" A voice pierced through the high-pitched sound at the edges of her mind.

Jasmine stopped to listen. Luc appeared several feet away, gasping for breath, and stopped when he saw her, his eyes wide with disbelief. Reality seeped into Jas, cooling the bloodlust, and her grip loosened.

What the hell was wrong with her? She let go of the boy and he stumbled back a few feet, where he fell onto his hands and knees, gasping for air.

Luc started toward Jasmine but then stopped and

picked something up off the ground. The boy's knife. He paled and spun around, facing the boy.

"What the hell are you doing here?" Luc demanded.

The boy just stared up at Luc with a mixture of pain and resolve on his face.

Luc stood over him with the knife clenched in his fist. Oh God, was he going to hurt the guy because of her? This was all so wrong. The whining had stopped, and now Jasmine heard the familiar sounds of the city. Her hands still shook, and she could still feel the faint beating of the boy's pulse under her fingertips. The lust for blood was gone too, and she felt sick, like she'd just ridden a mega roller coaster.

Something horrible had taken over inside her, and the worst part was that it felt so natural.

"Luc?"

He glanced over his shoulder at her.

She saw the hesitation on his face.

The fear.

Was he afraid for her or *of* her?

"We're only doing what we must." The girl stepped hesitantly from behind a tree. Her palms were turned up to show she wasn't armed. "You of all people must understand that."

Luc growled at the girl, "Haven't they taken enough already?"

Jasmine looked from Luc to the girl. Did they know each other?

"We don't make the rules," she said with a shrug.

Her casualness seemed to make Luc even madder. "*I don't believe in your rules. That should be clear by now.*"

Jasmine watched the exchange, growing more confused by the second.

"You know how this has to end," the girl said. With a wary eye on Luc, she walked over to the boy and helped him stand.

They disappeared, and Jasmine sagged under the weight of what had happened. Luc wrapped his arm around her shoulder, pulling her against his chest.

"I don't understand." Jasmine felt as though she'd stepped out of a nightmare into that place where dreams and reality are still mixed together. "What just happened? Who were those people?"

"Shhh. It's okay." She couldn't help but notice how his voice shook.

Jas wanted to believe him, but it didn't feel like things were ever going to be okay.

How *was* this all supposed to end?

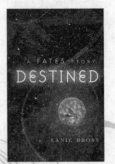

And don't miss this beautiful, romantic digital original prequel to *FATES*. Corinthe attends a beachside party at a glamorous mansion on Point Reyes, where she must help fulfill a mysterious—and potentially deadly—destiny. There she gets her first taste of the strangest human emotion of all: love.